To

The Dark Side
Darkening
Darker
Darkest

Sure Mastery
Unsure
Sure Thing
Surefire

The Hardest Word
A Hard Bargain
Hard Lessons
Hard Choices

A Richness of Swallows
Rich Tapestry
Rich Pickings
Rich Promise

What's her Secret?
The Three Rs

Totally Five Star
Chameleon
La Brat

Collections
Paramour: Re-Awakening
Jolly Rogered: Right of Salvage

Totally Five Star: Paris

LA BRAT

ASHE BARKER

La Brat
ISBN # 978-1-78430-559-8
©Copyright Ashe Barker 2015
Cover Art by Posh Gosh ©Copyright April 2015
Interior text design by Claire Siemaszkiewicz
Totally Bound Publishing

This is a work of fiction. All characters, places and events are from the author's imagination and should not be confused with fact. Any resemblance to persons, living or dead, events or places is purely coincidental.

All rights reserved. No part of this publication may be reproduced in any material form, whether by printing, photocopying, scanning or otherwise without the written permission of the publisher, Totally Bound Publishing.

Applications should be addressed in the first instance, in writing, to Totally Bound Publishing. Unauthorised or restricted acts in relation to this publication may result in civil proceedings and/or criminal prosecution.

The author and illustrator have asserted their respective rights under the Copyright Designs and Patents Acts 1988 (as amended) to be identified as the author of this book and illustrator of the artwork.

Published in 2015 by Totally Bound Publishing, Newland House, The Point, Weaver Road, Lincoln, LN6 3QN, United Kingdom.

No part of this book may be reproduced, scanned, or distributed in any printed or electronic form without permission. Please do not participate in or encourage piracy of copyrighted materials in violation of the authors' rights. Purchase only authorised copies.

Totally Bound Publishing is a subsidiary of Totally Entwined Group Limited.

If you purchased this book without a cover you should be aware that this book is stolen property. It was reported as "unsold and destroyed" to the publisher and neither the author nor the publisher has received any payment for this "stripped book".

LA BRAT

Dedication

This book is dedicated to John and Hannah, and to the beautiful city of Paris.

Chapter One

Required – Events Coordinator. Could it be you?

Eugenie grabbed at the page as it flicked past then she thumbed back through the magazine more slowly to find the job advertisement again. Had she been mistaken, misread it? No, here it was, a full color spread no less in the prestigious *Hotel International* magazine, the world's number one publication serving the high-end hospitality industry. She spread the page out on the low glass table in front of her to read the notice properly.

Totally Five Star Paris, a flagship hotel in this renowned international chain, is seeking a dynamic new member to join our senior management team. You will have experience of organising high-profile events and functions, a proven track record in managing complex budgets and juggling competing priorities, and you will be accustomed to getting things done. For the right candidate we offer excellent salary and other benefits, a chance to live and work in the most iconic part of one of the world's most beautiful cities, and the opportunity to be a part of the Totally Five Star continuing success story. More details and instructions for applicants can be downloaded from our website.

Closing date: 28th February 2014

The advertisement was illustrated with a range of wonderful images depicting the glamour and sophistication that were the hallmark of every Totally Five Star hotel anywhere on the globe, though Eugenie would have insisted that Totally Five Star Paris was the jewel in the crown of one of the most recognized international chains. The hotel's brand of magic was famous the world over, the most luxurious surroundings, the most efficient, the most comfortable, no detail overlooked, no effort spared to ensure guests enjoyed the very best that money could buy.

Eugenie had never actually ventured inside the Paris hotel, but she knew it well enough. She had passed it frequently when she was a student in Paris and to make ends meet had worked as a waitress in a café bar off the Avenue des Champs-Élysées. The hotel was in the next street, an imposing, elegant presence gracing the entire avenue. A continuous parade of the rich and the famous was regularly seen trotting in and out of the sliding glass doors, as often as not across the sumptuous red carpet the staff would roll out to welcome their exalted guests. They would be aided by the traditional English-style butler, who greeted all who came and went with the same quiet courtesy.

Eugenie pored over the ad again, rereading the seductive words. Could she? Might it be possible?

She ran her gaze over the essential requirements again, mentally checking off her qualifications.

Experience of organizing high-profile events and functions? Well, she'd done some of that. Complex budgets, competing priorities? She sighed. *Yeah, tell me about it. Anyone who works in the public sector these days knows about that. Getting things done. Er, well, yes, probably. Depends on what things they meant exactly.*

"Miss d'André? Mr. Metcalfe will see you now."

Eugenie startled at the voice alongside her. She closed the magazine and laid it back on the coffee table with the rest of the literature artfully displayed there to keep visitors entertained while they waited to see the head of corporate affairs at Newcastle International Airport. The smartly dressed executive secretary picked up Eugenie's coffee cup and gestured for her to precede her along the spacious corridor toward the executive office suites. Eugenie started to do just that then turned.

"I wonder, could I take that magazine I was just looking at, please? There is an ad... I mean an article in there I was reading. I do not mind paying you for it, of course."

The other woman stopped too and smiled, perhaps at Eugenie's very obvious French accent. Her English was perfect, but her continental origins unmistakable.

"Of course not. You're welcome."

Eugenie picked up the magazine and slipped it into her briefcase. She would have a proper look later. Now, she had work to do.

* * * *

The meeting with the CEO at the airport went well. The international corporate functions suite seemed to be more than adequate to hold the two hundred plus delegates expected at the launch of North East Now, the council's latest foray into presenting Northumberland and the northeast of England as a suitable location for films, entertainment and cultural activities.

It was a new take on the tourism trail, this time aimed at a younger, more technically savvy market. The more traditional venues such as city center hotels or outlying conference centers wouldn't cut it, whereas the ultra-modern environment of the airport would. Their rates were steep but just about within budget, if she cut back somewhere else.

Mr. Metcalfe was also keen to secure the business so he was ready to include catering and refreshments in the price—a considerable savings. Eugenie was pleased and knew her boss would be too. She stood and they shook on the deal. She promised to email him within twenty-four hours confirming the agreed price and their exact requirements as just discussed. Mr. Metcalfe declared it a pleasure to do business with her and pressed the buzzer on his desk to summon his PA back again.

A few minutes later, Eugenie was in a taxi on her way back into Newcastle city center. She should really have been going over the notes from the meeting with Mr. Metcalfe. Instead, she pulled out the magazine and reread the ad. Maybe she was feeling a little buoyed by her recent success, but she made up her mind.

Why not? She was experienced. She did have a track record. And she was successful. Well, today she was. She could try. And if she got it—a big if—but even so... If she got this wonderful job in Paris, she could finally say goodbye to the wreckage that was her life here in England. She could leave La Brat behind and start over.

She hadn't always been a brat. Or more accurately, not so much of a brat as she had become in the last year or so. She used to be biddable, acquiescent, the perfect submissive. Well, some of the time she was. She must have been good, or at least had shown potential. Otherwise, Aaron Praed would never have looked twice at her. He could have had his pick of all the submissives at The Basement, the fetish club she'd discovered soon after moving to England. But he'd chosen her. He'd invited her to scene with him the first time she'd ventured there, shy and on her own, not sure what to expect.

Eugenie laid the magazine on the seat beside her as she let her mind drift back to that first scene with Aaron, nearly three years ago now. He'd been good, by far the best Dom she'd ever played with—before or since. It had been on the tip of her tongue to decline his offer of a spanking, but there had been something compelling about the tall, blond Dom with the vivid blue eyes. Instead, she'd accepted and followed him across the dungeon to a cubicle that housed a padded bench and a rack sporting an assortment of paddles and leather straps.

* * * *

Then

"Take your pick. Or if you prefer I'll just use my hand."

"That one. If you please." Eugenie pointed to a pretty little lemon-colored paddle made of flexible silicon. She honestly had no idea if she was making a good choice or not, but her limited experience had at least taught her that the difference would be made by the skill and intent of the Dom, not the implement used. If this man wanted to hurt her, he could and he would. If it was too much, she could stop him by using her safe word.

Sure enough, his next question addressed that issue. "What's your preferred safe word for this, Miss...?"

"Eugenie. My name is Eugenie d'André. And my safe word is Maupassant."

At his raised eyebrow, she felt moved to clarify. "He is one of my favorite authors. He was French."

"Ah, right. Excellent choice. Very classical. My name's Mr. Praed — Aaron — though you will address me as Sir."

"*Naturellement*, Sir."

His tight smile was his only further response. He gestured for Eugenie to lean on the bench and lift the short skirt she was wearing. She did as instructed, quashing her natural modesty, which had no place here. Even so, she appreciated his choice of the cubicle as it did offer a degree of privacy.

"Would you like me to remove my thong also, Sir?"

"That's up to you. It makes no difference to this."

"Then I will leave it in place. Thank you, Sir."

"Ten strokes okay?"

"Yes, Sir, ten will be fine." Eugenie wriggled against the soft leather padding on the bench, making herself comfortable as her handsome playmate for the evening positioned himself behind her. Now that the initial embarrassment was behind her, she was glad that she'd taken the plunge, so to speak, and accepted his invitation to play.

"I'll start when you tell me you're ready."

"I am ready, Sir — Ooh!"

The first stroke fell immediately, sending a sharp burst of pain across her left buttock.

"Too hard?"

"No, Sir. That is perfect."

Mr. Praed made no comment. He proceeded to deliver the remainder of the ten strokes, pausing for a few seconds between each. Eugenie presumed this was to allow her the opportunity to use her safe word if she wished, and she silently appreciated his care. There would be no safe wording, though. His technique was heavy but controlled, the slaps just painful enough to elicit a squeal or two by the time he reached eight and a definite scream at the tenth. Eugenie was impressed. By the time he offered her his hand to help her to stand upright once more, her bottom was smarting and her pussy moist. She began to wonder at the wisdom of retaining her thong, but it was done now.

"Thank you, Sir. I enjoyed that." Eugenie was careful to assume a suitably submissive posture, her head bowed, hands clasped behind her. She liked this Dom, wanted to make a good impression. Perhaps he was a regular here. If so, she would certainly be returning frequently.

"My pleasure, Miss d'André — or do you prefer mademoiselle?"

"Either is quite all right, Sir. Just as you please."

He gave a low chuckle, as though he knew exactly what was going on in her head. Perhaps he did — some Dom's had that knack, she'd found. She had no idea how they did it, where they learned that peculiar brand of telepathy. Were they born with it? Or did they perfect it by going to classes or some such thing? Probably the latter. She was aware that good Doms would read about BDSM, fact as well as the fiction that she was so fond of. They would practice, they would finesse their art before laying a hand or anything else on a submissive. Aaron Praed certainly had all the skills. She had felt safe with him. If so, all the more reason to give him no cause not to want to scene with her again.

"Is there anything else I can do for you, mademoiselle? Do you have further plans for this evening?"

"No, Sir, not plans as such. I just, I... This is the first time I have been here. I do not know the facilities well." *Please take the bait. Please.*

"Miss d'André, is that your way of hinting that you'd like me to give you a tour?"

"Yes, Sir. If you are not too busy, and if you have no other—commitments."

"I think I can make time for you. One word of warning, though—and I will not be repeating this—I don't appreciate hints. If you want something from me, in future come right out and ask me. I may say no, but you'll have to take that chance."

"Yes, Sir. I apologize," Eugenie uttered, head still bowed, her gaze fixed on a point about a yard in front of Aaron Praed's feet. Inside she was singing. *'In future'. He said in future.*

"Are there any more items of equipment you might like to sample here, whilst we're still in the dungeon?" He gestured beyond their cubicle to the public area where couples and groups milled about in various states of dress and undress. Prior to Mr. Praed's offer of a spanking, she'd already checked out the St. Andrew's Cross at the far end, the stocks set up in the center, as well as the many and various straps and hooks affixed to the walls and ceiling. Shelving and racks held an assortment of paddles, whips, crops, canes, and Eugenie knew that electrical aides such as vibrators could be supplied on request. In truth, she had more than a passing interest in all of those, but felt intimidated by the audience she would have here in the communal room. She appreciated the safety offered by the public setting, but had no taste for voyeurism herself. Her natural modesty was a powerful inhibitor.

The choice of location for a scene, and whether or not it would be conducted in public, would usually be the Dom's call, but Eugenie knew nothing would happen that she did not consent to — this was the first rule in the BDSM code book. To her way of thinking, though, it was not that simple. If she did not consent to whatever Mr. Praed had in mind, he could and would simply shrug and wish her a good evening — and go look for a sub more to his taste. He would have no trouble finding one, she was convinced of that.

So really, she had no choice at all.

"Yes, Sir. Anything. All of it."

"My my, you are ambitious, to say this is only your first visit. For myself, I prefer to take things more slowly. I'm thinking one of the private rooms might be more suited to our requirements right now."

Dom intuition again. Amazing. Eugenie gave a quick, grateful little nod.

"Follow me, please." Aaron turned on his heel and strode away from her across the dungeon. He never once looked back to see if his companion was behind him. He didn't have to.

The room he led her to was small and unfurnished apart from a solid wooden chair in the center and a drinks fridge and shelving unit against one wall. The shelves were empty except for a couple of straps and a length of rope. The fridge contained several bottles of mineral water, both still and sparkling. The chair had no arms though the seat was padded, the back straight. It looked very utilitarian, as indeed Eugenie knew it was. It was a spanking seat, designed for a Dom to use when administering an over-the-knee spanking. That must be his intent then. Her buttocks were still tingling from her experience downstairs, but she found her pussy moistening again in anticipation of a repeat performance.

He seemed to be in no rush, strolling across the room to help himself to a small bottle of sparkling water. He turned and offered to Eugenie.

"Still or sparkling?"

She shook her head. "Neither, thank you. I am fine just now."

He snapped the top off his bottle and took a long drink. Eugenie used the brief interlude to cast her gaze around the room again. This time she spotted a metal ring suspended from the ceiling. There seemed to be no restraints attached to the walls, a fact that struck her as odd.

"I prefer to keep things—uncluttered—when I'm getting to know a new submissive. Just you and me, and a few basics. Strip please, Miss D'andré."

The command was delivered in a clipped, matter-of-fact tone that brooked no argument. Even so, Eugenie hesitated. She knew the score, had known exactly what would happen when she agreed to accompany Mr. Praed into a private suite, but still the terse instruction unnerved her.

"Problem, Miss d'André?"

"I—no, Sir."

"Do it then. When you're naked, I want you to stand under the ring and reach up, grasp it with both your hands." He turned, appeared to be selecting something from the not exactly extensive array of items on the shelves.

Stung by his apparent lack of interest in watching her undress, Eugenie obeyed his instructions anyway. She resented his arrogant tone, her irritation simmering as she removed her skimpy vest top and skirt. She reached behind her to unclasp her bra, glancing at Aaron as she did so. He was at least looking at her now. She tilted her chin up as she bared her breasts for him, proud of her body.

If he was impressed, he concealed it admirably.

"I like the shoes. Those can stay."

"And my thong?" Silly question, really.

"What part of naked is not entirely clear to you?"

Eugenie's thong joined the rest of her discarded clothing in an untidy heap beside the chair and she stepped over to position herself directly beneath the metal hoop. She found that if she stretched up she could just manage to reach it, though without her high-heeled shoes she would not have been able to. No doubt, he'd worked that out. Damned cocky know-all Dom.

Aaron came over to stand in front of her. When she would have dropped her gaze, he tipped her chin up with two fingers, forcing her to look him in the eye. Eugenie's mouth went dry. She wished she'd accepted his offer of a drink a few minutes earlier.

"I'm going to tie your hands to the ring, then you will stand still and be quiet whilst I explore your body. I intend to touch you everywhere, in any way I choose. I may hurt you. I may pleasure you. If you feel a need to orgasm, you will ask my permission. If you want me to fuck you, you must ask for that. If you've earned it, I may oblige you. Is this all absolutely clear to you, Miss d'André?"

Eugenie drew the tip of her tongue across her lower lip before curling it inward to chew on it. It was a mannerism she couldn't help and one that always betrayed her. She berated herself for allowing him to see how nervous she was, how deeply he intimidated her, though at some level she appreciated his skill in being able to reduce her to this with just a few words. How would she react when he did actually lay his hands on her?

"Miss d'André? Eugenie? Do you understand what is to happen?" His voice had gentled a little, the difference almost imperceptible but somehow enough to restore Eugenie's flagging confidence.

She nodded.

"Excellent. You have your safe word, but other than that, I don't want you to talk to me unless I ask you a direct question. You may make other sounds, of course. I suspect you will be quite vocal as we get to know each other this evening. You may wish to close your eyes and I have no objection to that. If at any stage I want you to look at me, I'll tell you so and you will obey."

As he spoke, he attached leather straps to her wrists, binding them together, then fastening the straps to the ring. It was the work of moments, but when he stepped away, Eugenie was securely tied, stretched out for his perusal and whatever else he had in mind.

Eugenie eyed Aaron as he leaned against the bare wall, his stance one of studied nonchalance. He seemed to be in no hurry, whereas with every second that passed, she felt more and more strung out with nerves. The longer he made her wait, the more apprehensive she became. She wished he'd just get on with it.

A couple of minutes slipped by before he took a bottle of still water from the shelf and walked toward her. She watched him, her eyes widening. She was silent, as he'd instructed, keen to obey. Aaron unsnapped the cap on the bottle and held it to her mouth. He didn't ask this time if she wanted the refreshment, just put it to her lips and tipped the bottle up. She sucked greedily.

"If you want a drink, at any time, you may ask for one." He withdrew the bottle from her mouth. Eugenie licked her lips and smiled at him, both grateful and wary.

He circled her, unhurried, then returned to stand before her. "Nice tits. A little small but we'll manage. I love your arse, especially as it's still so pretty and pink from the paddle just now. I expect we'll brighten it up still more, though. What do you weigh, Miss d'André?"

"I, I am not sure. Perhaps nine stones."

He shook his head. "Nearer eight, I'd say. You're too thin. We need to build you up, Miss d'André."

Circling her once more, he stopped behind her, this time trailing his fingertips across her shoulder and tracing the shape of her clavicle. Her long brown hair fell in soft waves to her mid back. He wound it around his hand and tugged until her head tilted back. Turning her face toward him, he leaned in to brush his lips across hers. Eugenie was conscious that this was the first expression of intimacy between them. Not much, but sufficient to reassure her that he was pleased with her so far. Or so she hoped.

Eugenie allowed her eyelids to drop as she relaxed slightly. Perhaps he saw this and chose that moment to ramp things up a little, to throw her off balance again. He reached around to cup her breast. Eugenie gasped, gnawing on her lip again. He squeezed her breast, molding it in her palm before he took the small pink nipple between his finger and thumb. He rolled then pinched it, the tip hardening and swelling in his hand. He applied a little more pressure, enough to hurt, and she gasped again, jerking against him. He brought his other arm around her too, across her lower abdomen.

Even though he was holding her still, and really, she was not in any position to struggle or resist, he repeated his instructions. "Don't move, Miss d'André."

Her response was to stiffen in his arms. It was difficult, but Eugenie wanted to comply. She was making an effort, and hoped he'd realize and settle for that, this time.

Aaron continued to torment her nipples, first one, then the other, pulling, twisting, flattening them between his fingers. Eugenie whimpered, and tears dampened her eyelashes. She was suffering, but managing to endure because he'd instructed her to.

His next ploy was to slip his free hand between her legs, stroking through her damp, soft folds. Despite the pain of his touch her pussy was wet, proof of her arousal if any were needed.

He relaxed his grip on her swollen, distended nipples. He then parted her pussy lips, thrusting two fingers deep into her. No preamble, no warning, he penetrated her with his fingers and scissored them inside her. The walls of her cunt tightened around his digits. She let out a low moan.

"Do you like this, Miss d'André?"

She nodded.

"Answer me please, Miss d'André. Say it."

"Yes, Sir, I do like this."

"Would you like more of this then? Shall I continue?"

"Yes please."

"Yes please, Sir."

"Yes please, Sir. I am sorry, Sir."

"I believe you are sorry, but even so, I intend to punish you for that mistake. It'll help you to learn. A leather strap across your delightful derrière I think. Would that provide a memorable lesson, do you imagine?"

"Sir, I... Oh!"

Aaron chose that moment to twist his fingers and connect to her G-spot. He rubbed hard, applying pressure to just the right place to send her into a frenzy. He reached down and around with his other hand, too, to caress her clit.

"Sir, I'm going to come."

"No you're not. Not until I say so."

"Sir, I cannot help it. Please..."

"No." Aaron continued to finger-fuck her, his thrusts relentless now, hitting her G-spot every time he drove his digits into her. He drew the pad of his finger backward and forward across the tip of her clit, synchronizing the movements of his hands to focus the intensity. He seemed to know the moment she lost control, convulsing around his fingers as huge wracking shudders rocked her small frame. He didn't let up, drawing out her response, teasing every last tremor from her before slowing down. His hands still on her, in her, he leaned in to whisper in her ear.

"Oh dear, Miss d'André. I appreciate your enthusiasm, but you just earned yourself a serious thrashing. Was it worth it?"

"I believe it was, Sir."

Aaron chuckled. "Sassy little sub. I think I might come to like you. A lot."

"Thank you, Sir."

"That wasn't a question, Miss d'André. Silence please."

Aaron stepped away, returning to the shelves. This time he picked up a tube of lubricant, and returned to stand in front of Eugenie. She gazed at him, her head a confused jumble of conflicting thoughts and emotions. She was aroused, but anxious too, apprehensive, maybe verging on distressed. This scene was intense, much more than she'd experienced before, and this stern, implacable Dom didn't seem anywhere close to being finished with her yet.

"Are you still with me, Miss d'André? I don't hear any mention of French classical authors."

Eugenie was relieved. He might be harsh, but Aaron Praed did at least seem to be attuned to her responses, both spoken and nonverbal.

"I am fine, Sir. It is just…"

"What is it, Eugenie?" His tone was gentler, as though he genuinely wanted an answer, not more trembling.

"I don't want you to punish me. I meant no disrespect or disobedience, Sir. I tried to obey you but it was too intense."

Aaron cupped her chin in his hand, lifting her face up. He caught her gaze and held it. "We can stop this any time you want to."

Eugenie shook her head, her eyes tearing again.

"Eugenie? Tell me."

"If I use my safe word, you will let me leave, I know that. But you will not want to scene with me again."

"Would that be a problem for you? If I'd pushed you so far you had to safe word?"

She had no hesitation in her response. "Yes, Sir. I like you."

Aaron smiled. He leaned forward to kiss her, and Eugenie noted he seemed inclined to make a more thorough job of it this time as he slipped his tongue into her mouth. Eugenie's response was instant, the slight purring sound in her throat an indication that he was getting through to her. He explored her mouth, tasting and testing, and Eugenie couldn't resist starting to suck on his tongue. At last, he broke the kiss but remained close, his nose nudging hers.

"I like you too, little sub. And I will most definitely want to scene with you again, even if you do use your safe word. I hope you won't feel you have to do that, but you might. I want to know what your limits are, and to find that out I need to push you right to them. I need to know that I can trust you to protect yourself if it's too much. Can I trust you, Miss d'André?"

He waited, and Eugenie gazed at him. There was more to come, he'd hinted as much, and it was going to be just as intense as before. Possibly more so. She knew she was chewing on her lip again. Then her thoughts cleared. She smiled at him before giving an almost imperceptible nod. It was enough, though, and he got it. Aaron stepped back, still holding her gaze. And he winked at her.

Chapter Two

Eugenie's confidence soared. His wink made all the difference. Aaron was stern, demanding, a Dom to the core. But she took comfort in that he also seemed to know when she was struggling and just how to tap into her submissive instincts to bring her along with him and keep her in the scene. She drew in several long breaths, concentrating on her respiration as she brought her senses under control. Aaron did not hurry her. He seemed prepared to allow her the time she needed to collect her wits.

A couple of minutes passed. Eugenie turned her head to seek out Aaron as he leaned against the wall. "May I speak, Sir?"

"You may."

"Thank you, Sir. I am ready to continue now."

"Yes, I know."

"Then, I do not understand…"

"I'm just enjoying looking at you."

"Sir?"

"You are one sexy little sub, Eugenie. I thought I should mention that."

"Thank you, Sir." Eugenie's head was reeling again. She'd thought him less than impressed.

"You're welcome." He pushed himself off the wall and advanced on her again. His expression had lost the humor and warmth of just moments before as he shrugged on his Dom cloak once more. The effect on Eugenie was instant, her submission immersing her once more. She bowed her head, breathing slowly while he circled her again then came to a halt behind her. She remained motionless as he trailed the backs of his fingers down her spine, giving a slight, involuntary shiver when he reached her bottom. She was not sore exactly, but as he palmed her buttock, she was conscious of the residual tenderness from the earlier spanking. He must have known but made no reference to it.

He parted the cheeks of her bum with his hands, and Eugenie inhaled sharply. He was inspecting her.

"Arch your back, Miss D'andré. Show me your arse."

Eugenie obeyed, widening her stance a little, at the same time lifting her bottom up. Aaron ran his fingers down the crease between the rounded globes, exploring, seeking and finding. He reached her tiny puckered hole and pressed his finger against it. She groaned, knowing what was coming.

Aaron massaged her arse, working the tip of his finger inside. Eugenie closed her eyes, concentrating on holding still for him. This was not the first time she had done this, but she had mixed feelings about anal play. It was intense, intimate, and she found it ultimately humiliating. She supposed that was the point and would not normally have welcomed this the first time she scened with a new Dom.

Saying no to Aaron was not an option. In any case, Eugenie found she did not object on this occasion. She relaxed in his hands. Aaron was gentle but determined, easing past her sphincter, working his finger deeper inside.

She flinched as the cool slickness of lubricant hit her slackening hole. Aaron worked it inside, thrusting one finger fully into her. He twisted his hand to swirl his digit around, stroking her inner walls. Eugenie squeezed down, gripping around his questing finger.

"You tolerate this well. You've done this before, I think."

"Yes, Sir. I mean, I am sorry—was that a question?" She held her breath.

"It was. Relax, I'm not trying to catch you out. I want to learn about you. What about butt plugs? Have you had a plug in here? Or a cock?"

"A small plug, Sir. Just once. Oh!" She clenched her bum as he drove a second finger inside her. Her knees gave way and she was hanging from the metal ring, suspended there by the restraints around her wrists. Aaron caught her, his arm around her waist steadying her and taking her weight.

"Are you okay?"

"Yes, Sir. That was—a surprise. And a little intense." She locked her knees again. "I am all right now." She was by no means certain her legs were going to hold her up, but for now at least, they seemed to be doing their job

Aaron released her and resumed his rhythmic finger-fucking. Eugenie gave herself over to the sensation, for the first time actually liking this experience. With Aaron, it seemed not so much humiliating as intimate and erotic. Her pussy was wet, hot and clenching round nothing. She wondered if he might fuck her, if she asked him very nicely. He did tell her, right at the onset, to ask him straight out for whatever she wanted from him.

"Has anyone ever fucked your arse, Miss d'André?"

"No, Sir. Not yet."

"Good answer. We'll work on this some more then, though perhaps not tonight. It'll be something to look forward to."

"Sir, I—oh. Oh!" Eugenie let out a little shriek when he twisted his fingers inside her, at the same time reaching around to take her clit between his finger and thumb. Eugenie groaned. Her knees threatened to give way again.

Aaron rubbed her clit then flicked the tip, hard. Her orgasm was just moments away.

"Sir, I need to come. Please. Please…" She was close to despair, expecting to be refused. The beating to follow would be a mere formality.

"Go ahead."

"Pardon? Sir?"

"You have permission to come, Miss d'André. Do it now."

"Thank you, thank you, thank you… Oh, Sir." Eugenie convulsed as her climax seized her, rocking her nervous system as wave after wave of pure sensual pleasure washed through her. Aaron continued to stroke her clit, finger-fucking her ass with a steady, forceful rhythm while she convulsed around his hand.

Her head cleared and Eugenie became aware of her surroundings again. Aaron chuckled, the sound coming from close to her ear, soft and very sexy, full of promise. Eugenie's pussy clenched. She needed to ask him, needed him.

"Please, Sir, I would like it if you would fuck me."

"Mmm, I bet you would. Are you hoping to distract me from delivering the punishment you've earned."

"No, Sir. I just…" Eugenie was unsure how to proceed, or even if she should persist. Desire and caution warred within her. Desire won out. "Sir, please punish me, then fuck me. Please."

"As you wish, Miss d'André, since you've asked so nicely." He reached up to release her restraints, sliding an arm around her waist to catch her when her body crumpled. He lowered her to the floor then crouched beside her. "When you're ready I'd like you to get up and stand by the chair. Lean over it. You can put your hands on the seat."

Eugenie nodded and attempted to push herself up. Aaron stopped her with his hand on her shoulder.

"Not quite yet. Take your time. We're in no hurry. Well, I'm not. You may disagree. The sooner your discipline is administered, the sooner you'll have my cock inside you. I suppose your powers of recovery now will demonstrate how much of a slut you are."

Despite his crude words, Eugenie knew he had a point. She was near enough desperate to have him inside her, but despite her inexperience she understood that rewards had to be earned in this demanding lifestyle. He would exact his punishment then, if he was satisfied she was truly sorry and had learned from his attentions, he'd deliver the prize he'd promised her. Despite her enthusiasm for what was to come, eventually, Eugenie was glad of the reprieve. She did need a few minutes to flex her straining muscles, to loosen up her shoulders, and most importantly to let her legs solidify again. Aaron Praed had a most profound impact on her equilibrium, she was finding.

Minutes later, she pushed herself onto her knees then got to her feet. Still a little unsteady, she made her way to the solitary chair in the center of the room. She stood in front of it then leaned forward to grip both sides of the seat.

"I take it you're ready?" The low drawl came from across the room. Eugenie turned her head to face him. He was still leaning against the wall, a leather strap dangling from his right hand. It was looped in the middle, the two ends clasped within his fist. He quirked his upper lip in a half smile.

Eugenie suppressed the urge to glower at him. She did not relish what he intended to do to her. Maybe she was a fair-weather submissive, a cherry picker who loved the fabulous orgasms and some of the heavier stuff, but resented the discipline aspect. Whatever, this was a means to an end and that end was very much in sight.

"Yes, Sir. Thank you for waiting."

"No problem. So now, let's do a tally-up. You forgot to refer to me with the proper respect. That earns you six strokes. And you came without my permission, for which I'm minded to add a further ten. So, sixteen strokes, Miss d'André. Do you agree this seems fair?"

Eugenie felt the blood drain from her face. She'd expected six strokes perhaps, ten at most. Ten slaps was the most she had ever managed previously and that with a Dom's bare hand. And, of course, downstairs earlier, but that had not been a punishment. She should have known that Mr. Praed would be more demanding when it came to discipline.

"Sir, I… If you think that is appropriate."

"You disagree?"

"No, Sir. It is just, I have never…"

Aaron pushed himself away from the wall and strolled across to stand behind her. His palm on her buttock was warm, gentle as he massaged her rounded cheek. "If you think it's too much, you may say so. I will listen to you."

Eugenie sighed, loving the feel of his hands on her body despite the circumstances. His words gave her confidence. Perhaps there was negotiation to be conducted here.

"I think I can manage ten, Sir. I have before, but that was just a spanking. It was a punishment, though, and hard."

"How long after that punishment before you were able to sit comfortably again?"

"Two days, Sir. And I could not sleep for the first night."

"Mmm, that was hard. I wonder what you did to deserve it?" He appeared not to require an answer as he continued immediately, "What I intend for you will hurt here and now, but you will not experience such lingering effects." He leaned in to whisper to her. "You will lose no sleep over this, Miss d'André."

"Thank you, Sir."

"And I think eight strokes will be sufficient. I appreciate that you've been forthcoming and have told me about your previous experience. For this, I'm prepared to halve your punishment this evening. How does that sound to you?"

Eugenie turned her head, straining her neck to look at him. Aaron helpfully moved around into her field of vision.

"Thank you, Sir. I — thank you." She was at a loss for words, had not expected such a concession and this just for being honest and saying what was in her head.

Aaron grinned at her. "We'll see if you're still inclined to be so grateful after you've felt the strap against your bum a time or two. So, we start then?"

Eugenie nodded, tightening her grip on the seat.

The first stroke was excruciating. There was a whooshing sound as he swung the strap toward her then a resounding crack as it connected with her right buttock. Eugenie stepped forward a pace, unable to prevent herself. She managed not to cry out.

"Remain still, please. Arch your back more, if you would. I want you to lift your bottom up for me."

Oh. God. Screwing up her eyes, Eugenie did as she was told. The strap whooshed through the air again, this time landing across her left buttock. She held her position, biting back her squeal of pain.

The next two strokes were delivered quickly, striping her bottom just below the first two. He seemed to be a master at this and accurate in his work. Eugenie knew he was deliberately not hitting the same spot twice and appreciated his skill.

"Halfway there, Miss d'André. Are you all right?"

"Yes, Sir. Please, just finish this quickly, if you would, Sir."

"Of course."

He was as good as his word, dropping two more strokes onto her quivering bottom just moments apart. She was no longer able to remain silent and let out a little squeal with each blow, clenching her buttocks hard. The final two were landed across the backs of her thighs, and Eugenie screamed aloud at those. They really hurt, her backside and thighs felt to be on fire. Regardless of his reassurance, Eugenie was sure that she'd feel the effects of Aaron Praed's strap every time she sat for the next few hours at least.

After the final stroke, she waited, unsure whether to stand or remain in place until instructed to move. Caution was called for. Her hunch was right. Breathing heavily as pain bloomed across her smarting buttocks, she turned her head again to watch Aaron Praed stroll back to the shelf unit and drop the strap onto one of the shelves. He returned to her and laid his hand on her right butt cheek.

"Hot. That'll be hurting, yes?"

"Yes, Sir. Thank you, Sir."

"Good. So, what have you learned?"

Eugenie drew in a long breath, schooling her body not to flinch from his touch. "I will always remember to call my Dom Sir. And I will try harder not to orgasm unless I have permission to do so, Sir. I am sorry I did not manage to achieve those things for you this time, but I will not make the same mistakes again."

"A pretty enough apology, and I do believe you mean it. I expect you will make the same mistakes, but perhaps less often. Controlling your orgasms will improve with practice. Are you still desiring a fuck, then?"

"Yes, Sir! You promised. You—" She caught herself before she started to remonstrate with him. So much for contrition. If she wasn't careful, she'd be receiving another eight strokes, at the very least.

Aaron chuckled. "Hmm, your sassy mouth will get you in so much bother, girl. You've learned enough for tonight, though, I think. Stand up straight now."

Biting her tongue, Eugenie stood upright and stepped away from the chair. Aaron moved around her and sat on it.

"I'm all yours, little sub. Take what you want." He gestured to his jeans, his impressive erection clearly visible behind the zip.

Eugenie stared at it, uncertain what to do next. Up until this moment, she had been entirely passive in the scene.

"If it's my cock you're interested in, you'll need to get it out then straddle me. Get on with it, girl."

"Yes, Sir." Eugenie needed no further encouragement. She leaned forward to undo the button on his jeans then lowered his zip. As the fabric parted, his cock sprang free, jutting proud and solid from his clothing. Eugenie wrapped her hand around it, and with the other she reached into his jeans to palm his balls. They were heavy, filling her hand. She squeezed them slightly as she started to pump her small fist up and down his shaft.

The head of his cock was wide, flaring just above the rim. The shiny, smooth surface was already coated in pre-cum, which was emerging from the slit in the end in a steady stream of droplets. Eugenie ran the pad of her thumb across the head to smear the natural lubricant about, and flirted with the notion that she might lean forward a little farther and lick it.

"I'll fuck your beautiful mouth next time, girl. Right now, I want you to sit astride my lap and sink my cock into your pussy. Get on with it." He hitched one hip to reach into the front pocket of his jeans, retrieving a condom wrapped in foil. He handed it to Eugenie, who opened it and unrolled it over his erection with a deft, practiced movement.

Her preparations made, Eugenie gave a brief nod and stepped forward, his legs now between hers as she stood over him. She released his balls and used that hand to steady herself against the back of the chair beside his shoulder while she guided the head of his cock toward the entrance to her pussy. She bent her knees to sink a little lower, enough that she could place his cock between her pussy lips."

"Look at me, girl." The command was curt.

Eugenie raised her eyes to meet his dark gaze when she lowered herself onto him. He was big. Despite being so hot and wet and ready for this, her cunt was tight, stretching around him. She paused, chewing on her lower lip as she adjusted to his size.

Aaron placed his hands on her hips, though he didn't press her downward. Neither did he thrust up. He waited, his eyes holding hers until she steadied. Then she sank slowly down the full length of his shaft with a long, low groan.

The sensation of fullness was overwhelming. This was just what she'd been craving and yet so much more. Her sore bottom was forgotten when she squeezed her inner muscles around him and prepared to lift herself up again. Aaron's hands on her hips stopped her from moving.

"Kiss me, girl." His voice was near enough a growl, the words low and husky.

Eugenie leaned forward, stretching her body to reach his mouth with hers. She kissed him, stroking her tongue between his lips to caress the backs of his teeth. Their tongues tangled and danced, and Eugenie let go of the chair to tunnel her fingers through his hair. Her other hand was on his shoulder, then around his neck. She deepened the kiss. Her nipples scraped the fabric of his shirt, sending delightful tingles through her body. She repeated the motion, reveling in the crackle of electricity that seemed to shoot straight to her cunt. She gasped, rocking her hips to seat him more deeply within her.

Aaron reached up to grasp the tangle of her hair, fisting his hand in it and lifting her face away from his. "Ride me, girl. Now."

Eugenie straightened and obeyed. She lifted her body and lowered herself onto him again, trying to keep the motion slow and smooth. Aaron quirked his upper lip.

"You fuck like a girl."

"I am a girl, Sir."

He narrowed his eyes. "Fuck me like you mean it, Genie."

"Like this, Sir?" She lifted her body and this time slammed her weight back down, sending waves of pleasure through her pussy. She couldn't contain her groan.

"Better. But I was thinking more like this." He placed his hands on her hips again, taking her weight, taking control. He lifted her then dragged her back down sharply at the same time as he thrust upward. The stroke was hard, driving deep, and Eugenie cried out at the sheer carnality of it. Her pussy walls started to convulse, her orgasm gathering low down in her body.

"Christ, Sir, yes, yes! May I come? Please, I need..."

"Yes. Come when you like. This is your reward, enjoy it." He punctuated his words with more sharp upward thrusts, each one sending shivers of delight through Eugenie, waves of pure pleasure washing over her.

She looped her arms around his neck and hung on when Aaron took over the action. Her legs turned to jelly. She could not have maintained the motion even if she'd wanted to. If he'd permitted it. Aaron lifted her effortlessly and drove his cock into her again and again, each plunge sending her closer and closer to the edge. Suddenly she was there, spinning, weightless while he pounded his cock inside her.

No sooner did she come down from that high than he was pushing her again, this time by sliding his hand between their bodies to rub her clit. Eugenie clung to him as he angled his cock. He rotated his hips slightly to increase the friction. His thrusts shortened, became more concentrated, and somehow he found that sweet inner place where all her nerve endings seemed to meet. Her pussy spasmed beyond any conscious control of hers as Aaron fucked her, his skill and unerring control obvious. He played her body like a violin.

"Sir, Sir... Oh, God, *Cela se sent tellement bon...*" Eugenie started to convulse again as her third orgasm bubbled and swelled to consume her senses.

"It sure does, honey, *putain, c'est parfai*t." Aaron's low growl rumbled against her ear as he tightened his grip on her. He lengthened his strokes, shuddering when his own climax loomed. He drove his cock deep into her one last time then held still, the head of his cock nudging Eugenie's cervix for an instant before the hot swill of his semen pumped from him to fill the condom.

They lay still for several minutes, neither having the energy to move. At last, Aaron tapped Eugenie on the hip before lifting her from him. He dealt with the condom, knotting the end and dropping it on the floor to be disposed of later. Then he turned her, so she was cradled in his lap, and smoothed the tangled hair from her face.

"Are you satisfied now, my beautiful *petite salope*?"

She snuggled in, gripping the front of his shirt with her fists. "*Oui, monsieur, très satisfait. Merci.*"

Aaron nuzzled the top of her head, loving the sweet smell of her hair. It had a sort of citrus tang to it, very sensual. He breathed her in as she shifted in his arms.

She leaned back, peering up at him. "You spoke to me in French, Sir. And you understood what I said."

"Mmm, I did."

"You speak French?"

"Evidently. Not as fluent as your English, but good enough to keep up with you."

She grinned. "You knew the swear words too."

"Ah yes, but that's what every English schoolboy goes straight for. I've picked up a few more since and I've no doubt you could teach me some as well."

"You have been to France?"

"Yes, many times. It's a beautiful country. I particularly love Paris."

"Ah, me too. I studied in Paris, before I came to England. I would love to go back there. Perhaps, some day."

"Perhaps. For now, though, would you like to take a shower before you get dressed again?"

Eugenie glanced up at him. He gestured toward the small door discreetly situated in a corner of the room — the en-suite facilities.

"Yes, thank you. I would appreciate that."

Aaron thought she seemed reluctant to leave his arms, but made no comment on that. Neither did he hurry her as she uncoiled herself and got to her feet. He was gratified to note the unsteadiness in her gait when she made her way across the room — he liked to make an impression. He was even more impressed by the glowing stripes now adorning her soft, round little ass, precisely positioned about an inch apart, testimony to his skill but also to her fortitude. She'd remained still, even when he knew she must have been hurting like hell.

Oh yes, she was one sweet little subbie, his lovely Eugenie.

She disappeared into the en suite and Aaron got to his feet. He righted his clothing, fastening his jeans, then collected Eugenie's discarded items of apparel from the floor. He folded those and placed them on the chair then picked up the condom and followed Eugenie into the en suite. It was actually a wet room, so she was showering with no curtain or screen. He offered her a polite nod as he skirted the room to reach the toilet, careful to avoid the water splashing about. The last thing he needed was to parade through the club dripping wet, though it did occur to him that it might be fun to strip off and join her.

He decided against it. She was sure to be sore, both outside and in, and he didn't feel their relationship had yet progressed to the cuddling and touching without necessarily fucking stage. He could work on that, though. He smiled at her and left her to enjoy her shower alone.

Minutes later, she emerged, draped in a towel, her damp hair tied on top of her head in a messy knot. She started as she saw him still there, leaning against the far wall in what he supposed had become his customary position. These sparsely furnished rooms were very effective for the sort of scene he liked to start a relationship with—no frills, just testing and exploring boundaries. But they offered no creature comforts at all.

"I… You waited."

"Of course."

"I did not expect you to still be here. I thought, when you did not come in the shower with me, that perhaps you did not want..."

He loved the way her face flushed, such a pretty pink. Aaron walked over to her and looped an arm across her shoulders, pulling her to him. He dropped a quick kiss on her lips.

"I did want, but you've had enough for tonight. You must be feeling the effects."

Her face colored even more, but he noted she didn't deny it. Instead, she smiled, and glanced around the room for her things.

"Oh, you picked up my clothes. Thank you, Sir."

"You're welcome. And when you're dressed, what are your plans for the rest of the night?"

"I do not have plans, Sir."

"Not in a hurry to be away, then?"

"No, Sir. I am not at work tomorrow."

"Good. In that case, will you join me for a drink?"

Her brow wrinkled in puzzlement, though, rather than annoyance. Then her face brightened and she smiled at him, the first proper, brilliant smile he had seen since he'd first laid eyes on her downstairs. It lit up her entire face.

"Yes, Sir, I would love that."

Chapter Three

Now

"That'll be four pounds thirty-five, miss."
"What?"
"Four pounds thirty-five." The taxi driver twisted in his seat to peer at her over his shoulder. Eugenie glanced out of the window, astonished to realize they were back, parked outside the county council headquarters in Morpeth—and the driver wanted to be paid. She scrabbled in her bag for her purse and handed him a five-pound note. He fumbled about, pretending to look for change, obviously hoping she'd tell him to keep it. No such luck. She intended to claim the fare back, so she wanted her change and a receipt too. She waited for him to hand it over—however reluctantly—then she got out of the cab.

Eugenie checked her watch—twenty past five. She might just catch her boss before he left for the day. She could fill him in on the deal she'd struck at the airport, bask in his praise for a bit then rush off home to fill out her application. It occurred to her that it might be considered disloyal to be looking for another job when this one was going so well, but she quashed that notion. Everyone was entitled to their dreams and this Paris opportunity looked to be a dream worth chasing.

And the closing date was in just two days, so she needed to crack on with it.

* * * *

Back in her smart apartment in Newcastle, Eugenie fired up her laptop to download the job details and application form. From the look of it, the whole lot could be done online, which pleased her. It made things easier, simpler. And it was quick. Time was not on her side, but she could meet that deadline if she got on with it.

As she read the full details, she became even more hungry for the job at the Totally Five Star Paris. She drooled over the slideshow tour of the hotel, the public function suites, which she supposed would be her terrain, as well as the private guest accommodation. Even the staff apartments were pleasant and ultra-modern.

And, above all, this was Paris. Beautiful, vibrant, exciting, sensuous Paris, the city Eugenie had loved when she'd lived there briefly. Desire for this gnawed at her stomach. She studied the person specification, tried to frame her somewhat meager experience around it. She convinced herself she could manage this and had actually done most of the things they seemed to expect. Her track record included the breadth of experience required. It was just that Eugenie hadn't been at it for long. There would be other, more experienced applicants. Self-doubt would get her nowhere, though. What she might lack in experience, Eugenie could more than make up for in enthusiasm.

Before starting to complete the form, Eugenie did some more research. She checked out guest feedback and trade press, Totally Five Star's own marketing and financial announcements. To have any real hope of success it would be vital to get under the skin of this company, work out how it ticked, its culture, the values that drove it. Eugenie would need to convince the interview panel that she was just the person they were looking for, and to do that, she needed to understand them. Her strategy now was a simple one—immerse herself in the language of the high-end hotel industry, absorbing the passion evinced by Totally Five Star for offering the very finest, the most luxurious environment for their discerning clientele. This hotel was expensive, but it was the best. Absolutely. It was that simple. So Eugenie had to be the best, too.

She spent the first evening on her research, making notes, bookmarking web pages, assimilating all she could about the prestigious hotel chain that she so badly wanted to infiltrate. She felt like a fraud at some points, was sure they'd see through her finely honed prose and know her for the jumped-up little wannabe she really was. Then she pulled herself up short, delivered the talking to she needed.

She was a genuine applicant and truly believed she could do this job and do it well. She was keen, intelligent. She could learn and would give it her all. The Totally Five Star Paris would have no cause for complaint if she could just convince them to give her a chance. The first hurdle was to get as far as an interview, so her application had to shine to ensure she got in front of them. Eugenie pored over the essential requirements listed in the person specification and double-checked her notes to make sure she had something to say on all of them, some evidence to offer that might help to demonstrate that she was exactly the person they were looking for.

The following day—Saturday—was devoted to filling in the online forms. And even setting aside her desire to impress, Eugenie felt as she read it all back that she had done herself justice. There was nothing more to say that might boost her chances. There had been no opportunity yet to talk to her boss about a reference, but she felt he'd be fine. She closed her eyes and pressed send.

Four days passed, and apart from the automated acknowledgement she'd received within seconds of submitting her application, Eugenie had heard nothing from Totally Five Star. She checked her personal email several times a day. Surely even if they'd decided she was just too young, too raw, they'd do her the courtesy of saying so.

Another two days passed and it was almost the weekend again. HR departments in international hotel chains didn't work on weekends. Did they? If she heard nothing by close of business on Friday, she'd be left stewing all weekend. Still, the ball was not in her court. She could do nothing but wait. As well as crossing her fingers, toes and anything else she could find.

She emerged from the shower on Saturday morning to hear her mobile trilling. It rang off before she could reach it. Probably someone from work looking for an extra to make up the numbers for a tennis match, or maybe a drink later on. She left the phone in her bag and went to get dressed.

It rang again minutes later, and this time Eugenie got to it in time. As she tapped the 'accept' icon, she noted that she had three missed calls. Someone must be desperate for her company. Or maybe it was just one of those firms offering to reclaim her payment protection insurance for her— Christ, those calls got on her nerves.

"Hello, Eugenie d'André speaking."

"Good morning, Miss d'André. I hope I am not disturbing you. I apologize for calling on a weekend. Is this a convenient time?"

The soft female voice spoke in English but Eugenie was not sure if she detected a faint accent. She struggled to know, as English was not her first language either, and accents were difficult to pinpoint. "No, that is quite all right. How can I help you?"

"My name is Madeleine Lambert. I work with the recruitment and selection team at Totally Five Star. You applied to us recently for a position at our Paris hotel."

Eugenie sat down, hard. Her mouth went dry. With her brain on autopilot, she made the polite responses. "Yes, yes, I did. No, this is quite convenient. Do continue. Please."

"We were very impressed by the information you provided for us. The interview panel would love to meet you. Would you be available to come to Paris next week? We hope to hold the interviews on Wednesday. I realize this is short notice, but the hotel manager is about to go on three weeks' leave and we would very much like to make the appointment before she goes."

"What? Yes, Wednesday. Yes, I can be there..." Eugenie was frantically trying to recall what was in her diary for the coming days. Had she any important meetings she just couldn't miss? Would she be able reschedule?

"We will interview in the afternoon, but, of course, if you need overnight accommodation, we will be happy to provide that. You are currently in—the north of England, I think?"

"Yes, I live in Newcastle. In Northumberland." Eugenie did a quick reckoning in her head. A train to London then on to the Channel Tunnel in Kent, followed by the journey across to France. No way could she be sure of arriving in time for an afternoon interview, she would need to travel the day before. "Thank you. I would appreciate a room on Tuesday night, please. Of course, I would be happy to pay—"

"No, that won't be necessary. We are happy to meet your expenses. Travel too, naturally. If you could make the arrangements to suit you and let my office know, we will ensure that you are reimbursed. I will send you an email confirming all this, but given the short timescale, I felt it was important to discuss with you, make sure you could attend next week."

"Yes, of course. Thank you."

"The interview panel would like to see you at three-thirty in the afternoon on Wednesday. The formal interview will take perhaps one hour, and three members of the senior management team in Paris will be present. They would like you to make a ten-minute presentation to them outlining your top three priorities for the first year in the post—should you be the successful candidate. A laptop and projector will be available if you require them. The interview will be conducted in French and in English, as fluency in both languages is a requirement for this post. Will that pose any problems for you, Miss d'André?"

"No, none. That all sounds fine." Eugenie hoped her voice was not shaking, despite the fact that her head was reeling. A presentation to prepare, travel arrangements to be made, her boss to be told, her diary to reshuffle. Christ, she needed to get cracking.

"I will email conformation in the next thirty minutes or so, but may I just wish you all the best for a pleasant trip. And, of course, my best wishes for next week. It has been a pleasure speaking to you today, Miss D'andré."

"And to you, Madame Lambert. *Merci.*"

"*Merci, et au 'revoir.*"

The call ended, and Eugenie sat motionless for several seconds, absorbing this latest development.

An interview! They wanted to meet her. They actually liked the sound of her and wanted to meet her. She'd done it. Or at least, so far so good.

The rest of the weekend passed in a blur of activity. Eugenie went online to book her Eurostar ticket for Tuesday. She would be arriving in Paris in the late afternoon, and would have an opportunity to relax and drink in the atmosphere of the Totally Five Star, perhaps experience it as a guest would. She intended to make good use of the chance. Her research had been copious and detailed, but there was no substitute for firsthand experience.

She also treated herself to a new outfit, a smart but sensually understated silk suit in a deep shade of blue. The calf-length skirt was flattering but very proper, and the jacket almost military in style. She offset the slightly austere look with a loose and flowing pale lemon blouse. She posed in front of her mirror on Sunday evening, and thought she'd managed to strike just the note of sophistication that she wanted—

feminine but businesslike, efficient but without seeming too prim. Yes, she would do.

Monday saw her presenting herself at her boss' office explaining that she needed three days off. She had to tell him why and was delighted by his response. He hoped she didn't get it and he would find her difficult if not impossible to replace, but he wished her all the luck in the world. And, of course, she could rely on him to come up with the goods as far as a reference was concerned.

She spent Monday evening working on her presentation and decided not to avail herself of the IT facilities on offer. In her view, those just complicated things and she wanted their attention on her, not on any fancy graphics. She set out her points, made brief notes that she could rely on to prompt her through the ten-minute slot and decided to trust to her natural instincts. She was a good communicator and could do this.

* * * *

At six-thirteen on the Tuesday, Eugenie exited a taxi in the dropping off bay at the main entrance to Totally Five Star Paris. She shoved three ten-euro notes at the driver, who seemed content with that. He wished her a pleasant stay in Paris and hurtled back out into the teeming traffic.

Eugenie reached for her overnight bag, only to have it taken from her by the quiet but insistent butler who had swept down the front steps with majestic grace to greet her. He gestured for her to follow him, issuing the standard, practiced words of welcome as he ushered her into the spacious, cool reception area. A long, gleaming counter ran the length of one wall and uniformed staff milled in the lobby. As soon as the butler escorted her through the plate glass doors, a young woman headed in their direction, a friendly smile plastered across her face.

"Good afternoon, you wish to check in, *oui*?"

"*Oui. Je suis Eugenie d'André. Je suis ici pour une entrevue d'emploi.*"

"Ah, yes, I have the information. Please, follow me."

Eugenie trailed after the vibrant receptionist, who disappeared behind the long desk to rummage beneath it for a sheaf of papers. She found what she was after and laid the documents on the shining counter.

"I will need your passport, if you please, Mademoiselle d'André."

"Of course." Eugenie handed it over and waited patiently while the necessary formalities were dealt with. It took a few minutes, but soon she was on her way up to the eighth floor where a suite had been reserved for her.

The porter, who insisted on carrying her bag and pressing all the elevator controls, explained that the hotel had four award-winning restaurants and food and refreshments would be available twenty-four hours a day. She would find menus in her room. There was a spa she could use, a lounge bar where she could enjoy live entertainment, a movie theater for the use of guests, a fully stocked library and, of course, two swimming pools, one indoor and one on the rooftop. Eugenie had read up on the hotel before she'd set out and was fairly familiar with the amenities offered but still listened with care as the porter waxed eloquent about the casino and the gym. His pride in this establishment was obvious, and Eugenie wondered if all the staff felt similarly engaged and committed. If so, this was a good sign, hinting at skilled leadership and enlightened management. More than ever, she wanted to make her future here.

As the porter guided her along the hallway on her floor, her sandals sinking into the plush carpeting, he informed her that hotel transport was available to take her wherever she might like to go, whether she wished to explore the city, or to shop perhaps. Or maybe she would prefer to make use of the hairdressing salon, or enjoy a manicure? Or, if it would be more convenient, the hairdresser or a masseuse would come to her room. The usual housekeeping services were available, complimentary drinks were provided in her suite and the flowers would be changed daily.

As they entered her suite, muted classical music greeted her, which the porter explained she could turn off via a concealed console. Or she could make other selections if her tastes ran to something raunchier. A whole system of home entertainment was provided, including a plasma screen television that seemed to take up most of one wall, and naturally Wi-Fi was available throughout the hotel. As if this were not enough, she would find facilities to charge any electrical items she might have with her.

As he bustled about the room, opening windows and stacking her bag on the neat trolley provided, he assured her that Totally Five Star hoped to anticipate any needs she might have. Even so, if there was anything at all that she needed and could not find, she was just to phone down to reception who would be delighted to oblige.

Eugenie thanked him and held out a ten-euro note. He offered her a respectful bow and declined, inviting her instead to leave any gratuity she felt might be appropriate when she checked out. The staff who had served her would share it. He wished her a very pleasant and comfortable stay then slipped back out into the corridor.

Eugenie sank onto the bed, somewhat in awe at her surroundings. She'd known this place was smart, upmarket, the best of the best. But she'd assumed it all applied primarily to the physical environment, the superbly appointed rooms, the elegant architecture, the graceful pieces of French art displayed in the public areas. And, of course, to the Michelin-starred excellence of the food they would serve, as well as the quality of the entertainment to be enjoyed here. She was impressed to learn that Totally Five Star excellence extended to her personal needs and comfort too. It included the understated but efficient welcome, the speedy transition through reception, her questions answered before she even thought of them.

Eugenie lay back and stared at the ceiling, her head a pleasant jumble. She was here. She was really here. This was actually happening. Now all she had to do was make it last.

Chapter Four

Eugenie spent the next few minutes unpacking her bag, not an arduous task given she'd only brought a couple of outfits with her. By this time tomorrow, she'd be checking out. But she wanted her interview outfit to be fresh and uncrumpled, so she hung it carefully on the front of the wardrobe before setting off to explore the suite.

The marble tiled bathroom was fabulous, the complimentary toiletries all neatly arranged on the vanity and stamped with the Totally Five Star crest. She found a fluffy bathrobe and slippers inside a large closet, along with a huge pile of towels and a hairdryer.

Her balcony was small, but offered a view of the Champs-Élysées, and she could just make out the top of the Eiffel Tower, well within walking distance. Maybe later, she'd take a stroll around the city. Tomorrow, perhaps, before she left for the station. Tonight was her chance to soak up the atmosphere of this sumptuous hotel, make sure she was as prepared as she absolutely could be for her interview.

She splashed cool water on her hands and face, retied her hair in a soft pile on top of her head and pocketed the key card. She left her room, intending to visit the guest facilities. There would be nothing quite like a spot of mystery shopping to get a proper feel for the hotel and the Totally Five Star experience. A tour of the conference and banqueting facilities was part of her itinerary for tomorrow so she would concentrate elsewhere this evening. Maybe she could even find some aspect where she might actually suggest improvements, though she somehow doubted that. This whole place was the epitome of perfection.

She glanced through the door of the main restaurant, La Maison, first. She knew this already had three Michelin stars and the hotel was hoping to be awarded a fourth soon. It was usually necessary to book at least three months in advance. The staff was preparing the dining room for evening service, the atmosphere one of sedate and controlled industry, everyone knowing their job and performing it to perfection.

Two further eateries offered a more relaxed, informal ambiance, and their all-day service offered the traditional staples of French cuisine, a range of quiches, steaks, seafood and crêpes. One was decorated in an art deco style that Eugenie loved, the other more modern with stainless steel furniture, the walls and flooring tiled in bright primary colors. But it was the fourth restaurant that made Eugenie catch her breath. This was situated on a shady patio surrounded by a leafy, lush garden. The food was simple and understated, but she knew it would be exquisitely prepared and presented. Eugenie found a free table and took a seat there, intending to enjoy the floral and slightly woody scents of the honeysuckle trailing up the wall beside her. In moments, a waiter appeared with a jug of ice water and a glass. He offered her more refreshments if she wanted them, but assured her she was welcome to just sit and enjoy the evening sunshine.

The aroma of spicy tomato soup proved irresistible, and the next hour or so passed in peaceful enjoyment of her meal. Eugenie usually felt self-conscious about dining alone, but this place made her feel so at home, so relaxed she barely gave it a thought as she ordered her meal. After the soup, she opted for a main course of chicken chasseur and a half bottle of crisp Chardonnay. She declined the desserts but accepted the offer of a *café au lait* to round it off. She surveyed her fellow outdoor diners over the rim of her cup, noting the ready attention of the staff who hovered around the edges of the patio. They were discreet, unobtrusive, but alert to any signal or gesture, rushing across to tend to each and every need.

A family with two young children were having difficulty choosing. The burger, which the eldest boy wanted, seemed not to be on the menu. Nevertheless, one was produced, followed by plain and simple ice cream.

An elderly gentleman requested a newspaper, and his waiter procured one. Nothing was too much trouble. Eugenie was impressed and more than ever, she wanted to be a part of this.

She signed the tab, thanked the staff for her meal and moved off to continue her excursion. She strolled around the intimate little garden, loving the serene, shady nooks as well as the bright tinkling fountain gracing the center of a manicured lawn. The garden wasn't large, but she hadn't thought such an oasis could ever be found in the heart of Paris, not a ten-minute walk from the Place de la Concorde. She adored it.

Back inside the Totally Five Star, Eugenie made for the main lounge bar where a pianist and singer were providing soft background music to accompany the subdued chat of the few guests there at this time. She ordered a sparkling water and perched on a barstool to savor the relaxed mood. As in the terrace restaurant, the staff was attentive, but without the pushiness she so often experienced. No one seemed overenthusiastic, there was no hard sell, but whatever she wanted would be provided.

She left her empty glass on the bar and strolled off in search of something more vibrant, and discovered it in the form of the live bar. Here a comedian was just concluding his set, a performance that seemed to have gone down well with the guests. This room was crowded, the piped music loud, the voices raised over it. Eugenie settled herself at an empty table to wait for the next show to start—a troupe of dancers who did something astonishing and clever with lights. These, too, were popular with the audience, and the bar was full to overflowing by the time Eugenie decided to move on. Her final stop, before turning in for the night, was the library. She hadn't come across such a facility in a hotel previously and was intrigued to see what they might stock.

The room was breathtaking. Carved wooden shelving lined all the walls, and a balcony skirted the room with further shelving above. The titles encompassed a range of international classics in various languages. Signs invited guests to make their selections and scan any books they wanted to borrow into an automated system. They were urged to take books away with them, and if they checked out before they finished to post the book back later. Or if a guest simply preferred to read there, they could avail themselves of the huge leather armchairs and low tables. A coffeemaker was provided for their further comfort and convenience.

Eugenie had the place to herself and settled into one of the chairs to thumb through a book on French antiques of the seventeenth century. She passed a contented half hour or so then felt it was time to turn in. She needed to get plenty of sleep.

Tomorrow was to be a big day.

* * * *

Sleep eluded her. Her brain was whirling, her head full of warring thoughts. She was excited about the coming interview and terrified as well. So much depended on how she might perform in that hour or so tomorrow afternoon. She'd done her homework and was prepared. Why then did she not feel more confident? She was here to carve out a brilliant new career for herself, wasn't she? This was just the beginning.

It was more than that, though — much more. She so did not want to return to Northumberland and her old life. Here, in Paris, she could make a fresh start. No more La Brat.

As she lay in her queen-size bed listening to the low hum of the air conditioning, her mind drifted back to the man who started her on that path. Aaron Praed.

Eugenie had loved him. She now realized it, though at the time she'd not recognized it. Their relationship had progressed fast from that first delightful encounter at The Basement. After the scene, they'd sat drinking coffee together for perhaps a couple of hours before Eugenie had eventually given in to the urge to yawn. She hadn't been bored, just bone-weary. The scene had been demanding and she'd needed to sleep. Aaron had driven her home, kissed her forehead as she'd clambered from his car then taken her mobile number. He'd said he'd call.

All the next day — a Saturday — Eugenie's phone had never been more than a foot away from her hand. He hadn't called. He hadn't said when exactly he'd be in touch, but by the time she'd been undressing for bed, she was in despair. She'd loved their encounter and believed he'd had a nice time too, but in the cool light of day, he'd obviously thought better of continuing their acquaintance. She really should not have been so disappointed, but she hadn't been able to help it. She'd resigned herself to the reality that she had been just a one-off to him. Nice, probably, but not to be repeated.

* * * *

Then

The tinkle of a text was unexpected. She nearly missed it. She checked her phone — an unknown number — and tapped the screen.

Lunch tomorrow? Then my place? A

Eugenie hugged the phone to her chest, forcing herself to take a few minutes before replying. It didn't do to look too eager, desperate even. Then she replied.

Love to. Where and what time?

He replied swiftly.

I'll pick you up at twelve. No underwear.

Eugenie sent her response immediately.

Thank you, Sir. I understand.

He picked her up at exactly the time he'd promised and took her to a pub with a beer garden where they enjoyed a leisurely Sunday lunch. Both knew what was to follow, and there was no rush.

Eugenie had considered carefully what to wear and eventually settled on a loose cotton skirt that fell to just below the knee. As she was wearing no panties, she didn't want any unfortunate wardrobe incidents to occur due to a sudden and inopportune gust of wind. She wondered if Aaron's no underwear rule extended to her bra as well. She could have texted him back for clarification, but opted for a cautious approach. She was therefore braless too under her tight vest top, and could see his appreciation of that fact in Aaron's sexy smile.

They left the pub and strolled across the car park in the direction of his vehicle, a sleek, dark gray BMW.

"You still up for this?"

"Yes, Sir, of course."

He tilted his head in silent acknowledgement as he opened the car door for her. The journey was not long—just ten minutes or so—before he pulled into the driveway of a large semidetached house. Vaguely surprised, Eugenie had expected him to have a flat, as she did.

Aaron got out and came round to open the door for her. She exited the car and took the hand he offered her. He led her up a couple of stone steps to the front door and let them both in. Eugenie hardly had time to glance around the wide hallway before Aaron turned and pressed her face first against the door. He was not rough, but she knew she was not to move.

"Put your hands on the door and lean forward, arse out." He sounded different, curt, commanding. She was fast coming to recognize his Dom voice and knew she would obey whenever she heard that tone.

She did as instructed, clenching her buttocks as he lifted her skirt up around her waist.

"Hard and fast first. Slow comes later."

He didn't wait for her to agree or to comment. Eugenie had no expectation that he would. In accepting his invitation to come here at all, she handed control to her Dom. She was in Aaron's hands now and wanted to be nowhere else.

He parted her buttocks and slid his fingers along her exposed pussy lips. She was wet, had been since she'd first caught sight of him through the door entry CCTV at her apartment. He inserted one long finger into her and swirled it around. Eugenie gasped, clenching her inner muscles.

"So wet. You are one dirty little slut. You want me to fuck you?" The snap of foil punctuated his words.

"Sir, please, I do. Yes, yes, oh…" Her words ended on a moan as he drove his cock full-length inside her, his hands on her hips to hold her still. He withdrew and set up a rhythm of short, rapid thrusts that drove Eugenie wild. She squeezed her pussy around him, trying to grip, gyrating her hips in an attempt to intensify the friction.

He slapped her arse cheek, hard. "Keep still. I'll tell you if I want you to move."

Gasping, Eugenie managed to comply. Her arousal spiking fast, she knew her orgasm was not far away. Recalling the consequences of coming without permission, she groaned. She had to ask.

"Sir, I need…"

"You are to come. Do it now."

Thank God. "Thank you, Sir. I…oh, oh…"

Aaron reached around to pinch her clit between his thumb and fingers and she was gone, convulsing in helpless delight as her body shook with the pleasure of what he was doing to her. He lengthened his thrusts, fucking her hard as he chased his own climax. Moments later, the heat of his semen warmed her inner space. He drove his cock deep and held still, his arm wrapped around her waist to prevent her from moving. Eugenie could feel her heart racing. She panted, acutely conscious of Aaron pressed up close to her back.

He slid his cock from her and lifted his hand to tangle it in her hair. He dragged her head back and around so he could meet her eyes. "Good start, *ma petite coquine*. Upstairs. Now."

Eugenie spent the next two hours in Aaron's bed, or perhaps more accurately spread across it, naked, her wrists and ankles strapped to the posts. She writhed and screamed. She shrieked, begged, pleaded, swore and begged some more as he clamped her nipples, slapped every inch of her body with a suede flogger, spread honey on her pussy lips and proceeded to lick it from her—sloppily. And all the while telling her what the consequences would be if she allowed herself to orgasm again. He pointed out that he'd been kind and considerate enough to take the edge off for her by the front door, but now she could fucking well wait.

And wait she did. For what seemed like hours, he teased and tormented her, playing with her body, bringing her again and again to the very brink of release then hauling her back from the edge. Eugenie wept, she growled her frustration, but he was unmoved, this Dom with iron will and vise-like control.

She'd almost resigned herself to a self-induced climax back at her apartment before he finally allowed her the orgasm she craved. And it rocked her world. The waiting sucked, but Christ, the rush of the eventual release. Eugenie was not sure if she might have passed out at one stage, the intensity of the sensation was so deep, so moving it overwhelmed her. Aaron was inside her, his cock filling and stretching her as the waves of her climax washed over her like a tsunami.

She needed to hold him. Intuitive, he released her hands at the exact right moment and she clung to him as though he were the only solid entity in a world of shifting vapor.

Afterward, he freed her ankles too, and they lay together on his bed, his arms around her as she snuggled in as close as she could get without actually being a part of him. He murmured sweet, reassuring nonsense into her hair, and she knew a bone-deep sense of wellbeing.

That first day at his house set the pattern. They would go out, usually to eat, occasionally to see a film or to the theater then back to his home or sometimes hers for hours of sensual play. They occasionally went to clubs together, fetish clubs like The Basement, where he insisted she wear a collar for the evening to mark her as his.

He hurt her, he spanked her, and she loved it. He whipped her breasts and she begged for more. He clamped her nipples then teased them with ice or hot wax until she pleaded with him never to stop. Aaron tapped reserves of sensuality Eugenie had no inkling she even possessed. He found them all with his voice, his touch, his wicked imagination. At a word, a look, a tilt of his eyebrow, she dropped to her knees at his feet. She was his, utterly.

She'd known, she supposed, that he met needs of hers that went far beyond the sensual. Eugenie was ambitious, driven in her work as well as her personal life. She often came home exhausted, her head buzzing with tomorrow's issues, problems she had to solve, obstacles to find ways around, difficult people or situations she somehow had to manage. She had lain awake on occasions planning, analyzing and, as often as not, just plain worrying.

Aaron put a stop to that with his hands, his flogger and occasionally his whip across her shoulders. Each shuddering climax, each screaming orgasm was a release of her pressure valve, as though he'd unscrewed her lid to allow her inner tensions to fizzle out and cascade harmlessly away. He relaxed her. He grounded her. He kept her sane.

He, too, had a stressful job. He was a police officer, a chief inspector no less. She'd been astonished at that when he'd first told her. He couldn't be more than thirty-two. How had he reached such an exalted rank so quickly? Aaron explained to her that he was in fact thirty-four and went on to fill her in on the police graduate entry system and the accelerated promotion it offered. He had a degree in international law and he'd joined the police straight from university. He was an inspector by the time he was thirty and had just been promoted again. It seemed he was destined for great things.

And still he had time for her.

Eugenie's feelings were hopelessly conflicted as far as Aaron was concerned. At the time, she just felt confused as she hurtled from the heady extremes of passion to the bitter resentment of his discipline.

He was exacting and quite implacable on some things. He insisted on punctuality and the courteous obedience that was the hallmark of a D/s relationship. Without fail, she called him Sir in private—several severe spankings had drilled that into her. She would strip and kneel on command—no argument there. When they were together, he expected her to slip into the submissive mindset, and she invariably did. She had only to step through his door or slide into his car, and her mind shifted into that space where she could do anything—would do anything—he commanded. Pleasing him became all-important. She craved his approval.

In fairness, while she would have willingly allowed her life to revolve around him, he was considerate of her wider responsibilities. He knew her work meant a lot to her, he never expected her to compromise on that. He encouraged her to prioritize her career when she needed to, which might mean days spent away from him on training courses or at conferences. He wanted her to socialize with others, to spend time with friends and colleagues as well as with him. He accompanied her to corporate events on occasion and was able to blend in seamlessly. She knew he cut an impressive figure and that did her embryonic career no harm at all. She appreciated him at the same time that she resented his easy charm around others, which contrasted so sharply with the stern demeanor that he reserved just for her.

His own job meant he kept erratic hours, often working nights and weekends. His routine was unpredictable, and he often had to contact her to reschedule their time together if some emergency called him away. He headed up the Special Operations division, which meant he was in charge of the police dog handling section, underwater search and rescue, the helicopter and the mounted section. He laughingly referred to his domain as the police equivalent of Toys R Us, but the work he was involved in was deadly serious. His teams were called out whenever a child went missing or a body needed to be recovered. He dealt with major crowd control incidents and natural disasters. Eugenie was in awe of him for more reasons than just his whip hand.

His relaxed approach and natural confidence meant that he could hardly be described as possessive but even that wasn't enough. She wanted to be possessed, she wanted to feel he cared, that he craved her even a fraction as much as she lusted after him. His control irritated her. His unflappable calm perplexed her. He could make her scream, whereas she couldn't seem to ruffle his composure at all.

She started to act up, just to get a rise from him. She would arrive late, having spent ten minutes sitting in her car outside his house. He'd know—he had eyes and windows. Occasionally, he'd spank her for it, but usually he didn't, as he knew that was what she was wanting. He wouldn't be manipulated.

She might drink too much on her occasional nights out with her friends, despite his clear instructions that she not do that. Afterward, he always asked her, and she always told him the truth. Then he did spank her, hard. Her personal safety was important to him. He wouldn't compromise that or permit such carelessness from her. On one occasion, she drove home after four glasses of wine. Of course, she confessed to it, and he was livid. He made her wait for nearly thirty-six hours until his anger cooled sufficiently before he was prepared to lay a hand on her. Then he bent her over a chair, tied her in place and thrashed her naked bottom with his belt while she screamed and writhed and begged him to stop. He did stop, eventually. Eugenie was uncertain as to whether she'd ever be able to sit again. Her ass felt to be on fire, her every muscle stiff from her desperate struggles and her throat ached from screaming. She hadn't used her safe word, though.

Her face was wet with tears, and she shivered uncontrollably as he finally released her. Then he carried her to his bed and lay with her, holding her until she stopped crying and her body was still again. He laid her face down and massaged cream into her flaming buttocks, his fingers cool and gentle as they touched her tender skin. She apologized, cried some more and swore never to drink and drive again. He kissed her, then made slow, leisurely love to her. The matter was closed.

Eugenie knew she'd never drive after having so much as one glass of wine again.

Chapter Five

Now

Eugenie woke, feeling remarkably refreshed. She stretched and opened her eyes, blinking at the unfamiliar room that greeted her.

Totally Five Star Paris. She was here in a guest suite, enjoying the understated luxury as she prepared to be interviewed for the job of a lifetime. She sat up, planning her day even before she was fully awake. Shower, dress, breakfast, then perhaps spend an hour or two prowling the lounges and public areas. She could learn a lot from watching the other guests, listening, observing their reactions to the hotel, their needs, the attentive staff. She could use these remaining hours to deepen her understanding of how this place ticked, which would be all to the good later.

The afternoon she would spend back here in her room. Maybe she would shower again before dressing for the interview. She'd apply her makeup, subtle of course, since she was going for the natural look. She would arrange her hair in a neat, businesslike coil at the back of her head, fastened with a wooden claw she'd bought just for this occasion. She may have had only a few days' notice, but she'd used the time well. Her planning had been meticulous.

She was realistic enough to know that she may not succeed today, that there might be other candidates more impressive than she. But Eugenie was determined that she would not look back on this and berate herself that there was anything more she could have done. She would review her notes then probably run through her presentation a couple more times in front of the mirror.

Practice makes perfect, and perfect was what might—just might—get her this job.

* * * *

At precisely three twenty-three, Eugenie presented herself at the entrance to the hotel's executive management suite. The door was marked Staff Only with a button to gain admittance. She pressed and waited.

A buzzer sounded, followed by a smooth female voice. "*Bonjour, puis je vous aider?*"

"*Bonjour, madame. Je suis Eugenie d'André…*"

"*Ah oui, nous vous entenderons. Entre, s'il vous plait.*"

The buzzer sounded again, followed by a quiet click. Eugenie pushed the door. It opened and she stepped inside.

She stood in an empty, carpeted corridor. Double doors ran all down one side. The other side sported a series of prints. She thought she recognized one or two of the artists, Lowry certainly, perhaps Monet. Constable's The Hay Wain was unmistakable.

As she contemplated which direction to head in, a middle-aged woman appeared from a door about halfway down the hallway and bustled in her direction.

"Mademoiselle d'André, how nice to meet you." She spoke in English so Eugenie answered in like manner, accepting the proffered hand for a brief shake.

"Thank you, it is lovely to be here."

"You are welcome, very welcome. My name is Elise Rougin. I am the general manager here at the Totally Five Star Paris. I am chairing the interview panel today. I will introduce you to my colleagues in a few minutes, but first, may I offer you some refreshment?"

"A glass of water would be nice, if that is not any trouble."

"None at all. Please follow me." She gestured Eugenie into a small side room where a bottle of chilled water and several glasses sat on a low table. There was a leather couch, too — clearly some sort of waiting area.

"Please help yourself to water. Your interview will commence in ten minutes. First, you might like to glance at this..."

She handed over a sheet of paper. "This is the list of questions we will ask you at the interview. It is our intention to get the best from you, so we want to hear all you have to tell us about yourself. By letting you know what we intend to talk about, you have an opportunity to collect your thoughts, even make a few notes should you wish. You only have ten minutes, so not sufficient time to browse the Internet or phone your friends. Enough, though, to know that we have no surprises lurking. There are no trick questions. We are not looking to catch you out.

"Also, if there is anything you really want to share with us that we have not included in our topics for discussion, please feel free to mention it at the end of the interview. There will be an opportunity to ask us questions and, following the interviews, our security team will conduct each candidate on a tour of the conference and banqueting facilities if you would like to take advantage of that."

Eugenie was astonished and impressed. She'd never come across such a practice before, but it made perfect sense. And it chimed completely with her desire to be as prepared as possible for this. She could not have asked for a better start.

"Thank you. I—"

Madame Rougin raised a hand in friendly dismissal. "Please, make yourself comfortable. I will be back in ten minutes." She closed the door quietly as she left.

Eugenie poured herself a glass of water and wasted no time in perusing the list of questions. Relief washed over her. She could offer a decent response for all of these issues.

She had several ideas about how she'd approach growing the corporate events side of the Totally Five Star Hotels. She had read up on recent and current trends in the hospitality industry and was familiar with the main areas of European Union legislation relating to public safety. And she could manage the equality and diversity stuff readily enough. She had a list of her own training needs, which she had already recognized for herself, and by asking her about this, the Totally Five Star chain seemed intent on developing their employees' skills.

The final question delighted her. They intended to ask her to imagine herself five years in the future. Those had been the best years she could possibly hope for both professionally and personally. She was to look back and pick out for them the reasons why those years had been so good, what had gone well, what had she done to create such success? And what did she intend for the following five years?

It was a clever way to ask the question, engaging candidates' imaginations and flair as well as their professional skills. Eugenie knew she could craft an impressive response. She spent the next few minutes scribbling feverish notes on the reverse of the sheet and looked up in surprise when the door opened again.

"We are ready for you now. Please come with me." Madame Rougin stood in the doorway holding the door open for her.

Eugenie put the cap back on her pen, picked up her notes and the sheet she'd brought with her outlining her presentation, then she followed Madame Rougin.

* * * *

The interview had gone well. Better than well—it had been a dream. Eugenie knew she'd done herself justice and could tell by the reactions of the panel that they were impressed. She was particularly encouraged by the quiet, friendly smile and occasional nods from the hotel's medical officer, introduced as Fleur Mansouri. She seemed especially interested in Eugenie's ideas for adding childcare and play facilities which would enable delegates to bring their families to events. The other member of the panel, Pierre Rivaux, was in charge of finance and admin, including human resources. He quizzed Eugenie carefully regarding her projected out-turn figures, and he was keen to explore her grasp of promotion and marketing. He seemed well satisfied with her responses.

Madame Rougin concentrated on the development and strategy aspects of the interview, and was forensic in her questions on that final topic. Eugenie was glad of her notes and felt she gave a good account of herself. As the interview drew to a close, she asked a couple of questions of her own about the management structure and Totally Five Star's policies on conservation and carbon emissions. Not her central area of concern, but these were important matters to her even so.

"Thank you, Miss d'André. That concludes all our questions for you. Do you have anything else you'd like to mention before we finish?" Madame Rougin smiled across the interview table as she rearranged her notes into a neat pile.

Eugenie had observed that the hotel manager had been writing a lot during her interview, and she took it to be a promising sign. "No, I think that's everything I wanted to say. Do you know when you'll be making your decision?"

"Soon. Today, probably. We have another candidate to see and we met with three before you. We are hoping to be able to let the successful candidate know by tomorrow or the day after—subject to getting verbal references. Do we have a mobile phone number for you, Miss D'andré? Ah yes, here it is, on your application form."

Her smile remained pleasant, but Eugenie knew the interview was concluded and the panel had to move on now to the next and final candidate. She would not outstay her welcome by stretching out the time. She stood and held out her hand to Madame Rougin.

"Thank you for inviting me here to meet you. This is a beautiful hotel. May I wish you every success, whatever your decision."

The hotel manager shook her hand, her smile unwavering. Eugenie took her leave of the other two panel members as the door opened at her back.

Madame Rougin glanced toward the door. "Ah, thank you. Miss d'André, you did say you wanted to make a tour of the conference and business center facilities, did you not?"

"Yes, I would appreciate that."

"You are honored. Our director of security is here to conduct you personally, it would seem. May I introduce…"

Eugenie turned. The smile of welcome died on her face.

Aaron Praed.

"Miss d'André and I have met before. In England. You look well, Eugenie."

His slow, easy drawl drifted across the room, the modulated tones in sharp contrast to her own breathless stuttering.

Stunned, incoherent, Eugenie could only gape at him. The careful, perfectly orchestrated poise that had served her so well for the last hour deserted her entirely.

"Aaron! What? I mean, how…? I thought you were in England, in the police." She stood rooted to the spot, staring at him, incredulous. So much for not wasting any more of the panel's time.

"I decided on a career change. Are you ready for the tour?"

"I, what…?"

"Miss d'André, are you all right? If you'd prefer a different escort, I am sure Monsieur Praed could assign another member of his staff...?" Doctor Mansouri, her face etched with concern, had come around the table and now touched Eugenie's elbow.

"No. Yes, I mean... That is..." Her sophisticated persona lay in tatters. Eugenie could have wept were it not for the absolute certainty that this would only serve to convince the panel that she was in fact a total idiot, nothing more than an overemotional impostor attempting to hoodwink them into thinking she might be able to hold down a responsible position in their pristine, slick organization. Certainly, that was how she felt in that moment, confronted by a man she never expected to see again.

A Dom she'd loved. And lost in such spectacular fashion.

It was ironic in the circumstances that Aaron should be the one to rescue her, to salvage her pride. Or maybe he always had. He closed the distance between them in seconds to place his hand under her elbow. "Would you like to follow me, Eugenie? I'm sure you'll find our facilities of interest—and impressive too. The TFS ballroom holds eight hundred guests, sufficient for more or less any gathering. Smaller suites offer more intimate surroundings..."

He propelled her from the room, all the while murmuring his cover story of a sales pitch, which she realized was intended to distract attention from her until she could recover her wits. She exited the room beside him to be ushered along the carpeted hallway and out of the executive suite. Once back in the public lounge, Aaron guided her to a low couch at one end of the room. He gestured to one of the waitstaff, and in moments a jug of ice water and a glass materialized in front of her. He poured her a drink and sat back while she sipped it.

"Better now?" He took the glass from her.

Eugenie met his eyes for the first time since that initial flash of stunned recognition. "Thank you. Yes. You surprised me, that's all. I hadn't expected to see you again."

"Evidently. Not so much a surprise as a shock, I'd say. Am I still so terrifying to you?"

"No." *Yes.*

"Well, that's good then. Shall we continue?"

Eugenie was beginning to think there really was no point in pursuing the tour. Even if she hadn't entirely ruined her chances with that ridiculous display back in the interview room, Aaron was sure to be consulted about his opinion and he wasn't likely to give her a glittering testimony. She could imagine it now.

A promising candidate, were it not for her propensity to take dangerous risks and refuse to accept the consequences of her mistakes. Won't even submit to a well-earned caning. Given to episodes of violence when provoked.

It was true enough, fair comment even. She had broken the cardinal rule in the submissives' handbook. Thou shalt not attack thy Dom — especially not with his own cane.

Despite her fatalistic acceptance that this glorious dream was to end in ignoble failure, Eugenie followed Aaron as he conducted her through the conference and events suite. She hadn't really listened to his remarks as he scooped her from the interview room so he repeated the patter, drawing her attention to the dimensions of the ballroom, the flexibility of the various other meeting and banqueting facilities. All were tastefully furnished, provided with audio and HD video facilities, staging, a range of seating styles and, of course, ready access to refreshments. Despite her inner turmoil, Eugenie was impressed. The video tour she'd watched back in her apartment did little justice to the real thing. Totally Five Star Paris was quite simply superb.

But it was not for her. Not now. Not ever. Aaron would see to that. If he hadn't already.

Chapter Six

Aaron took more pleasure than he'd expected he would in seeing Eugenie again. She looked to have lost weight, but she was still a sexy little package. He wondered if she was still in the lifestyle but thought probably not. He hoped not, if her last encounter with him was any indication of her approach. Submission did not come naturally to Eugenie d'André. Which was a pity, but it couldn't be helped.

"You didn't seem surprised to see me. You knew I was one of the candidates."

It was a statement, not a question. Aaron paused at the door to the small lecture theater to answer her. "Of course. As Head of Security, it's my job to run background checks on all the candidates."

"Yet I was still invited for an interview. Why?"

"Elise was very impressed with your application. You look good on paper." *And in the flesh.*

"They won't offer the job to me now. I made an absolute fool of myself."

"Not absolute, I'd say."

"I would. And even if I hadn't…"

He was interested in the play of emotions flitting across her face—annoyance, frustration and disappointment? Yes, disappointment dominated. She met his eyes again, squaring her shoulders. "I need to go back to my room now. I have to pack and check out."

He lifted an eyebrow. "I see. What time's your train? You are on Eurostar, I assume?"

"Yes. Eight o'clock."

He knew she was lying. Her claim for travel expenses had passed across his desk as part of the security check. He knew full well her train didn't leave until after ten. Clearly, she was desperate to get away from him—and not for the first time. He inclined his head and gestured her toward the lift.

He had to admire her powers of recovery as she made her way across the expanse of deep pile carpet. The seductive sway of her hips had lost none of its allure. The determined set of her chin was familiar too. She held her back ramrod straight, the very picture of dignity in defeat, though why she appeared so convinced her application would fail was beyond him. As far as he was aware—both from what he'd read of the candidates and the comments of his colleagues as they'd agreed on the short list—she was the standout candidate, the one to beat.

It was clear to him that she thought he intended to derail her efforts, that a bad word from him would put an end to her chances. In all probability, she already believed he had done just that. Privately, he doubted he held such sway with the senior management team, but even if he did, that was never his plan. If she was the best candidate, if the interview panel arrived at the conclusion that she was the person they wanted to appoint, the job would be hers. It was that simple.

Or not. If she did come to work at Totally Five Star Paris, things would be far from simple. But whatever the outcome as far as their professional association went, their personal relationship was over. That final scene with her three years ago still haunted him and he could never risk such a thing happening again.

* * * *

Then

Eugenie was late. Again. She did this on purpose, he knew that. She could have left home in plenty of time but had chosen to cut it fine, hoping to provoke him into a solid bare-bottom spanking. She loved that, seemed to need it. He might well oblige her, but he was determined the choice would be his, not hers. He wouldn't let her manipulate him.

His mobile rang and he checked the screen. Eugenie. He took the call.

"I will be ten minutes, no more. Just leaving now."

"Then you'll be twenty minutes. Which will make you half an hour late, Eugenie."

"I apologize."

She didn't sound in the least contrite. He wondered if denying her an orgasm for the next two days or so might not be a more effective deterrent for the future. It probably would, but the effect would be to wreck his weekend too. Eugenie's orgasms were an utter delight, so he was loath to deny either one of them.

She was lovely, but she was a brat. She tested him continually, pushing, goading, manipulating. His beautiful little Genie was probably worth the bother, though there were times when he wondered.

He strolled into his kitchen to pour a cup of coffee. He sipped the bitter brew, strong and black, just as he liked it, and contemplated the coming scene. He had planned an hour or so of erotic play featuring a flogger and a rather sweet bullet vibrator. That would be followed by a shower, then they could share an intimate pasta at a bistro down the road. Maybe afterward he could indulge her yearning for a spanking—he'd noticed she always slept better if her bottom was red and sore.

His phone beeped. A text.

Two minutes.

Puzzled, he pried the slats of his Venetian blinds apart to check if her car was outside already. No, not a sign of her. He finished his coffee and poured another then waited out the two minutes.

Three and a half minutes later, the purr of her engine in his driveway alerted him to her arrival. He glanced from the window to see her smart little Volkswagen roll to a stop behind his BMW. Eugenie emerged from the car. She looked flustered as she leaned back in to grab her phone from the passenger seat. She reached into the back for her overnight bag and scurried toward his front door.

Aaron waited in the kitchen. The door was unlocked and she would let herself in. He was thinking, assessing the evidence, and not liking the conclusions he was arriving at.

How many fucking times did he need to tell her that her safety mattered? It mattered more than anything to him. He knew there was no way her first call could have been made as she was leaving her flat. She must have been already en route. And that text a couple of minutes ago—definitely. Christ, she liked to live dangerously. The copper in him responded to the law breaking, but it was the Dom in him that reacted to the sheer bloody madness of it. She could have been killed, or killed some other innocent road user. This had to stop.

He heard her voice in his hallway. "I'm here. I'm sorry to be late, but it is only about twenty minutes. I will stay longer tomorrow to make up for it."

She burst into the kitchen and dropped her bag to the floor before rushing at him, her face upturned for a kiss. He halted her with one imperious finger.

"Your phone, please, Eugenie."

She teetered before him, her expression uncertain. "My...?"

"Phone. Now." He held out his hand. Eugenie placed her phone in his palm. He switched it on, keyed in her passcode then started trawling through her calls log. He really had no need to go through the exercise. He knew exactly when the device had been used.

"You said you were just leaving?" He quirked an eyebrow at her, his face still lowered to study the small screen. "Where were you really when you made that call?"

"I, I..." She wasn't a fool. They'd talked about this before and she knew exactly where he was heading. She had the good sense to lower her gaze. "On the inner ring road. I had stopped at the traffic lights. I just... I did not want you to be worried about me."

Fucking hell. Has she no bloody idea at all?

"And the text?"

She shifted, her posture betraying her apprehension. "There was a hold-up. Roadwork."

Her tone was breathless now. He could tell she was nervous. He wondered if her lateness had been a ploy. In fact, on reflection, he was convinced of it and as such it wouldn't work. Arriving twenty minutes late wasn't going to earn her the spanking she seemed to crave. But her thoughtless disregard for his rules about safe driving? No, he didn't think that was Genie being manipulative. That had been a mistake on her part, a dangerous error, and one he intended to correct. She would not enjoy the consequences. Neither would he, but he was prepared to do whatever was necessary to get his point across and make it stick.

But not now. Now he was just too fucking angry to dare go anywhere near her. Certainly he was in no mood to deliver a severe punishment. He needed to be calm for that, in control. Tomorrow would have to do.

"I think you know the rules, but oblige me by repeating them now."

"Rules, Sir?"

"The Highway Code, particularly in relation to the use of mobile phones whilst driving."

"Oh, those rules. You are playing policeman with me, Sir?" She smiled, her expression coquettish.

"If I was playing policeman, I'd be writing you out a fixed penalty notice, not contemplating a whipping." His tone was harsh enough to break rocks, expertly modulated to maximum effect.

"A whipping, Sir?" Her playful smile evaporated. She stared at him, her eyes widening. "I am sorry and I have said so."

He noted with some satisfaction that the color had drained from her face. She was at last taking this matter seriously. He would ensure she was left in no doubt as to how gravely he regarded her carelessness.

He'd stopped her from drinking and driving, so now he would up the ante and make sure she never repeated this offense either.

"As I recall, you apologized for being late. I have no intention of punishing you for that. You know why you deserve to be disciplined."

Her eyes glistened with tears that she tried to blink back. "I phoned you whilst I was driving. I admit it and I am very sorry. Please, Sir, there is no need for this."

He stiffened his resolve. She could be so very appealing, but he had no intention of relenting. In any case, he was immune to tears. They came often enough with the Dom territory. "My call, not yours. But it'll have to wait. Go to bed now, Eugenie."

"Bed, Sir? But I thought—"

"Alone. You know where the spare room is. I don't expect to see you again until tomorrow morning. Then, provided I'm no longer so fucking angry with you, you will accept whatever punishment I decide on. After that, if you feel so inclined, you can apologize and I'll be listening. Now, do you have any questions?"

"I do not want to go to bed. At least, not alone. I came here to… It is only four o'clock in the afternoon, Sir. I am not a child."

"Believe me, I know you aren't a child, though you do behave like one sometimes. But you're a woman, and a submissive, so act like it. I expect you to obey and to be courteous about it. Also, I know what the time is. This is not up for discussion. Either you go upstairs and stay in my spare room until tomorrow, or you go home now and return here in the morning. Ten o'clock. Sharp."

She stood before him, clenching and unclenching her fists. Her jaw was set, her lips flattened in—what? Anger, frustration? All of that, he suspected. She might be lovely—his cock hardened every time he laid eyes on her—but she had a lot to learn about submission, about obedience and about the proper demeanor to display for her Dom. He waited with his arms folded across his chest as she appraised her options.

A full minute ticked away before she turned on her heel and marched for the door, bending to retrieve her bag as she went. She might have muttered something along the lines of 'arrogant bastard' as she left the room. Aaron let it pass. This time. The clatter of her feet on his staircase informed him of the choice she had made.

Tomorrow would not be easy—for either one of them.

* * * *

At around seven thirty that evening, he took her a tray of food. Nothing special, just some cheese sandwiches, a pot of tea and a bowl of tomato soup. He was no culinary genius—it was only some stuff he'd heated up from a tin—but he knew she must be hungry. Starving her had no part in his plan. She was seated cross-legged in the center of the double bed when he entered. She looked to have been crying.

"Please, Sir, I am bored. And lonely. I want to be with you."

"Tomorrow. After. I brought you this." He set the tray on the bedside table and turned to head for the door.

"Sir, please. I want to sleep with you. Please. Do not leave me here alone."

He paused. She was tempting. He loved the softness of her sleek body in his bed, especially since she'd managed to gain those few pounds she needed to fill out her curves. It wouldn't do, though. He turned his head to regard her over his shoulder.

"Eat up, then get some sleep, if you can. I'll see you in the morning."

* * * *

Eugenie padded into his kitchen just after nine o'clock. She'd obviously showered, her hair still damp, and she wore a pretty yellow sundress. It was one of his favorites and he wondered if it had been selected for that reason. But she still looked a wreck.

Aaron considered delaying her punishment. He'd decided on a caning, the most severe physical discipline at his disposal just now. If this didn't work, he wasn't entirely sure what would, though he was confident he could come up with something. He knew she'd struggle with what he intended to do to her — it was his absolute intention — but he doubted whether a decent night's sleep would have made any real difference.

He'd made her wait and he knew that being incarcerated on her own overnight was what had really taken its toll. Best just to get it done with now and let the pair of them move on. They might yet salvage something from this weekend.

"Good morning. You're early."

"Is that all right, Sir? I mean... I was hungry again. May I have some food?"

He noted that an air of contrition did at last seem to be creeping in. Her manners had improved since yesterday and the dress denoted a clear attempt to please him. Maybe he was starting to get through to her.

"Of course. Cereal? Toast? A yogurt?" He gestured at the fridge, indicating that she should help herself to whatever she fancied.

Eugenie selected an orange and mango fat-free yogurt then joined him at the kitchen table. Aaron passed a teaspoon across the table to her.

"Would you like some tea?"

"Yes, please."

He shoved the last of his own wholemeal toast in his mouth and stood to fill the kettle. Neither of them spoke until he set her steaming cup in front of her. He resumed his seat and waited until she'd finished her yogurt before he spoke again.

"Did you put on any underwear?"

She held his gaze over the rim of her cup. "Yes, Sir. You did not give me any other instructions."

"I think you know by now that I rarely allow you to wear knickers when we're here together." So much for trying to impress him.

She lowered her eyes. "I am sorry, Sir. I did not think."

Aaron got to his feet again. "When you've finished your tea, join me in the dining room. Leave your panties in here." He strode from the room without a further glance in her direction.

Ten minutes later, the door to the dining room opened and Eugenie slipped inside. She closed the door quietly and leaned back against it, watching him from across the room.

"I am here, Sir. As you instructed me. What is it that you intend to do?"

Always that note of belligerence, of challenge. Despite her exquisite responses when they scened together, he did wonder if she was truly submissive at heart. Today might help to clarify that. Aaron straightened, shifting his weight from where he'd been leaning against the dining table. As he moved, Eugenie's gaze was drawn to the narrow rattan cane laid on the tabletop.

She lifted her chin, her eyes wide. She shook her head quickly.

"No, Sir. Not a cane. We have never —"

"What's your safe word, Eugenie?"

"You know what it is. Maupassant," she whispered her response, all the time shaking her head.

"Your safe word stops this. Nothing else will. Ten strokes." He gentled his tone. "It will soon be over. I suggest we get on with it."

"No. No. This is not fair. I thought... I expected..."

"No, Eugenie?" Aaron's tone was soft, but he made no move to approach her. She had to submit to this without any coercion from him. He would never force her.

"Please, Sir, why are you continuing with this? I have said I am sorry."

Aaron schooled his features to be as inscrutable as he could manage. In truth, he took no pleasure in these sorts of interludes, but he wouldn't shirk his responsibility to her as her Dom. "I know this seems harsh, but you need to learn. And it's best you learn before you kill someone, quite possibly yourself." He paused for a few seconds then added, "I do care about you, Genie. I'm not doing this because I want to hurt you, but I do intend to teach you a lesson. You have to obey me in this matter, and the cane today will help to ensure that. So, unless you intend to safe word, I'd appreciate it if you'd bend over the table and lift your skirt, please."

She made no move to do as he'd instructed. "But, I thought that today we might—we might be together again. That we could scene, have fun. A caning will hurt me—really hurt. I do not understand why you insist on this."

"I know it'll hurt. But you will survive it. You might not survive a head-on collision if you carry on driving as you have been." He moved to the side of the table, his arms folded. He captured her gaze and held it. "We did talk about caning when we first got together. I asked if you wanted to put it on your hard limits list. You said no, so here we are. We'll proceed at your pace, of course. I'm in no hurry. But neither of us leaves this room until the ten strokes have been administered. Are we clear?"

Long seconds ticked past as she glared at him, conflicting emotions warring across her face. He wasn't at all sure she was going to go through with this.

At last, she stepped forward, started to make her way toward him. She crossed the room slowly, her eyes fixed on the cane. Even as she rested her palms on the table, Aaron expected to hear her safe word.

Instead, she turned to face him. "I do not want to do this."

"I know that."

"But still, you insist. You are a mean bastard."

"I do insist. And in the circumstances, I'm going to let that last remark go, but watch it, Eugenie. My patience is not limitless. So now, safe word or bend over."

Her eyes blazing, Eugenie leaned forward. She took her time, but at last she was positioned across the tabletop, her arms outstretched in front of her. Her chest lay flat on the smooth surface, her back and hips ramrod stiff. Tension and—unless he was very much mistaken—fury radiated from her in waves.

"Your skirt, please. Lift it up around your waist, if you will, and bundle it underneath you."

He swore she growled, actually snarled as she obeyed his last instruction.

At last, she was ready, or as much as he supposed she was ever going to be. Her buttocks were pale, quivering and utterly beautiful. Despite her willful nature, he couldn't recall a woman who turned him on nearly as much as Eugenie.

She was scared, but was masking that beneath a veneer of simmering and very far from submissive rage. Oh yes, today's events were clarifying his view of what his little Genie's true nature was, and that being so, he was by no means convinced any more that he could, or should, continue. A submissive personality would accept what was about to happen. She might hate it, might scream and plead and struggle, but ultimately she would accept his right to discipline her and she would learn from it. If that was not Eugenie's innate character, her reactions would be different. Unpredictable even. Worse still, if he was correct in his suspicion that she was not submissive at heart, then what he was about to do would be no more than abuse?

And if he was right about that, what the hell had they been doing these past few weeks?

He reached for the cane and opened his mouth, intending to tell Eugenie that she could leave. He never got the chance.

Afterward, he would reflect that whatever tenuous hold she had on her self-control snapped in that instant.

"No!" Eugenie screamed the word as she grabbed for the cane before he could get his hands on it. She pushed herself from the table, whirling to face him as she did so. She hurled herself at him, slashing at his chest with the cane. She landed one searing stroke before he grabbed her wrist. There was a brief struggle before the rattan clattered to the polished wood floor, but Eugenie was not done. She continued to fight him, flailing her fists, kicking at his shins with a ferocity he would not have dreamed she could lay claim to. Acting on pure instinct, he wrapped his arms around her, preventing further damage, eventually wrestling her to the floor and pinning her there.

She lay under him, bucking against his weight, her expression furious. "Let me go, you vicious bastard. I hate you. You can go fuck yourself."

"I'm beginning to think it may come to that, love. I'll let you go, but no more throwing punches. Right?"

"*Lâches-moi. Je te deteste.*"

"Evidently. Okay. You can get up." He released his grip on her wrists and levered himself from her, paying close attention to those lethal feet of hers.

As soon as she was free, she scrambled to her feet, breathing heavily. She fixed her eyes on the cane, lying underneath the table now.

"Oh no, don't even think about it." His tone was low, ominous and sufficiently commanding to get her attention. She seemed to abandon her plans to resume her assault on him with his own cane and started to back away instead.

"Eugenie, we need to talk about this, about what just happened."

"I do not want to talk to you. I never want to see you again. You are cruel, and...and a bully. I loathe you."

"Genie, sit down, please."

"No. No. No! I am leaving. Now. You cannot stop me."

"Honey, you're free to go, though I think you should stay. At least until you feel more calm."

"*Bâtard!*" She turned on her heel and flung herself toward the door.

Aaron made no move to stop her.

She clattered upstairs to emerge a couple of minutes later with her bag. Aaron was waiting at the bottom of the stairs when she came down. Eugenie barged past him without a word, heading for the front door.

"Genie, please." Aaron knew their relationship lay in tatters. There would be no coming back from this. Even so, he would have preferred her not to leave in this mood. Short of manhandling her to the floor again, though, the choice wasn't his. She flounced out of his house, slamming the door behind her. A few seconds later, her car roared from his driveway.

That was the last time he saw her.

Chapter Seven

Now

Back in her apartment, Eugenie lay in her bed and stared at the ceiling. She'd arrived home around midmorning the day after her interview, and had gone straight to bed. She'd managed a couple of hours sleep on the Eurostar crossing, but was still exhausted. Now, it was late afternoon. She was awake, more or less, and felt utterly miserable. The loss of the shining opportunity at TFS Paris was painful, intensely so, almost like a bereavement. Her entire glittering future canceled. She knew she should never have allowed her imagination such free rein, should never have fallen into the trap of actually envisaging herself in Paris, working in those elegant surroundings.

She should not have let herself dream. And she should definitely never have let herself believe, not for one moment, that the dream could become real.

Except it had. Almost. She knew in her heart that she'd nailed it. She'd been sure, quietly confident as the interview drew to a close, that they were likely to offer her the job. Her efforts had been worthwhile, she'd done the work and the prize was hers—until she had turned and seen Aaron Praed standing behind her. Her nemesis.

As she lay there, contemplating the pattern on her wallpaper, she remembered her sheer terror as she had faced him across his dining room three years earlier, her eyes drawn to the cane he'd apparently intended to use on her. His handsome features had been so calm, so implacable as she'd pleaded with him.

But he had been so merciless, intent on meting out the punishment he'd decided on. She vaguely recalled that he'd offered her the chance to use her safe word, and she was not entirely sure why she hadn't taken him up on that. He would not have forced her. Nothing ever happened in a BDSM context that the submissive did not consent to. She knew that, had known it then, but somehow none of that had registered.

She'd been scared, rigid with fear, then furious. She had been enraged by his arrogance, his sheer bloody-minded conviction that he was right and that he was entitled to punish her as he saw fit. The precious law he worked for would have been far less harsh—a fine and a couple of points on her license at the most. But no, he was judge, jury and fucking executioner.

She had been confused too. She had thought she'd known the rules, understood their deal, but apparently not. He'd continued to punish her, first by banishing her to the spare room then with his cane. It had been relentless, never-ending. It had seemed to her she could do nothing right, could find no way to atone for her mistakes. Or that's how she had seen it then.

Not now. If she was entirely honest, she knew he had been right. His actions that weekend were stern but not disproportionate. Such a pity she hadn't seen it that way at the time.

As she'd bent over his dining table, her bottom bared for the caning, she had been overtaken by what she might now describe as some sort of red mist, a sense of righteous anger, bitterness at his intransigent attitude and an overwhelming urge to retaliate. Some sort of temporary insanity had taken over and she had struck him in anger, several times. First with the cane, then, when he'd disarmed her, with her fists and feet as she fought him. He'd overpowered her with ridiculous ease, which had enraged her even more. She had felt impotent, vulnerable, a coward, afraid. All of those things had bubbled and boiled within her, until they'd erupted in that burst of white-hot fury that had resulted in her striking out at her Dom as she had.

She had fled his house, sobbing as she'd driven away, whether from rage or grief, she had no idea even now. She'd gotten as far as the end of his road before she'd stopped and curled up in her seat to let her emotions flow freely. She'd wept for what had seemed like hours, but in reality, it must have been a few minutes. Eventually, her face a red, blotchy mess, she'd managed to drive herself home. Once there, she'd locked herself in and turned off her phone. Three days later, when she'd returned to work and had had no option but to switch it back on, she'd found she had three missed calls from Aaron. He'd left two voicemail messages, each one asking if she was all right and to please call him. She'd deleted the messages, and his number for good measure.

A week later, she'd bitterly regretted her decision. As her temper had cooled, and the shock of what had happened in his dining room receded, she'd begun to realize that she missed Aaron.

Emotionally, physically, intellectually — she'd loved his company and finding herself alone was like having a limb missing. He might scare her, but shit — he excited her too. As Eugenie began to view the incident more rationally, she'd overreacted. And how.

Eugenie couldn't explain, even to herself, why she hadn't safe worded when he'd given her that chance.

They would have talked, compromised. Or maybe Aaron could have convinced her to go through with it. He might have been able to find the words to boost her confidence enough to be able to accept his discipline.

Her instincts had screamed at her to apologize, to ask if he'd let her try again. It would involve groveling and that ten strokes of his cane would no doubt multiply. She hadn't cared. She'd do whatever was needed to get him back.

Deleting his number had felt good at the time but it meant she hadn't been able call him, or send a text. She'd known where he'd lived, though, and in desperation, she'd gone to his house. He hadn't been there so she'd pushed a note through his letterbox. She'd written that she was sorry and wanted to meet him to talk things through.

Three hours later, her phone had pinged with a text from Aaron.

Thanks for your note. Glad you're calmer now and OK. Not sure it would be a good idea to meet, though. We clearly have different needs. Be happy, and good luck for the future.

Eugenie had stared at the screen. She hadn't been able to believe it—he was dumping her. The polite finality of his text had chilled her. It had left no room for negotiation. Different needs? What the fuck did that mean? She'd texted him back.

Please, Aaron. Sir. I am sorry. Please let me have a chance to explain.

I'm sorry too, but no.

She'd left it a few days before trying to contact Aaron again. The outcome had been the same. He did not want to meet her, and neither was he interested in her explanations or apologies. He'd wished her well and advised her to think carefully before embarking on another D/s relationship. She needed to be sure this was really the lifestyle for her.

It was this final piece of unwanted advice that had set Eugenie on the self-destructive course that resulted in *La Brat*. She'd applied for membership of every fetish or BDSM club within a hundred miles of Newcastle, not all of them especially salubrious, but she didn't care. She'd known Aaron was likely to avoid The Basement, as he might expect to run into her there, and clearly, this was not on his agenda.

But he was a Dom, and Eugenie reckoned he had to go somewhere. He'd be out there, active in the fetish scene, and sooner or later, she'd meet him again. This time, she'd make sure he had no illusions about what he'd given up, what he was missing. She'd be the sexiest, most desirable submissive on the scene.

And she'd make sure he knew she could have been his. He'd be left under no illusion about what he was missing, what he'd thrown away when he refused to give her a second chance.

Most weekends she'd haunted kinky clubs, parties, munches. She'd widened her networks and played with any Dom who had invited her. She had not been short on offers. At least, not at first. She hadn't set out looking for a replacement for Aaron, or not consciously. Even so, she'd compared every other Dom she'd scened with to him and they had all come up wanting. Too harsh, too soft, the wrong voice, the wrong physique. She'd been looking for her idea of the perfect Dom, and that was Aaron Praed. Others were pale imitations.

Her quest had become more desperate. She'd tested her Dominant partners, acting up to provoke them, to manipulate them into punishing her. She had been looking for someone who could affect her as deeply as Aaron had, a Dom who could bend her will and gain her unfailing obedience. So she'd disobeyed to force their hands. She was the 'make me' girl. She'd earned herself punishment spankings, paddlings, even on one occasion a public caning.

She couldn't believe she'd done that. The one thing that had so freaked her out when Aaron had been about to do it, she'd eventually submitted to in full view of dozens more kinksters. It had hurt like fuck, but she'd weathered it.

None of the Doms she'd tried out had impressed her, and it hadn't been long before she'd stopped impressing them. She still got her kink, but increasingly at the impersonal hands of a house Dom or dungeon master.

She was unfulfilled, at last realizing what she needed and craved wasn't the sex, or the play. It was the D/s relationship itself. She desired the intimacy, the trust, the permanency of a real connection with another person. She wanted a Master. She'd had one, but had thrown it away.

Maybe she'd been too young when she and Aaron had gotten together, certainly too inexperienced. And now it was too late. Despite her frantic searching, it seemed he was nowhere on the scene, and her reputation as *La Brat* had pretty much destroyed any chance she might have had of truly connecting again.

Basically, she was stuffed—until Paris—and now that dream was wrecked too.

* * * *

Eugenie got up at around six in the early evening. She wandered into her living room then switched on the news while she fixed herself something to eat. She ate with her microwaved meal-for-one balanced on her knee in front of the television, and started to plan the rest of her life.

So Paris wasn't happening. That was a shame, but it had demonstrated that, Aaron Praed aside, she was capable of getting an interview for a good job and of performing well. Maybe she could win herself a promotion, or there would be other jobs. Not of the Totally Five Star standard probably, but good enough. She began to wonder if there might be recruitment agencies out there, executive headhunters she could register with. Perhaps she should revisit her CV, or look for some training in the hospitality industry. That would enhance her prospects, surely. Oh yes, there was a lot she could do if she set her mind on this. Her future was hers to control and it was time she got on with it.

She dumped her empty plate by the sink and went to fire up her laptop.

She had twenty-seven unread emails. Three were from the TFS group. The first of these, which had been waiting for her since ten seventeen that morning, was from Madeleine Lambert. The second was from Elise Rougin, and the third was from Aaron.

Eugenie knew the protocols. Madame Lambert would be emailing to tell her that she'd been unsuccessful but to thank her for her interest in Totally Five Star Hotels. Madame Rougin would be wanting to offer her the opportunity to seek feedback on her interview performance. God only knew what Aaron wanted. She'd start with Madame Lambert.

From: Madeleine Lambert
To: Eugenie d'André
Date: 27 April 2013
Subject: Events Coordinator, TFS Paris

Dear Ms. D'André,
Thank you for attending the interviews earlier this week in relation to the above post.

I am pleased to inform you that the panel has instructed me to make you an offer of employment. You will find the principal details attached to this email. Please could you let me know within five working days if you intend to accept this offer? If you have any questions regarding the contractual arrangements, please direct those to me. All other queries can be dealt with by senior staff at TFS Paris.

I understand that Elise Rougin will be in touch with you to agree on a start date and discuss the induction arrangements.

Finally, I would like to take this opportunity to welcome you to the Totally Five Star Group.

Yours sincerely,
M. Lambert

Eugenie stared at the screen, rereading the short message three times before its meaning sank in. An offer. They were offering her a job. *The* job.

Holy fucking shit!

She ignored the attachment for now and went straight to Elise Rougin's message

From: Elise Rougin
To: Eugenie d'André
Date: 27 April 2013
Subject: The Job

Dear Eugenie,

I trust you had a safe and pleasant journey home.

You have received an email from our HR department confirming our offer of the post. May I just add my congratulations on your stunning performance in the interview, and say what a pleasure it was to meet you yesterday. You were the unanimous choice of the panel. Rarely is any recruitment decision so simple.

I hope you will accept our offer, and I look forward to welcoming you to our team.

Some formalities. Your application states that you must give one month's notice to your current employer. On that basis, and to allow for the necessary exchange of paperwork, contracts, etc., may I suggest we agree a start date five weeks from Monday?

If you require it TFS Paris can provide accommodation in our staff apartments, or you may prefer to make your own arrangements. Please let me know. Your starting salary and other particulars are in the documentation provided by Madame Lambert. I will be on leave from tomorrow for two

weeks, but please don't hesitate to contact my PA if you need to know anything else.

Best regards, and once again, welcome to TFS Paris.
Elise Rougin

'Unanimous choice'. 'Stunning performance'. 'Simple decision'. Eugenie replayed the accolades in her head. She knew she'd done well at the interview, but had not expected such lavish praise. And no mention at all of the final couple of minutes when her brain had turned to porridge and she'd stammered like a broken record. And neither, it seemed, had Aaron undermined her efforts with any comments of his own regarding her less than stellar past. Which brought her nicely to his email. She clicked on his name in her inbox.

From: Aaron Praed
To: Eugenie
Date: 27 April 2013
Subject: Congratulations

Genie,
It was lovely to see you again. You looked well.
I gather we are to be colleagues. And neighbors — your office is next door to mine.
See you in a month or so.

Aaron

Christ, not a hint of bitterness, nor any of the acrimony she'd expected from him. Perhaps he was prepared to let bygones be bygones. The office next door — shit!

The next hour or so she spent in a flurry of activity as she downloaded her proposed contract, the offer letter, her terms and conditions of employment. She read those, found nothing unexpected or untoward, replied to Madeleine Lambert accepting the post, then to Elise Rougin thanking her for her comments and agreeing in principle to the suggested start date, though that would be subject to agreement with her current employer. She would hand in her resignation tomorrow.

Her final email of the evening was to Aaron. She took much longer to compose it, uncertain what she wanted to say to him. Eventually, she settled on the truth.

From: Eugenie d'André
To: Aaron Praed
Date: 28 April 2013
Subject: Thank You

Hi Aaron,
Thanks for your note, and for the congratulations.
It was a shock to see you yesterday, I think you know that. I owe you my gratitude, first for not letting me make a bigger fool of myself than I already did, then for not saying anything about what happened between us in the past. You could have ruined my chances of being offered the post and you did not. I do appreciate that. This job means a lot to me. I am so pleased to have been offered this opportunity and I intend to make a success of it.
I will be starting work in about five weeks. I hope it will not be a problem that I am in the next office, but if so I could request a move.
We will be colleagues, as you say, and neighbors, perhaps. I hope too that we can be friends in time.

Yours,
Genie

She hit send and started to compose her letter of resignation, ready to hand it in to the personnel department of the council in the morning. A few minutes later, the new message icon appeared in the corner of her screen.

From: Aaron Praed
To: Eugenie
Date: 28 April 2013
Subject: No new office will be required

Brief and to the point. And exactly what she'd wanted him to say.

* * * *

The next few days passed in a blur as Eugenie put in place the arrangements for her relocation to Paris. She had to give notice to her landlord, send emails to countless utilities and official departments, complete endless change of address forms. Her boss declared himself sorry to be losing her, but assured her his reference would be a glowing one. He applauded her decision and the initiative she had shown in landing herself this plum prize. He wished her every success.

Her other colleagues took much the same attitude, and Eugenie knew she would miss the friends she had made there.

Most of them. She went online to discontinue her membership of the various kink clubs she had frequented, preferring not to appear in person anywhere on the scene. She was embarrassed, not proud of her behavior over the last couple of years. Sexual promiscuity was not really a concept that meant much in her circles, but even so, she wished she'd been a little more discerning in her choices.

She owed herself more respect, let alone the Dom's she'd used in her self-destructive antics.

But that was done with. Over. She was starting afresh. *La Brat* was history.

Chapter Eight

She was here. She'd arrived. It was real.

Eugenie sat heavily on the bed in her studio apartment in the staff wing of Totally Five Star Paris and gazed around her. The fitted furniture was modern and sleek. Gleaming whitewood doors fronted the wardrobe and drawers waiting to be filled with her stuff. The place was compact, but perfectly adequate. It was also ridiculously inexpensive for a self-contained flat in the most sought after district in one of the world's most sophisticated cities. She was not a stone's throw from the Champs-Élysées, could take a morning stroll through Les Tuileries if she wished, the Eiffel Tower was no more than twenty minutes or so from where she now sat.

She'd brought a large suitcase with her and arranged for a few other possessions and the rest of her clothes to be sent on. She busied herself putting her things away, opening and shutting drawers, checking the contents of the kitchenette. Although utensils and cookery were provided in the furnished studio, she could see she would need to buy some provisions quickly. She'd ask at reception where the nearest mini market was. She didn't expect to be doing much cooking as staff could get a discount at any of the hotel restaurants. Eugenie suspected she'd be a regular at the garden bistro. In fact, she wondered if they'd be open now.

It was Sunday evening. She'd been traveling all day and was tired. She was also hungry, and her stomach won out. She changed into a fresh skirt and blouse, tugged a brush through her hair and set off in search of sustenance. She hoped no one saw the little happy dance she did along the corridor leading to the lift. She had a dignified position to uphold now and she was a member of the senior staff at one of the most prestigious hotels in the world. But still…

* * * *

The following morning, at eight o'clock on the dot, Eugenie presented herself at the desk of Elise Rougin's PA. She was ushered straight through into the general manager's office, where a crowd awaited her. Elise came across the room to meet her and launched into a round of introductions.

Pierre Rivaux she had met already. Eugenie's smile of recognition was warm as she shook his hand. Next, she was introduced to Claudette Leclerc, a statuesque woman who she learned was in charge of marketing and public relations. Jean Raymond, a middle-aged man with hair just starting to turn gray at the temples, managed customer services, which he went on to explain meant anything to do with the reception staff, entertainment, spa facilities—pretty much everything that wasn't connected with eating, drinking or sleeping. Eating and drinking was the domain of a gregarious Italian called Antonio Alecia, an accomplished chef who now presided over all the hotel's restaurants and bars. A small, bustling woman, Annette Giraud, was in charge of all matters related to housekeeping and the creature comforts enjoyed by guests. Fleur Mansouri she had met at the interview, and of course, she already knew Aaron Praed who, Elise explained, was responsible for keeping the guests and staff safe.

Eugenie reckoned he'd be good at it.

This group made up the entire senior management team, and now Eugenie was part of it. Elise explained that it was their regular habit to meet each Monday morning at eight to go over the events of the coming week, address any issues, and generally keep in touch with each other. The meetings were informal and brief, but a necessary part of the routine. She would be expected to make them a priority. Eugenie had no problem with that.

They all took their seats around the circular meeting table in Elise's office. Eugenie was told to sit anywhere. The first few minutes were spent on a quick round of news and highlights from each department. Eugenie tried to take notes but soon abandoned that and opted to listen instead.

Anton had decided to change their fresh meat supplier for one more local and known to adhere to compassionate farming methods. Elise nodded, and explained to Eugenie that this was an important principle at TFS Paris. Annette Giraud chipped in that she was hoping to recruit three or four more maids later in the week, and Fleur confirmed that defibrillators were now installed on each floor and staff trained in their use.

The round-up completed, Elise turned her attention to the most pressing matter on their current agenda — *the* wedding.

For Eugenie's benefit, she explained that Lucas Belanger, the captain of the French football team and a center forward playing in the top flight of the Italian league, was known to be looking for a venue for his wedding to Farah Ajram. The bride was less high profile, but probably substantially wealthier as her father owned half the oil production in the United Arab Emirates. This was to be the wedding of the decade, and Totally Five Star Paris wanted to land it.

Lucas and Farah were due at the hotel in two days' time, complete with their usual entourage, and Elise was pretty sure the hotel was among the final one or two venues they were still considering. Their location was an asset. Farah had studied in Paris and loved the city. Transport links were as good as any in the world, which would be a significant factor in assembling guests from every continent. The facilities offered here were known to be superb, their reputation was second to none, and now that they had an accomplished events organizer on the team, this might just swing it.

The Arab contingent had voiced concerns about security, so Aaron too would have his work cut out to convince Farah's family that their little princess would be protected at all times. There had been terror threats, and unrest in the Arab world was always an issue, though the UAE was stable enough.

Elise's expression was deadly serious as she directed her attention first at Eugenie then at Aaron. "I need you two to get your heads together and work out how to dazzle them. The hotel wants this wedding. If we can pull this off, it will be the highest profile event on the social calendar for months to come. We'll be inundated with inquiries from every bride who wants to be a princess for a day. Aaron, do you perceive any issues we should be considering?"

Eugenie glanced at Aaron sitting across the table from her. He looked incredibly handsome in his sharp business suit and crisp white shirt. His red tie looked perfect for restraining a submissive, and despite her best intentions, Eugenie couldn't help wondering if he had another sub now. She supposed he must have.

He sat forward, his elbows on the table as he replied to Elise's query. "There are issues, but none that are insurmountable. We would have to instigate additional checks on all guests, staff and suppliers whilst the wedding party is here, and I'd recommend we limit all other bookings for that period too. I'll schedule sweeps and searches of the premises at random intervals, and staff should expect to be searched as they come and go. Ideally, guests too, but that could prove tricky, which is why I suggest we limit the numbers. Only staff who need to be there will have access to any of the wedding party's suites. Our standard passkeys and ID checks should be thorough enough, but I'll review those and let you know if I find any aspects that need tightening."

"Excellent. I'd like you and Eugenie to lead on this. Pull out all the stops to secure the business then make sure it goes without a hitch."

Aaron nodded. Eugenie gaped.

The wedding of the decade. Here. And Elise was looking to her to organize it. Talk about hitting the ground running.

"Problem, Eugenie?" Elise looked at her, a slight frown furrowing her otherwise unruffled brow.

"What? No, no of course not. What information do we have about what they're actually looking for? Is there any theme? Number of guests?"

"No theme that we know of, but it is posh. Catwalk stuff. Think of the Oscars red carpet, and you'll be about there. The Muslim ceremony will be held first, in her uncle's palace, and will be a massive affair, I gather, though largely hidden from the press and paparazzi. This second ceremony is to satisfy that more public appetite for celebrity glitz. Number of guests is to be confirmed, but won't be fewer than five hundred, so we'll need the ballroom for the actual ceremony, and the banqueting suite for the formal meal to follow. We can handle those numbers, but they'll be looking for that something extra, that sparkle that sets us apart from any other places they might be considering. That's your job, to come up with the hook that lands them."

"Of course." Eugenie murmured the words, her mind racing with possibilities. She was itching for the meeting to conclude so she could find her way to her new office. She needed to start planning her campaign to get Lucas and Farah to tie the knot at Totally Five Star Paris.

* * * *

The list seemed endless. Every time she closed her eyes to visualize the wedding she came up with yet another possible theme. Colors, eras, vintage, rock music, rustic, more outlandish ideas such as pirates or fairies, or perhaps a sporting theme would be more appropriate. Or the arts. Maybe the bride would like something romantic, a bit whimsical. Without knowing more about the personality and lifestyle of the couple, Eugenie really had no idea.

Lucas Belanger was easy enough to research. A Google search came up with literally hundreds of results, though primarily concerned with his prowess on the football field. Successful, skilled, one of the top players in the world, and the most expensive. His earnings put him in the multi-millionaire bracket, though he was still only in his mid-twenties. He'd clearly enjoyed the lifestyle that went with his wealth. He was pictured in top nightclubs, driving the sexiest cars and lounging on the most exclusive beaches. As far as Eugenie could tell, he'd never been embroiled in any of the scandals that seemed to attach themselves sports personalities, or maybe he was just more discreet than most. His playboy lifestyle seemed to tail off in the last eighteen months or so, possibly due to the influence of his bride to be.

On Farah Ajram Eugenie could find almost nothing. There was a record of her having attended the *École Normale Supérieure*, Paris' most prestigious seat of learning, where she obtained her master's degree in the history of art. Eugenie whistled under her breath, Farah must be bright as well as beautiful. But apart from this little nugget, the bride seemed shrouded in mystery. Who knew what sort of wedding might suit her, or even whether she wanted it to be themed at all? And given that she would already be married under Islamic law by the time this second ceremony took place, what was she actually seeking from it?

At the back of Eugenie's mind, something gnawed at her. She sat back in her chair, eyes closed, and let her mind drift. What was it about this couple that seemed so obvious, yet so elusive? A squeaky-clean footballer, his lovely, exotic, and oh so secluded bride—what were they coming to Totally Five Star Paris in search of?

Privacy. Of course. And sheer, unadulterated excellence. Eugenie wouldn't mind betting Farah wanted to satisfy the paparazzi, make her entry into the high-profile world of footballers' wives and girlfriends, but be the WAG with panache. What if she aspired to quiet and discreet sophistication? Totally Five Star Paris could provide that. It was the hallmark of this hotel, its unique selling point.

As soon as it occurred to her, Eugenie knew she was right. If Farah and Lucas wanted a circus to please the media, they would have said so already. Prospective venues would have been scrambling to sell them shabby chic or retro or movie-themed wedding madness. Instead, the couple gave no clues. Maybe they weren't even sure themselves, but they'd know what they wanted when it was presented to them.

Rather than trying to inject some new, untested and in her view quite ostentatious quality into the affair, Eugenie would showcase what they did best. She would offer them quiet, understated elegance. She could promise perfect service, a serene atmosphere, food and drink that was unequalled anywhere.

Add to it all the confidence that every detail of their big day would be planned and coordinated by Eugenie personally, that nothing would be left to chance. Aaron's enhanced security measures would ensure the safety and smooth running of the whole process. Farah and Lucas could relax. They could enjoy their day knowing they were in safe and capable hands. It was a simple plan, but Eugenie's gut instinct told her it would work.

"Taking a little nap? Are we tiring you out already?"

Eugenie snapped her eyes open at the masculine drawl from her office doorway. Aaron leaned against the frame, arms folded, grinning at her. She sat up straight, smoothed back a stray tendril of hair that seemed to keep escaping the neat clasp at the nape of her neck. What was it about him that always put her on edge? She fought the urge to stand and lower her gaze.

"I was thinking. Planning." Was that a defensive note in her voice? She hoped not.

"The wedding?"

"Yes."

"Me too. What are your thoughts?" He came right into the room and took the chair opposite her desk. Eugenie didn't recall having invited him in, but hell, he was so good to look at. She knew her knickers were moistening and she shifted uneasily in her seat.

"Are you okay, Genie?"

"Fine. Yes." Now she sounded snappy, waspish. Shit. She hadn't reckoned on him still having the same effect on her. Their relationship had been hot and intensely sexual, but it was over. Long dead. Or so she'd thought. Her pussy seemed to disagree.

"Good. So, what are your plans then? How do you propose we reel in this footballer?"

"We don't need him. We need *her*. Farah will decide this, not Lucas."

"You think?"

Eugenie nodded, her certainty growing. "Yes, I'm sure of it. And she's not looking for anything over the top. There's a reason she never appears in any of the celebrity magazines or tabloids. No one has ever heard of her because she's intensely private. I reckon she's looking for a secluded, intimate and above all *tasteful* wedding. Glamour, yes, sophistication, definitely. Elegance—off the scale. We have all of that, so we need to make sure she sees it, that she appreciates all the finer details and is absolutely confident in us. By us, I mean you and me. You to keep her and her guests safe, me to be on top of every detail for her, to make sure everything she wants is there, even before she knows that she wants it."

Aaron's expression never changed. He regarded her carefully, assessing. Eugenie sat still, hoping she'd said enough to convince him but ready to marshal further arguments if need be. Her panties continued to dampen as he scrutinized her.

His face cracked into a brilliant smile. It lit up her room. "I think you may be right. In fact, I think you may be a bloody genius. Holy fuck, girl, Elise was right about you."

"What? I mean—Elise?"

"She said you were gifted, a true talent. You haven't even gotten to your first coffee break yet and already you've accomplished more than the rest of the team have in months of thinking about this. So, how do you suggest we sell it to them?"

"Who? Sell it to who? The management team?"

"No. Elise delegated it to you, and to me. She'll trust us to come up with the best strategy. We'll tell her what we intend once we've worked out the details a bit more. I meant how should we sell ourselves and Totally Five Star Paris to Farah Ajram?"

"Ah, right. Well, we need a timetable for every part of their visit. They'll be here for two days so…"

Eugenie spent the next couple of hours mapping out a detailed program. Aaron contributed, clarifying points and supplying details she had yet to learn about the hotel, the facilities, the staff. He asked questions, drilled down into the detail, identified gaps that Eugenie plugged. By lunchtime, they had their strategy in place.

"We'll need to brief everyone that they are likely to come in contact with — every waiter, every chambermaid, every porter. All need to exude the same quiet, efficient charm, the same attention to detail and desire to please. Everywhere they look I want Farah and Lucas to see excellence."

"That's your department. I need to make sure my security team is invisible, but doing the business behind the scenes. I'll get on it." He shuffled his notes into a pile and stood. "Have lunch with me, Genie?"

"What?"

"You heard me. I want to have lunch with you."

"Why?"

"Why not? Maybe just because it's been a busy morning, we've worked hard and now we're hungry. But if you insist on having it spelled out, how about because you're a new colleague? I want to make you feel welcome. And if that's not enough, how about because you're a beautiful companion, creative and intelligent, and I've enjoyed your company this morning? You're a pleasure to work with. So have lunch with me. Please."

Well, when he put it like that... Eugenie smiled up at him. "Thank you, Aaron, I would love to have lunch with you."

* * * *

At Eugenie's suggestion, they ate at the terrace bistro. Aaron admitted it was his favorite too. They ordered soup and rolls and, as they waited for their lunch, Eugenie contemplated her companion.

"About what happened..." She blurted out the words before she had an opportunity to think through what she actually wanted to say to him.

"Yes? What about it, Genie?" To his credit, he made no pretense of not understanding what she meant.

"When I, when I..."

"When you attacked me with a cane?"

She cringed at the memory. "Yes. *That*. It was unforgivable. I am *so* sorry."

Aaron shrugged. "Not entirely unforgivable. I forgave you years ago. It's in the past now. We've both moved on."

Well, he might have. Eugenie gaped at him, her jaw dropping. "You forgave me? How? Why? I hit you. It was the one thing a good submissive should never do."

Aaron's grin was warm, as though he found some humor in the recollection. "I reckon there are lots of things a good submissive should never do, and yeah, calling your Dom a bastard and laying into him with a cane is probably on the list—near the top, in fact." He paused, his face taking on a more thoughtful expression. "But a good Dom should have read your signals better than I did that day. We both made mistakes, and we need to learn from what happened perhaps, but not agonize over it."

"You were a good Dom. It was me—"

"No, I wasn't. Not that day. I was in control, not you, so I was responsible for how our scene turned out. I should have realized how distressed you'd become and talked to you, understood better what was happening with you."

"I should have used my safe word."

"Yes, and that would have stopped the scene. But you gave off enough signals even so. You weren't in the right headspace, so you wouldn't have learned from being caned. You'd have hated me. You did hate me, at least for a while."

"I was angry, and humiliated. I felt so stupid and shocked at what I'd done. I couldn't face you again. Well, not at first. Then when I could, you wouldn't talk to me."

"I tried to contact you a couple of times in the few days that followed, to check you were okay."

"I know. I deleted your messages. Why wouldn't you talk to me after that, though? I came to your house. I left a note."

"You wanted to get back together, but it was too late for that. I hadn't meant to hurt you, but I had. I don't mean physically, but emotionally, and I would have again. We were looking for different things. I'm not convinced you wanted a Dom at all, and if you did, he wasn't me."

"Not you? That is ridiculous. I loved you."

Aaron frowned, tilting his head to one side as he regarded her critically as though considering his next words with care. At last he spoke, "No, Genie. You liked having sex with me—most of the time. I certainly liked fucking you. But you didn't trust me, so you couldn't truly submit to me. Sooner or later, we would have split up. It was probably for the best."

"I... I would have. I mean, I needed to learn, I *was* learning. I would never have done anything like that again."

"I believe you, especially if I'd taught you the lesson you deserved for attacking me. Assuming you managed to accept my discipline the next time. But I needed your submission to be given freely, not dragged from you with the help of a cane. That would have just been cruel, and not my style. Whatever you were looking for, whether from a Dom or not, I couldn't provide it."

"Maybe not then, but I've changed." Was that a note of desperation creeping into her voice? Of pleading, even. She had not intended to reveal so much.

"So have I. If anything, I'm even more exacting of my submissives now than I was then."

"You are still in the lifestyle, then? On the Paris scene?" Eugenie couldn't miss the pang of jealousy that shot through her like a barb at the mention of other submissives, presumably good, compliant submissives who obeyed their Master and liked nothing better than a decent whipping. Why couldn't that have been her?

"Of course. Are you angling for some introductions?" He treated her to his ready smile again.

"I..." Eugenie was about to accept his offer from sheer force of habit, but hesitated. She'd quite deliberately and consciously left *La Brat* back in England. Was she about to start the whole self-destructive cycle again, rushing from club to club, from Dom to Dom, seeking the connection she'd only ever managed to find once before? Especially when the one Dom she had ever felt connected to was right here in front of her, telling her they were incompatible. Eugenie made a decision. In that moment, she knew that if she could not have Aaron Praed, no other Dom would fill his place.

"No, thank you."

"No? Have you thought better of it, then? No longer into kink?"

Not with just anyone. Not anymore. "It's not that. I intend to concentrate on my career for the time being. I'll be very busy. I need to make a success of this job so

TFS Paris is going to get my undivided attention. If—when—we convince Farah to hold her wedding here I won't have any time for clubbing, or socializing."

Aaron nodded. "Probably a wise decision. Ah, here's our soup." They fell silent as the waiter laid their meal out for them. As the server sauntered back in the direction of the kitchens, Eugenie couldn't help asking the question that was provoked by Aaron's words of a few minutes before.

"What did you mean just now when you said you weren't sure whether I was looking for a Dom or not? Why would you have thought that?

Aaron tore a bread roll in half and took a spoonful of his minestrone soup. At first, Eugenie thought he might not intend to answer her. He laid his spoon aside, though, and met her eyes.

"There were times—just a few times, but enough—when I wasn't sure you were a submissive at all. Not at heart. I'd give you an instruction and you'd bristle, answer back perhaps, inviting discipline like a brat, but hating it when it was delivered. That last time was the most extreme example, but there were several other incidents. You were defiant, and resentful, I think, a lot of the time."

"I was scared a lot of the time. And confused. I loved most of the things you did to me, but not all of it. I was learning, though. I could have tried harder. I would have tried harder if you'd given me another chance."

Aaron reached across the table to take her hand. He squeezed it. "A D/s relationship is never easy for either partner. You tried it, and you did try hard. It just wasn't for you. I see that more clearly now."

"So you thought I was a rotten sub, then? Why did you put up with me for so long?" She hated the telltale tremor in her voice, could feel tears threatening.

"No, Genie, you weren't a rotten sub. You were hard work, a challenge certainly, but rewarding enough. A lot of the time you were sweet and responsive, and you were so fucking gorgeous you took my breath away. You still are."

She gazed at him, her eyes widening. "Then, why not…?"

Aaron wouldn't let her complete the request. "Let it go, love. We're colleagues now, and I hope we'll be friends in the future. Leave the past where it is."

He squeezed her hand again, curling his lips in a lopsided grin. Eugenie managed to mirror his expression, though she felt something brittle and delicate cracking deep inside her. She managed to quash it, though, forcing herself to accept what was on offer—friendship, professional respect. Aaron even seemed to like her, a bit. She'd settle for that.

They exchanged pleasantries as they ate their soup. Aaron insisted that she have the last bread roll, observing that she had lost weight. Eugenie accepted it with a smile, recalling that he had always seemed concerned that she was too thin. She'd thought his 'I know best' attitude had as much to do with his profession as it did his Dominant nature. Which reminded her of something that had been puzzling her.

"May I ask you a question?"

"Of course." He laid down his spoon to give her his full attention.

"Why did you leave the police? I thought you loved your work."

"I did. Then. I was still heading up Special Ops, I think, when we were together?"

"Yes. The police dogs, horses and helicopters."

"One helicopter. Singular. But yes, I did enjoy that."

"You never mentioned you were considering a move. That you might leave the police altogether."

"I wasn't, but things change."

"I hope it had nothing to do with me."

Aaron shook his head. "No, none of your doing. You remember I was on the graduate program—accelerated promotion and all that?"

Eugenie nodded.

"About six months after we split up, I was promoted to superintendent and transferred to headquarters in Gateshead. That was the last I saw of real policing. Instead, I found myself playing politics, juggling budgets and under constant pressure to reduce the costs of policing the county. I hated it. So when I was approached by an old friend from college about this opening that had arisen with Totally Five Star Paris, I was interested. My friend had become an executive recruitment consultant, a headhunter if you like. I spoke the language, and I was ripe for a new challenge. The pay they were offering was tempting, but if I'd been happy in my job, I doubt that would have swung it. I wasn't, and it did. I was headhunted, and here I am."

"Have you ever regretted it? Surely, this is not as exciting as the dogs and horses. And helicopter."

"Maybe not, but I'd already parted company from my toys. That was perhaps my mistake. Leaving the police to join TFS was a good move. I like Paris, I've found I like hotels and I particularly like this one."

"I do too. I intend to be happy here. I am grateful to you for not mentioning what happened in the past."

"I would never have done that, love. Apart from anything else, I value my privacy too." He brushed a few stray crumbs from his lap. "So, shall we get on with planning how we're going to charm this bride into coming to Paris for her wedding?"

Chapter Nine

Eugenie waited in the vast expanse of the hotel, her gaze riveted to the glass doors and the red carpet beyond. Monsieur Dubain, the butler who would greet her honored guests as they exited their limousine, was under strict instructions to signal her the moment their car came into sight. She would be there, at the top of the steps, ready to welcome Farah and Lucas to the Totally Five Star, and set the scene for the rest of their visit. Nothing would go wrong, nothing had been left to chance. Every detail of the next two days, every aspect of this visit had been anticipated, rehearsed, planned and prepared for.

TFS Paris ran a polished enough show as it was, Eugenie had simply brought everything to an even brighter sheen. She had Elise's total support, and all staff were under instructions to cooperate fully. And they had. Eugenie was impressed. From the most senior managers down to the elderly gentleman who tended the gardens, all were equally committed to this shared goal.

The place sparkled. Annette Giraud's staff had been on overtime to ensure there was not a surface that didn't shine, not a window or mirror with so much as a smudge to mar its glistening perfection. Glassware gleamed, the carpets and floors were spotless. The assorted pieces of art and antiques that graced both public and private areas were arranged and lit to their absolute best effect. The hotel was, quite simply, magnificent.

The building was ready. Now she had to hope the staff was too.

A nod from Monsieur Dubain, just visible on the other side of the plate glass door, alerted her. The show was about to start. Eugenie stepped forward as the pane slid soundlessly aside to allow her to pass through. She took her position beside the austere butler, arranged her features into a quiet, efficient smile of welcome, just the right blend of confidence and desire to please — she hoped.

She was vaguely conscious of Aaron's quiet presence behind her and to her right, and that of his team. He had a man at the entrance to the street, monitoring all vehicle access, and another at the foot of the steps ready to open the door of the limousine. That guard posed as a doorman, but she knew better. Often Aaron placed his security staff in innocuous positions, blending in with the fabric of the place but ever vigilant. There were more just now, new staff appearing in the restaurants, the kitchens, the casino, the bars. They had been drilled to perform their cover roles as efficiently as the genuine staff, while also providing the eyes and ears that Aaron insisted on having everywhere.

He also used new technology to the best effect. The CCTV throughout the entire hotel had been upgraded and intruder alarms installed in sensitive areas. He would know if so much as a fly landed anywhere within the suite to be occupied by Farah and Lucas—though it was unlikely such a creature would find its way through his ring of protection. He had been in close liaison with the security teams protecting both Farah and her fiancé, and had ensured that there would be no breaches at his end. This place was as tight as possible to make it without installing turrets and machine guns.

Not that Aaron would have balked at such measures had he thought them necessary. And if so, it would have been Eugenie's job to wrap his turrets up in the quiet veneer of sophistication that showcased everything about the hotel to its absolute best. Their teamwork on this quest had been seamless.

What a pity such rapport had escaped them three years previously.

Shrugging such misplaced reminiscences aside, Eugenie allowed the bubble of anticipation in her stomach to swell. The tingle of nerves would sharpen her performance now, the adrenaline flowing to hone her instincts. She welcomed it as she stepped forward, her hand outstretched to greet the couple now ascending the short flight of steps.

Lucas was the first to shake her hand, his broad smile softening his otherwise sharp features. He was a handsome man, quite stunning in fact, and from his first emergence as a center forward in the Premier Division had been much courted by the paparazzi. His blond good looks were perhaps a little too classical for Eugenie's taste, but even so, the prickle of attraction was undeniable. She defied any woman with a pulse not to experience it.

Her attention shifted to the darker, smaller presence beside him—Farah Ajram, Arab princess and heiress to an oil fortune worth billions, it was rumored. And Eugenie's true target.

She smiled and bowed her head. "My name is Eugenie d'André. I am in charge of corporate and social events at Totally Five Star Paris. I will be your hostess for this visit. I will take care of you and show you all the facilities we have to offer here. I will deal with any questions you may have and make sure your stay is as comfortable and fulfilling as possible. So, welcome to Paris, sir, madam."

"Thank you. We've been looking forward to coming back here." Lucas' polite reply was non-committal.

"I will show you to your suite. Monsieur Dubain will see to it that your luggage is unloaded and taken to your rooms. Would you like some refreshment after your journey?" Eugenie gestured them to precede her through the doors into the reception area, where the atmosphere was one of comfort and calm. A couple of guests, carefully vetted by Aaron, lounged on the couches, served with drinks by silent, efficient staff. The lighting was set up to accentuate a display of antique Moroccan vases, but without detracting from the businesslike efficiency of this central hub. This was the core of the Paris hotel, the first impression, the nerve center. Eugenie knew this moment could make or break her campaign.

Farah gazed around her, assessing. Eugenie saw this and realized she was holding her breath.

"Perhaps a glass of water, before we go up. Sparkling if you have it. It has been a long journey, and quite hot." Farah's tone was quiet, her words undemanding on the face of it. Eugenie knew better. This was their first test.

She ushered the couple to an unoccupied bank of sofas, her unobtrusive gesture summoning a server instantly. A bottle of sparkling water materialized with two glasses. The waiter snapped the top and poured as Eugenie perched on the couch opposite. She had chosen a modest but smart business suit, knee-length straight skirt in a shade just short of navy blue, and a soft cream-colored top. The neckline draped in soft folds, sensuous without being overtly sexy. As she surveyed the pair opposite, Eugenie was pleased. She felt she'd judged her choice of outfit just right.

Lucas wore a sharp suit in a pale gray, the jacket open to reveal a pristine white shirt. The neck was open and he wore no tie. Farah also wore trousers, but in the form of a feminine and loosely flowing pantsuit in muted purples and yellows. She arranged the kimono-style jacket around her as she reached for her glass. As she sipped her water, Eugenie was aware that Farah was scanning her surroundings, taking in every detail. In contrast, Lucas appeared utterly relaxed. He leaned back, extending his arm along the backrest to drape across Farah's shoulders.

Farah glanced briefly at her fiancé before turning her attention fully on Eugenie.

"We were very interested in what we saw on our last visit here, but we do have one or two remaining issues still to resolve. We have not yet made our final decision, you understand." Her voice was quiet, the timbre modulated to perfection. This was a woman accustomed to giving instructions. There was nothing strident in her tone, no hint of authority. Just a quiet certainty that her wishes would be obeyed.

Eugenie inclined her head, warming instantly. Farah was a woman she could respect. She knew instinctively that this was no highly strung, nervous bride. Farah had nothing to prove, no one she needed to impress except herself. There would be no histrionics, no hissy fits over flowers or invitation cards. Farah's requirements would be made known and that would be all that was needed. Eugenie would deliver.

"Of course. I and the rest of our team here are entirely at your disposal. I am sure we can address all your questions." She wanted to exude openness, willingness and absolute confidence in the quality of the hotel.

Farah smiled, her expression softening, warming. "Yes, I am sure. Thank you for the water. Could we go to our suite now to freshen up properly?"

"Of course. I'll have the drinks brought up too."

Another discreet hand gesture from Eugenie, and the waiter scooped up the glasses and half-empty bottle, stepping back to allow Eugenie to lead the little party to the lift.

She was gratified that the housekeeping staff had missed nothing. The honeymoon suite was presented beautifully, fresh flowers, champagne chilling, soft music greeting their entry. The couple's bags were already in the suite, and Eugenie offered them a maid to unpack for them.

"Thank you. That would be very welcome. Do we have time to shower, and I know my fiancé was hoping to make a few calls before we see the main function rooms?"

"By all means. I will leave you to rest. Please let me know when you are ready to look around our facilities. Is there anything else you need at this time?"

"No, we are fine, I think. Luc?"

Lucas had shucked out of his jacket and sprawled on the king-size bed, already flicking through channels on the wall-mounted plasma screen. He found Eurosport and seemed content. "Just some coffee, please. And some of those little pastry things they do here, if you have any?"

"I am sure we can find some for you, sir. I'll have a tray sent up. When you are ready, you can contact me through reception or on my mobile." Eugenie slipped her business card from her jacket pocket and placed it on the bedside table. With a smile and a slight bow, she left the room.

So far so good.

* * * *

The rest of the visit passed in a blur of seamless efficiency. Eugenie had laid her plans with meticulous precision, while somehow managing to allow for the couple to view the facilities at their pace. They lingered over the menus, debated the choice of vintage champagnes, visualized their guests arranged around the banqueting suite and contemplated the configuration of the master ballroom to accommodate the ceremony. Eugenie knew this was the crucial phase. Just like selling them a house, they needed to be able to see themselves there. They had to be able to imagine their wedding in this setting, and that scenario had to be the one they wanted above all the others on offer.

Eugenie was everywhere, never pushy, never overselling. Totally Five Star sold itself. All she did was show it off.

Although completely focused on the couple she needed to impress and convince, Eugenie was aware of Aaron's stamp everywhere. His security operatives served food and polished tables, they swept leaves and carried bags alongside the regular staff, their vigilance ensuring that nothing could go wrong. The couple's own security was very noticeable, surrounding the celebrity couple with their personal guards. Aaron's intensified security was discreet but pervaded the whole hotel.

Eugenie would glance up from some conversation with Farah to spot Aaron issuing instructions, talking to someone on his mobile, his expression intent. As far as she was aware, he was never in direct contact with Lucas and Farah, but he was in constant communication with their entourage. He gave off an air of calm certainty, utter control. She could not help thinking that his decision to make a career change must have been a great loss to the Northumbria constabulary.

* * * *

At last, the visit was drawing to a close. Farah and Lucas were in reception, their bags already loaded into the hotel limousine purring outside the main entrance, poised to whisk the couple to Charles de Gaulle Airport on their way to Dubai.

"I hope you have enjoyed your stay and found it helpful." Eugenie stepped forward, her hand outstretched. This time it was Farah she addressed. She had been spot on in her assessment of who would make this decision and knew whom she needed to convince. In response, Farah took her hand, but moved in to give her a quick hug.

"It has been wonderful. Your hotel is even more beautiful than I remembered and the service quite divine. We are very impressed, are we not, Luc?"

"Oh yes, babe. It's been great."

Farah shook her head in mock exasperation, her grin for Eugenie entirely conspiratorial. "Men. They know nothing. Thank you, Mademoiselle d'André. You have looked after us very well."

"Eugenie, please. And if there is anything else you need to know, you have my number. Please do not hesitate to contact me if I can be of any further assistance."

"Thank you, but I think we have seen all we need to. We will be in touch. *Au revoir.*"

Eugenie heaved a sigh of relief as Monsieur Dubain closed the limo door. She raised a hand in final salute to Farah as the vehicle pulled away.

"Well done, Genie." The words were murmured into her ear, Aaron's voice soft as he moved in behind her. She had not heard him approach, though in reality, she'd known he had never been far away.

She turned, feeling exhausted but content. "It went well, I think."

"Oh, yes. You played a blinder, love. Elise wants a word."

"Elise? Oh, right." Eugenie would have preferred a few minutes at least to prepare her debrief, but if the general manager wanted a report now, she could deal with that. She fell into step beside Aaron as they made their way across the reception area and into the executive management suite. The door to Elise's office stood open.

They went inside to find Elise and the rest of the senior staff already assembled. The manager got to her feet, her expression one of pure delight.

"Excellent work—both of you. The feedback has been entirely positive."

"Thank you. The visit went as planned. We managed to show them everything we wanted them to see, and I think we got our message across."

"I'm sure you did. Was there any indication when they would make their final decision?"

"Farah said it would be soon. I don't think they have any more venues to look at now."

"Well, we've done all we can. I could not have asked for a better presentation. Time for a little celebration, I think." Moments later, she produced a bottle of champagne and nine glasses. Elise invited Aaron to pop the cork then proceeded to pour everyone a drink. Standing, they toasted the hotel, then Eugenie, then Aaron.

Eugenie almost missed the brief vibration in her pocket, signaling that she had received a text. Juggling her champagne, she extricated her phone and turned it on—and gaped at the brief message it displayed.

The room hummed around her, the cheerful babble of her excited colleagues fading as she reread the text."

"Genie?" Aaron took her glass from between her fingers and placed it on the meeting table. He tipped her chin up with his fingers, a gesture once so familiar. "Are you okay?"

She stared at him, still clutching the phone.

"Genie?"

"We got it."

She'd whispered her reply, but he heard and understood immediately.

"Yes? Yes!"

Eugenie nodded, handing him the phone. He glanced down at it.

We will be getting married at TFS Paris. I wanted you to know straightaway. Will be in touch soon to sort out the formalities. Thank you so much. Farah.

Eugenie was aware of the cheers as the room erupted around her, the backslapping, the clink of glasses as more champagne was poured, even more sent for. Aaron seized her in a bear hug, lifting her from her feet to swing her around. He kissed her, but before she had time to register his kiss, she was grabbed and passed around the rest of the team for similar treatment. She was numb, overwhelmed and quite exhausted. But it had been worth it.

She'd done it. She'd actually bloody done it. Now all she had to do was carry off the main event.

Bring. It. On.

Chapter Ten

The wedding was to take place in six weeks' time. Aaron ran his fingers through his thick hair, contemplating all he still had to do to ensure the ceremony went off without a hitch. It would be tight, but he'd do it. He had to. It was that simple.

The click of the office door along the corridor signaled that Eugenie was in her office, just a wall separating them. If only that was all.

Not for the first time, he wondered what the fuck he'd been thinking of. That first day at the garden restaurant, she'd pretty much begged him to top her again. And he'd turned her down. Why? What the fuck was that about?

In the brief time they'd worked together—had it really only been three weeks—he'd had plenty of opportunity to observe his little Eugenie, and to recall in perfect detail all the reasons he'd been attracted to her in the past.

She was beautiful, the loveliest sub he'd ever played with. But he'd always known that. She'd also been complex and difficult, and he guessed she still would be. That was part of her allure. What might once have been brattishness, or mistaken for it, he now saw as discernment, the challenge presented by an intelligent submissive. Her obedience, and her submission, must be earned. Perhaps he'd expected more from her than he'd merited back then. Without doubt, he'd underestimated her, hadn't treated her with the respect she now commanded.

She was popular, had quickly established herself here. Elise was proud of her protégé, and rightly so. Eugenie's coup in winning the Belanger-Ajram wedding had cemented her position in the management team, and Aaron was delighted for her. Despite Eugenie's insistence that he had helped, he knew that essentially she was the architect of this success. He'd been the supporting act, no more.

They would be working together closely for the next few weeks as they prepared for the massive event. His cock twitched as he considered Eugenie's proximity, even as he told himself — again — that theirs was a business relationship. Nothing more. He'd said so, hadn't he? And she'd accepted that.

In any case, she'd made it clear where her priorities lay. She was devoting all her energies to her blossoming career from now on. Even if she did feel the occasional urge to be spanked, she would suppress it.

Which, he reflected, was not a good idea. Although not his preferred outlet, he had it on good authority that there was nothing quite like a decent spanking to provide focus and drive, to release tension and unlock inner creativity. Eugenie had found pain play helpful in releasing stress in the past, maybe he should offer?

Not that she appeared in the least stressed. She was in her element, on top of her job and clearly loving every minute of it. She'd fit in here and had made the role her own.

Footsteps in the corridor and a soft tap on his door heralded her arrival in his little domain. He called out to her to come in.

Christ, she was gorgeous. And that fragrance? Was it her or her perfume? A heady blend of fruits and soft floral undertones wafted across the room as she entered and took a seat opposite him. Her smile was artless, friendly. His cock swelled and hardened, and he was glad of his desk screening him from her view.

"Good morning. Are you busy?"

"No more than usual. What can I do for you, Genie?"

"I wanted to discuss the guest list for the wedding. It came through by email first thing. We need to identify any potential problems. I have a printout here and I was wondering if you had time for a coffee while we look it over?"

He held out his hand for the sheaf of papers. "I'll get someone to bring us a tray up."

"Couldn't we go out? Into the garden, I mean. It's a beautiful day and I just thought—"

"Not a good idea, Genie." He thought of his rampant erection, which would be obvious not only to her but to every guest and member of staff they encountered in the hotel. This was not the look he normally sought to cultivate in his professional setting.

"I'm sorry. I should not have suggested it. I will leave you the list and..." She made to stand, her expression embarrassed. And sad.

Aaron groaned inwardly. He'd given her entirely the wrong impression

"Please, don't go. That's not what I meant." Far from it.

"Oh? I thought I was disturbing you."

"You are, but not in a bad way."

Her face betrayed her confusion.

Aaron smiled at her. "You always did make a powerful impact on me. You're every bit as sexy as ever, Genie, and right now, imagining what I'd like to do with you and to you has given me a hard-on that would outrage half our guests and probably get me sacked. If you don't mind, it's probably best if I stay here for a while."

"I... Oh."

Her face reddened, but he spotted the little self-satisfied smirk, too. Still the bratty sub, but now he found he loved that quality about her.

"Aaron, Sir, I could... I mean, if you like..."

Sir? Now this is interesting.

"Are you offering to deal with my boner for me, Genie?"

"I am, Sir. If you would find that helpful."

Christ! "A delightful notion. And what about you? What would you like?"

"Anything, Sir. Or nothing. I would enjoy pleasing you, but I know that we are no longer..."

He watched in silence as her blush deepened. She really was the sexiest little piece. His cock threatened to burst from his trousers any moment now as he struggled to recall what his objections had been when she'd suggested resurrecting their previous relationship.

His mind was a blank. The only image he could conjure up was of Genie naked at his feet. He thanked the Lord for the security requirements, which meant that his was the only executive office with a lock on the door. A word from him, just one command, and she'd strip for him before dropping to her knees.

Then what? He'd fuck her, possibly offer her a spanking, if she wanted it. They'd have fun, then she'd go back to her office and he'd study the wedding guest list. They'd be colleagues once more, workmates who enjoyed an occasional kinky fuck. In work time no less.

So much for her ambitious plans of building a glittering career for herself. He could ruin that for her, annihilate her newfound professional self-image with just a few words and some well-aimed slaps on her delicious derrière. He couldn't do it. Wouldn't do it.

Aaron shook his head. It was a tempting prospect, but business was business for both of them. And if he ever let this attraction grow, become more than a quick scene behind the filing cabinet, what would that lead to? What might she expect? What would she be entitled to expect?

He'd been so sure they were over, so convinced their relationship was dead. He was not a Dom to be led by his cock, never had been. And whatever sort of sub Eugenie had been in the past—and now he was by no means certain he had understood her at all—she had matured into a beautiful, graceful woman, a woman to be treasured. She would be a submissive to savor, to take time over, her responses to be teased from her, drawn out by his touch, his words, the pain and the pleasure he could deliver.

As he regarded her across his desk, he knew he wanted that. He wanted her. Still. He had yet to convince himself of the wisdom of going back down that route, but in a flash of self-awareness, he knew that was only a matter of time.

"Not now, Genie. And not here. But soon."

"I see. Does this mean we are—I mean, have you changed your mind?"

"We need to talk. Again."

"Very well, Sir. This evening then?"

Aaron inclined his head. "Meet me in the library, say about eight? We should have it to ourselves by that time."

"I could come to your apartment, Sir. Would that not be better? My studio is very small."

"Neutral territory, I think. The library, and dinner later. I'll book us a table somewhere. Now, though, I have to review this list and you need to leave."

"Leave, Sir?"

"Yes, leave. Before anyone else comes in and I embarrass myself entirely." He shifted in his seat, attempting to rearrange his trousers to relieve the pressure. His attempts elicited a smile from Eugenie.

"I understand. My apologies, Sir. I will be next door if you require anything." She stood and made for the door. He was convinced the seductive sway of her hips as she left the room was affected just for his benefit.

It worked.

* * * *

"Nine o'clock. A table for two, please. Yes, charge it to my staff account. Aaron Praed. Thanks."

Aaron replaced the receiver and leaned back in his chair. His erection was somewhat subdued now, though he had no doubt Madamoiselle d'André would be able to rekindle it with one lick of her delectable lips. Christ, how had he managed without her for three years? For three minutes, even?

A more appropriate question would be, why?

Because she challenged him, unsettled him. Made him doubt himself, question his prowess as a Dom. The bottom line was — she baffled him.

Aaron closed his eyes, thought back to that day three years ago when he'd provoked her into losing her temper with him to such devastating effect. At the time, he'd been angry, but that soon passed to leave in its wake pure mystification. He had no idea what had made her lose it and turn on him. He had not been unduly harsh with her, and although he had never caned her previously, she'd had no reason that he could think of to believe he'd go too far. He'd punished her before that — frequently — and she had always walked away unharmed. Why her reaction on that day?

When she first brought up the subject of their past, he had urged her to let it go, to put it behind her. Now he knew they couldn't leave it at that. If they were to have any future together, or more specifically, if they were to resurrect their Dom/sub relationship, he had to understand her. He needed her to feel able to tell him what had caused her to snap, though he had a strong suspicion she wouldn't know the answer if he asked her.

So, where did that leave them? Him?

It left him relying purely on his Dom instincts. He would talk to her tonight, and tomorrow and the day after that. He'd keep on talking to her, probing her recollections of what had happened and how she had felt that morning. He would manage, somehow, eventually, to see the events through her eyes and identify the trigger.

If — when — he was successful, and knew what he'd done wrong the first time, he would invite her to replay the scene. This time he would get it right. Then they might be able to move on.

Chapter Eleven

Underwear? Yes or no?

Eugenie stood in front of her mirror, wondering whether to wear panties or not. Aaron had hinted pretty strongly that he wanted to scene with her, and he had a definite preference for an uncovered pussy. He always liked her to be accessible, but would she be making assumptions?

Well, perhaps she would, but she'd deal with the consequences if need be. If Aaron got as far as discovering her pantieless state, she suspected he'd be inclined to applaud rather than take issue. Now, could she also manage without a bra, or was that just too obvious?

It was a couple of minutes after eight o'clock when she slipped into the library. Aaron was already there, at ease in one of the large leather winged chairs, a tray of coffee on the low table in front of him. He glanced up and smiled as she entered.

"I am sorry to be late. I had a call just before I left — Elise."

"No problem. I ordered coffee for us. And I booked a table at La Mignon for later. Nine o'clock all right?"

"Yes, that will be lovely." Eugenie sat in the chair at Aaron's right and accepted the cup he handed to her. She took a sip and placed it on the table, then folded her hands in her lap.

"You look wonderful. I like that dress."

"Thank you." She reached for her coffee again, conscious of his pensive stare.

"Miss d'André, are you wearing a bra?"

"No, Sir."

"I see. Knickers?"

"No, Sir."

He nodded, offering no further comment as she proceeded to drink her coffee. At last, Eugenie could bear it no longer.

"Sir, I apologize if I overstepped the mark. I just thought it best to make my position clear."

"Your position?"

"Yes, Sir. As your submissive. If you'll have me back."

"Well that's plain enough. I appreciate a forthright subbie. It saves a lot of trouble. And time. You weren't always given to such plain speaking, though."

"No, Sir."

"Which gives rise to our current predicament. So, here's my position. I do want you back, but not until we've talked. Really talked. We should have done this years ago. It's my fault we didn't, but I intend to set that straight right now."

"I see, Sir. What is it you wish to discuss?"

"I wish to discuss what happened the last time we scened together. I want to know why you reacted as you did. Can you enlighten me at all?"

"I was—angry. Very upset, Sir. But no matter how distressed I was, I should never have done such a thing. I do appreciate that. I would be grateful if you could overlook my outburst and allow me to atone for my behavior. If you have a cane, Sir, I would be honored to accept the ten strokes now. Or more, if you think it appropriate."

"I see. A generous offer—I may take you up on that. And yes, I could lay my hands on a cane if need be. You mention being angry and upset. Distressed too. What about scared? Were you frightened of what I intended for you?"

"Maybe. A little. That is not what I mainly recall, though."

"So, what had so upset you?"

"I had made you angry. You were disappointed in me. Again."

"And? That's hardly a reason to lay into me. Just the opposite, really."

Eugenie stared at her fingers, lacing them together in her lap. "This is difficult. I am not certain. It was just... I felt—frustrated. I was so often in trouble. I made many mistakes."

"A lot of them on purpose. You wanted me to spank you."

"I did, but that is not such a bad thing, surely."

"I would have preferred you to just ask me. Tell me what you wanted. I can't read minds, and I don't like being manipulated."

"I apologize. I am making you angry again."

Aaron leaned across and took her hand. "No, Genie, you're not. I'm trying to understand. Whatever you say to me this evening, I won't be angry. I want to know what's in your head. So, back to that morning. You say you felt frustrated, and that suggests to me that you expected something different from me. I had told you I intended to punish you."

"Yes, Sir. You did."

"So why did you find it frustrating when I did just that?"

"Because... Because I thought you would be nice to me in the morning. If I stayed in the spare room all night, alone, as you told me to. I came downstairs early, but you didn't seem to mind that. You gave me food and I thought you would hold me, perhaps tell me I was a good girl for waiting all night. Then you would fuck me. But you didn't. You just seemed to want to carry on punishing me, even though I had obeyed you and I had apologized. You still were not satisfied and I felt...let down. I wanted it to end and I thought it had ended, then you ordered me into the dining room and made me lean over the table."

She fell silent, tears pricking her eyes as she relived the intense emotion of that morning. She felt again the dismay at realizing her punishment was to continue, the uncertainty that she could ever satisfy this implacable Dom. And above all, the sheer bloody unfairness of it all.

"Genie, you said I seemed to want to carry on punishing you. But I hadn't started."

"What more did you intend? Would it have continued all day, and for another night perhaps? And another? I could not bear that."

"Another night? What do you mean?"

"I suppose I thought you might make me spend another night alone. That was a cunning punishment to choose. I hated it, but I realize now that was what you had intended. It was awful, though, knowing you were in the next room but refusing to let me be with you. I wanted you to hold me, to forgive me, but you would not."

Aaron narrowed his eyes in concentration, then she caught the gleam of sudden awareness and understanding. "Oh, shit."

"Sir?"

"Fucking shit."

"Excuse me?"

"I never realized. Never even considered the effect a night on your own would have on you. I simply meant you to remain safe until I was cool enough to administer the caning. It was not meant as a punishment."

Eugenie stared at him, incredulous. "Of course it was. How could it not have been? I hated being separated from you. You knew that."

"I didn't."

"But you must have."

"Why would I? You lived alone. I worked long hours and so did you. We were often separated for days, weeks sometimes."

"Not at your home. When I was there, I was with you. Always. You never locked me in a room alone."

"I didn't lock you in."

"It was the same thing. You told me to stay there, even though I begged to come with you. To sleep in your bed with you."

Aaron's expression was now one of utter amazement, closely followed by dismay. "Christ, what was I thinking? God, sweetheart, I'm so sorry. I honestly never even considered that possibility. You did ask me. You did beg. I should have known."

"You did not know? You did not intend me to be upset by that?"

"No. God, no!"

"I... Oh."

"So, in the morning, you came looking for me, expecting aftercare. And I made you prepare for a caning. Christ, no wonder you were upset." He chuckled, a mirthless sound. "I think I got off lightly, considering."

"Even so, to do as I did..."

Aaron reached for her hand. "Maybe your reaction was over the top, but you were sorely provoked. I do see that now. I could tell at the time that something was badly off, but I convinced myself it was just that you weren't truly a submissive. I was wrong. I should have talked to you, or better still listened." He paused, his smile tinged with sadness. "For what it's worth, I'd already decided not to go through with the caning. You took matters into your own hands, though, before I could tell you that."

"You mean, if I hadn't lost my temper...?"

He nodded. "Just a couple more seconds would have done it. Better still, I should have pulled back earlier. It should never have got to the point where you felt desperate enough to hit out. I failed you, as your Dom, and I apologize."

"No, Sir. It was..."

"Genie, I was the one in control. I could have changed how that scene went. The worst thing is, I let myself believe the problem was down to you, that your submission was at fault. Or perhaps your lack of it. Shit, I even left you believing that too. I can't tell you how much I regret how it turned out, that morning and afterward You tried to talk to me, and I shut you out."

"But it is turning out all right now, *n'est-ce pas*? We are talking. We understand each other now."

"Well, we're certainly getting there. I'm just amazed you still trust me enough to even contemplate letting me near you again."

"I love you, Sir. I have never stopped loving you. So, it is simple, I think."

"Genie, nothing about this, about you, was ever simple. You challenge me at every turn, and there will be times I suspect when you'll just plain baffle me. But I want to try again with you and I swear I'll pay better attention in future."

"Then I accept your terms, Sir."

"Excellent. And now, I reckon our table at La Mignon should be about ready. Are you hungry?"

"Sir, I do believe I am."

* * * *

"So, Genie, about your underwear. Or lack of it."

"Sir?" Eugenie spread a smear of butter across her bread roll and regarded Aaron across the table.

"Your choice is very convenient. Please finish your roll. Then I'd like you to stroke your pussy and tell me exactly how wet you are."

"I see. Of course, Sir." Eugenie nibbled the roll, taking delicate little bites from it.

"I may have misread your signals in the past, but I'm pretty sure you're taking the piss now. I do not recommend it, Genie."

"I apologize, Sir." She finished her roll in two swift bites, dusted the crumbs from her fingers and proceeded to lift the front of her skirt. Her actions were concealed by the thick linen tablecloth, though she took the precaution of dropping her napkin across her lap too. The slide back into her old submissive headspace was effortless, felt natural. She was delighted that Aaron appeared intent on starting their scene immediately, and she was more than happy to comply.

She stroked her cunt, sliding her fingers between her moist pussy lips and dipping the tips of two of her digits inside herself. She swirled them around, caressing her inner walls, loving the sensation and luxuriating in the heat of his gaze as he watched her. She took her time about pulling her fingers out then held her hand up for him to inspect the juices coating it.

Aaron leaned across the table to take her hand, raising it to his nose to inhale the musky smell of her.

"Mmm, you seem very aroused, little sub."

"Yes, Sir."

"Is there anything you might like to request from me?"

"There is, Sir. I was hoping you might fuck me."

"I might. Eventually."

"Sir?"

"First, we have a dinner to enjoy. And you did offer to submit to a belated caning. I intend to invite you to join me in my apartment, where I can take care of all these matters to our mutual satisfaction."

"I see, Sir."

"Tomorrow's Sunday. Are you intending to work?"

"No, Sir, I was hoping to take the day off. As long as nothing urgent arises, of course."

"Of course. In that case, I expect you to remain with me all night. You will sleep with me, girl."

"I'd like that, Sir. Very much."

"And tomorrow? As you're taking a day off work, what are your plans?" He turned to smile at the waiter who had arrived with their main course, a fragrant *boeuf bourguignon* with a selection of vegetables and rice. The serving tureens were arranged across their table, but Aaron declined the server's offer to fill their plates for them. The waiter scurried off.

"You were saying, Genie, about your plans for tomorrow?"

Eugenie helped herself to *petits pois* and a few sliced carrots. "I usually walk on my days off, Sir. Perhaps along the Seine. Or maybe along the Champs-Élysées to la Louvre. Anywhere, really. I just love this city."

"Me too. Would you like company on this excursion of yours?"

"You want to come sightseeing with me?"

"Why not? We could hit the tourist trail together. I'll even treat you to an ice cream. Or a hot dog."

"In that case, Sir, I would love your company tomorrow. Please, would you pass me the potatoes? I think I may need the sustenance."

"I suspect you will, Genie. And you know how I feel about fattening you up." He piled a generous helping onto her plate. "Now eat up. I find myself rather keen to ask for the bill and get out of here."

* * * *

Aaron's staff apartment was on the floor above Eugenie's. It was not a great deal larger than hers, though his did boast a separate bedroom and his bathroom was more spacious, accommodating a bath as well as a shower. He also had a small balcony, though the view lacked the more spectacular vistas offered by the guest suites. Eugenie gazed around his living room.

"How is it you have more space than I do?"

"Seniority, sweetheart."

"You are not senior to me."

"No?" He raised one eyebrow, daring her to take issue with him on this. Eugenie felt discretion may be called for.

"Well, not at work. Here, yes, I accept that, Sir."

"Good. I'm glad we have that settled. In which case, lose the clothes and kneel."

Eugenie felt herself slipping yet deeper into the once familiar mindset as she unfastened the buttons on the front of her dress. She'd not been especially conscious of this sensation when she and Aaron were together in the past, but had been intensely aware of its absence as she'd scened with a succession of other Doms in the years since. A sort of calm descended on her, a quiet acceptance of his control, a willingness to obey and to serve him.

As the fabric slipped from her body to pool around her feet, she stepped into the center of the room and, without a word, sank to her knees.

She tucked her heels beneath her, spreading her legs a little, just sufficient to allow an unimpeded view of her swelling clit. Her hands lay on her thighs, palms up, and she lowered her gaze to a spot on the floor about a foot in front of her.

Aaron's footsteps behind her caused her to tense, though in anticipation rather than fear. She was not afraid of him, not in the least. He had mentioned a cane, and she had no doubt that if he said he could acquire one then he could indeed do so. She was content with that, would submit willingly, now or in the future. Privately she hoped he would not resort to it this evening, but that was not her choice and she would not mention any reservation she might have.

"I never forgot how lovely you are. If anything you're more beautiful now than you were three years ago." His voice was soft, his hand gentle as he stroked her hair.

Eugenie thought she might purr.

"I see you still wax. Is that especially for me?"

"It is now, Sir. I got into the habit with you as you required it, and I have come to prefer being smooth."

"I still require it. It lends a whole new level to naked."

Eugenie's stomach clenched in pleasure at his words. She hadn't realized until that moment how very desperately she wanted to please Aaron. She needed his approval so much she ached with it. And how fearful she had been that she might somehow fall short of his expectations. She couldn't bear that.

"So now, what do you want, Genie?"

"Sir? I want you. Just you."

"You will have me. What would you like me to do to you?"

"Spank me, Sir. I need that."

"Need?"

"I have missed your hand, Sir. I need you to make me scream."

"Ah yes, pain always seemed to have a calming effect on you. That and a few rocking orgasms."

"The orgasms would be very welcome too, Sir."

"I'm sure. I recall you used to be very supple. Can you still touch your toes, Genie?"

"I can, Sir."

"In that case, please stand and bend over."

Eugenie got to her feet, taking care to execute the move as smoothly and with as much grace as possible. She stole a peep at Aaron's face and took encouragement from his satisfied expression. So far so good. She bent over, placing her palms on the floor in front of her.

"Spread your legs. I want to be able to see your cunt."

"Like this, Sir?" She shuffled her feet apart, aware of the cool rush as her pussy was exposed to the air-conditioned atmosphere.

"Perfect. You're glistening, Genie. Aroused already?"

"Yes, Sir. It would seem so."

"Such a slut."

"Your slut, Sir."

"Mine." He drove three fingers deep into her cunt, causing Eugenie to rock forward and emit a small gasp. A sharp slap to her buttock turned the gasp into a squeal. "Keep still, girl. And be quiet."

He finger-fucked her hard, angling his thrusts to hit her G-spot. Eugenie concentrated on remaining in position and bit her lower lip to keep from crying out. She wondered briefly if all women were configured the same way, or had he managed to retain perfect recall of the geography of her body? He certainly knew his way around her.

As suddenly as he had started, he stopped. She groaned as he withdrew his fingers, but knew better than to complain. Instead, she shifted her feet and hands on the floor to settle more comfortably into her submissive, exposed posture.

She listened as his footsteps receded. He was moving away from her. She waited, heard him return. Then she winced as something hard and cool trailed across her bottom. The cane?

"You know what this is, little Genie?"

"I think so, Sir?"

"Any objections?"

She gulped, but schooled her voice to remain even. "No, Sir. Please proceed."

"Will you be able to keep still?"

"I'm not sure. The only other time I was caned, I was tied to a bench."

She thought he hesitated before asking his next question. "Tell me about that time, Genie."

She shifted again, concentrating hard on maintaining her balance. "It was a punishment. I had been very rude to my Dom. In public. So he caned me. In public. Twelve strokes."

Aaron whistled. "Twelve strikes, and a public caning at that. He must have been very pissed off."

"Yes, Sir. He was. I had called him a mean, controlling bastard when he rebuked me for orgasming without his permission."

"Mean and controlling—those traits are in the Dom job description."

"I realize that, Sir. I was in a bad mood. I should not have said it."

"And did it work? Were you suitably chastened?"

"I apologized, Sir."

"That's not what I asked."

"I know. I did not like him very much, Sir. And I do not believe he liked me. We only scened a couple more times after that."

"So, he caned you. In public. Then dumped you." It was a statement, not a question.

From his tone, she knew he did not approve of the conduct of this Dom from her past.

"I suppose he did, though I was not distressed at the loss. As I said, I did not like him."

"Do you like me, Genie?"

"I do, Sir. Very much. I never stopped liking you." She paused for a moment then continued. "I never stopped loving you, Sir."

Aaron paused, seemed to be considering her last remark. "I'm also a mean, controlling bastard. You must remember that about me. Especially now, when you're about to receive a caning."

"I love you, Sir. It is that simple. Really. And I trust you."

"Good answer. Let's get on with it, then. I won't tie you up, but would you prefer to lean on something for this?"

"If you would permit that, Sir."

"Of course. I'm finished admiring your pretty little cunt for now. You may straighten up."

Eugenie obeyed, relieved as the backs of her thighs were really starting to hurt. She stretched, rolled the stiffness from her shoulders before glancing at Aaron for further instructions. She could not prevent her eyes being drawn to the slender length of rattan dangling from his right hand. Was this the same one from before? Had he brought it with him to Paris from Northumberland?

"The chair. Brace yourself on one of the arms. I want your legs slightly apart and your bum lifted up for me. Tell me when you're ready."

"Thank you, Sir." Eugenie walked across the room to the chair and stood beside it. She placed her palms on the cushioned arm and lowered her shoulders. She arched her back to lift her bottom up, then decided she could do better and laid her elbows on the chair arm. She folded her arms and rested her forehead on them, the new position raising her ass farther in the air. She turned her head to face him. "Is this all right, Sir?"

"Fucking beautiful." Aaron followed her across the room to stand behind her. "I'm going to start with some gentle slaps to bring your blood to the surface, get you warmed up a little. I haven't decided how many strokes of the cane to give you. I'll stop when you stop liking it, so I'll be asking you frequently."

"Liking it, Sir?"

"Yes. Liking it. Despite your willingness to accept your caning from three years ago, this is not a punishment, Genie. I'll stop at any time, if you ask me. Or if I think you're looking distressed. So, are you ready?"

She nodded then closed her eyes to wait.

Aaron's palm connected with her upturned bottom, the slaps soft at first but gaining in strength as her skin started to tingle under his rapid taps. She wriggled, moaning her pleasure as he prepared her for the cane. By instinct alone, she parted her thighs, hoping he might take the hint and caress her pussy too. Maybe even drop a few slaps there.

Aaron picked up on her cues and landed a sharp swat on her throbbing pussy lips. Eugenie squealed, opening her legs wider.

"Ah, my lovely little slut. You like that?"

She nodded.

"More?"

"Please. More, Sir."

Aaron continued to rain quick, sharp swats across her now throbbing buttocks, delivering an occasional blow to her pussy or clit. Genie murmured her thanks for each strike across her cunt and wondered if she might come just from this.

"Not yet, greedy little subbie. You need to earn orgasms."

How did he always know what she was thinking? He'd said he was not a mind reader, but he gave a decent impression of one.

"I know that, Sir. I am sorry."

"Stop apologizing, Genie. You're doing fine." Aaron caressed her smarting skin, digging his fingers into the soft, rounded flesh of her buttocks. It felt heavenly.

The sensation changed. He laid the cane across her bottom, stroking her with it. Her breath hitched.

"Relax, love. Allow yourself to enjoy this."

His low, sexy tone calmed her, reassured her that whatever was about to happen would be fine.

Aaron tapped her with the cane, not hard, but still it sent a tingle through her sensitized skin. He repeated the action then did it again. Just as he'd dropped rapid slaps onto her rounded cheeks with his hand, now he did the same thing with the cane. The blows became faster, faster still, but remained light. Eugenie exhaled, realizing she'd been holding her breath in anticipation of the pain she was sure was about to explode across her ass.

Aaron pressed the cane into her bum, then raised it and dropped a single hard stroke across her right buttock. Eugenie screamed. Aaron caressed the spot, smoothing the pain away. She remained still, gasping as he massaged her bottom. The pain seemed to melt, soaking deep into her body, leaving a vague sense of anticipation in its wake. Of incompleteness. She wanted more.

"Again?" Aaron's low murmur penetrated her shuddering consciousness.

"Yes, please."

Moments later, the light tapping of the cane sent waves of quivering anticipation through her left buttock. He built the sensation, and Eugenie clenched in pleased welcome. As he pressed the cane into her skin, she drew in her breath and held it, letting it out in a sharp cry as the cane sliced across her soft curve.

The gentle caress of Aaron's hand followed, causing the hurt to sink deep into her flesh.

"Oh, Sir..."

"Enough yet?"

"No. More, please."

"Okay." He repeated the sequence, and Eugenie moaned in delight as he built the tempo across her right buttock again. He choose a spot below where he'd laid the first stroke, and this time she heard the soft swishing sound as the cane dropped for the final, hard stroke.

"Aargh. Oh, oh Christ, Sir." She was clenching and unclenching her buttocks as Aaron rubbed the sore spot. The sharp burning sensation subsided quickly to become a deep, throbbing ache.

"Genie?"

"Again, Sir. I need more." *Oh, Christ, it's been so long. So long.*

She groaned as he tapped her left buttock, knowing he would pick his spot with care to avoid the welt already striping her ass. She needed to hold still and benefit from his practiced accuracy, but shit, this hurt. It really hurt. Still, she wanted it. Her excitement built as he increased the speed and weight of his taps with the cane then the final whooshing slice that left a trail of fire across her rear. Eugenie screamed and collapsed forward as Aaron caressed the pain away. She was panting heavily as she absorbed the searing heat of the final stripe.

Aaron laid the cane on the seat of the chair, right in her eye line.

"Sir? I could manage more."

"Maybe you could. I prefer to leave you to thinking that, though, than have you safe word. Next time there will be more."

Despite her protests, Eugenie was relieved. And astounded. Her first erotic caning and he'd made it so hot for her. She'd felt cherished and completely safe. She lay still for a few moments, letting that realization take root. She turned her head to face him once more. "Thank you for showing me how good this can be. May I get up now, Sir?"

"Soon. First, though…" He moved behind her and dropped to his knees. He parted her throbbing buttocks with his hands to reveal her tight anus. "Ah, so pretty, and such a wet, needy little pussy we have here. Maybe while I'm in such a generous mood you might like me to deal with this for you?"

"Oh God, Sir, please. Please…" Eugenie spread her legs as wide as she could, her desperation mounting. She needed him to touch her, to fill her. She needed to come. She screamed again as he dipped the tip of his tongue into her pussy, slipping it between her swollen lips to swirl it inside her. At the same time, he trailed a finger along her slit to collect her moisture and used that natural lubrication to ease the way into her ass. He pressed one finger slowly into her, turning it as he did so to loosen the tight ring of muscle.

Eugenie sank deeper into her submission, relaxing her body to allow him total access. She felt to be floating outside her body, adrift in some dreamlike trance. Aaron sank a second digit into her ass. She welcomed it, loved the fullness, the wicked intimacy of it. He licked her clit, flicking the tip with his tongue. His strokes firmed as she stiffened, her orgasm moments away.

"Come for me, sweetheart."

His murmured command was all she required to release the dam that had been building. With a low, keening moan, Eugenie allowed her body to convulse, offering herself up in final capitulation. Aaron continued to lick her clit and pussy lips until the final shudders died away and only then did he pull his fingers from her ass. Eugenie's knees buckled under her. She lurched forward, but Aaron caught her as he got to his feet, scooping her up in his arms. He turned and carried her across the room.

Eugenie clung to him, her hands clasped behind his neck, reluctant to let go even when he laid her on her side across his bed. Aaron kicked off his shoes and rolled onto the mattress alongside her, hauling her across his body to arrange her face down on top of him. His arms were around her. He stroked her back, drawing large, comforting circles between her shoulder blades with his palm.

Eugenie shivered. He lifted his hips to raise the pair of them up enough to drag the duvet from under them. He wrapped that around Eugenie, snuggling her in close to him. Eugenie burrowed nearer still, loving the hard warmth of his body under hers, the solid strength and comfort offered by his arms across her shoulders, the smooth planes of his chest beneath her cheek.

"Do you still love me, little one? Even after that?" he murmured into her hair, nuzzling the tangled strands.

Eugenie kissed his nipple, tracing her tongue around the flat nub just visible through the thin fabric of his shirt. "Oh yes, much more after that, Sir. Thank you. Thank you. Thank you."

He chuckled. "Don't thank me too soon, love. I promised to fuck you and I still have to make good on that. Assuming you haven't changed your mind?"

She lifted her head, amazed. "I forgot. I was so, so…"

"So blown away by your first erotic caning?" He arched one eyebrow and seemed to find this amusing.

"Yes, Sir, that must have been it. Is it too late?"

Aaron rolled to face her. "That, sweet Genie, is one of the daftest questions I've heard in a while. Certainly from you. No, it is not too late. And I'm still taking requests, so do you want hard, fast, maybe a little rough, or slow and gentle?"

She peeped up at him from under the duvet, unable to prevent the smile that seemed to split her face. "It's been a while, Sir, so I'd normally suggest hard and fast. But I'm feeling a little delicate so I wonder if…"

"Slow and gentle it is, then. Can you lie on your back, do you think?"

Eugenie rolled into position, taking care not to put her weight on her tender buttocks. "Will there be marks?"

"Oh, yes, for a few days I should think. Your arse looks so well punished right now, little Genie. I'll show you. Later." The duvet slithered to the floor as Aaron stood up and pulled his shirt over his head, the buttons still fastened. He made short work of his trousers as well, grabbing a condom from the pocket before he dropped his shorts too. He was soon kneeling between Eugenie's thighs, rolling the latex over his cock. He placed his hands behind her knees and lifted her legs into the air, raising her off the mattress. The position was more comfortable and she murmured her thanks to him.

"Put my cock between the lips of your pussy, love. Show me where you want me to be."

Eugenie complied, reaching down to wrap her fingers around his erection, treating herself to a couple firm strokes along the shaft before angling him toward her moist and waiting cunt.

"Here, Sir. I want you here. Now."

Aaron surged forward, burying the length of his cock inside her. He stilled, allowing her the moments she needed to reshape around his thick, solid presence. She squeezed him hard, contracting her inner muscles as though she never wanted to let him go. Perhaps she didn't. She reached up to grip his shoulders, her nails digging into him as she shuddered with delight.

Aaron withdrew slowly, then sank deep again. Eugenie sighed, her pussy clenching hard. He repeated the motion, slow and deliberate, dragging out the pleasure. Eugenie began to wonder if she'd made the right choice as her body convulsed and she wriggled under him, seeking more friction. Maybe she should have gone for hard and fast instead.

"Keep still or I'll tie you up." The low growl put a stop to her writhing, at the same time sending a wave of lust through her. This was submission, this was surrender. This was what it meant to relinquish control. Her eyes closed, she allowed her head to drop back as he buried his face in her neck. His thrusts became shorter now, and he gyrated his hips to change the sensation slightly. Eugenie's pussy contracted again, quite beyond any conscious control of hers.

Aaron released his grip on her legs to slide his hand between them on an unerring path to her clit. He found it and rolled the sensitive bud between his fingers, pulling on it as Eugenie's moans increased in volume.

"Come now, little one. Come for me."

"*Oui, oui, je t'aime.* Oh, Sir…"

Aaron gave one last thrust, long and deep this time, the head of his cock nudging her cervix before he stopped and held still for a moment. She trembled, squeezing again as the welcome warmth of his semen filled the condom.

Chapter Twelve

They lay still, limbs tangled, Aaron's cock still buried inside her. He held her close, aware of the frantic pounding of her heart. Or maybe it was his. He was in no hurry to withdraw, but eventually knew he would have to deal with the condom. He kissed her mouth as he rolled from her.

"Hell, baby, I'd forgotten how tight and just how fucking hot you are. Shit, that was so good, so fucking good."

"Yes, I…"

He dropped the knotted latex onto the bedroom floor and turned back to her, tucking her head under his chin. Her hesitancy in speaking was not lost on him.

"What is it, love? Are you okay?"

"Yes, better than okay. I just… I did not want to embarrass you. Or put you in a difficult position. I don't expect anything from you."

"No? Well, you damn well should. What is all this?"

"I said I love you. Twice."

"I know. I heard. And it's been more than twice."

"You don't mind?"

"Mind? Why would I mind?"

"It is just that I have thought about this a lot over the years, since we've been apart. I knew that I loved you and I have always felt this way. I know that you do not love me, though, and I was not trying to trap you or push you, or —"

"Hush, love. I didn't think that, not for a moment. And you're right, you have had longer to get your head around how you feel, but I'll catch up. Give me time."

Eugenie pushed herself up on one elbow, her smile dazzling. "Do you mean that, Sir? Really? You could love me again after what happened?"

"Oh, I reckon so. What's not to love?"

"Everything. I'm a brat. Everyone says so, everyone thinks that."

Aaron was puzzled by the nervous expression on Eugenie's face. She may have said she was okay, but he knew there was more. "What everyone is this, then? Anyone I know?"

"Yes. No. Just, everyone. Doms. Other subs even, I guess."

"Tell me what you mean. What is it I'm missing here?"

He watched, noting the frantic play of emotions across her lovely face. She was nervous, scared even. He suspected he knew what she was struggling to tell him, but he waited, allowed her the time she needed to find the words.

"After we split up, I went a little crazy, I think. It must have been that because I can offer no better explanation for the way I behaved. I'm not proud of myself."

She found this difficult, he could see that. Her lips were pressed together in a thin, tense line and she closed her eyes as though considering carefully what her next words might be. It would have been easy to offer encouragement, or even to say it didn't matter, or it could wait.

He did none of those. He said nothing, confident she would get there in her own time. She had chosen to tell him now, so this must be the right time. For her.

A few minutes passed before she met his gaze again. "I was a slut. A real slut, not the nice sort as I am with you. And a brat."

"A slut and a brat? Sounds as though you were busy."

"You're making fun of me."

"No, but I am hoping to inject a bit of perspective here. You don't strike me, now, as either of those things."

"I am not. I swear it."

"Okay, so…?"

"After we parted, I went to a lot of clubs. Fetish clubs, you understand. BDSM clubs. I played with any Dom who asked me to — and quite a few did — at first."

"That doesn't surprise me. You're a beautiful submissive, Genie."

"Are you not angry? Jealous?"

"Are you angry and jealous about any of the subs I've been with since we split? There have been several. Would that make me a slut too?"

"Of course not. You are a Dom. You can do what you want."

He chuckled. "Hardly. But it's true I've not led an exactly celibate existence for the last three years, so I'm not about to take issue with you for doing the same. No double standards here, Genie."

"But, I was not a good submissive, not then. Not now, even. I was a brat. I would deliberately goad and irritate my Dom, doing what I could to make him punish me."

"Ah yes, I do remember that trait of yours. You were never easy."

"No. But I am trying to change. I will change. And you said you could love me, even now."

"I hope you won't be changing too much, because as I recall, you were pretty spectacular—complicated, demanding, downright bloody exasperating sometimes—but you were worth it. Well, most of the time."

"So, you liked being my Dom? Most of the time?"

"Fuck, yes!"

"Then, I do not understand. Why were you so determined not to forgive me?"

Aaron paused for a few moments, considering his next words. "It wasn't so much a question of not forgiving you, but of protecting you from my cack-handedness. I believed I was the wrong Dom for you. I couldn't get my head around what had happened, and that being so, I couldn't work out how to manage scenes with you in the future. I should have tried, or trusted my instincts better. Or even trusted you. I definitely should have talked to you—I see that now. You were owed an explanation. But I didn't do any of those things. All I have to say by way of mitigation is that I was less experienced then too."

Eugenie furrowed her brow, as she seemed to be trying to make sense of this. He knew in her apparent rush to blame herself she had not considered that he might assume at least some responsibility. He had been just as ready to blame her and he considered that unforgiveable. The least he could do to make amends was ensure she understood the reality of their situation.

She glanced up at him, her expression uncertain, but hopeful. "And now?"

He dropped a kiss onto the top of her head. "Now I do understand what happened, and what went wrong. What I did wrong, and why you reacted as you did. I'm grateful to have another chance."

Her face was transformed by the beginning of a smile. "Me too. I am so glad I saw that advertisement. I might not have, though. It was only by chance, as I waited to go into a meeting. I saw it as my opportunity to stop being La Brat. But I never expected to find you as well."

He kissed her again. It seemed the natural thing to do somehow. "La Brat? I reckon that suits you. Perhaps you can be my brat now, earn yourself a few more canings. And as for chance, I think maybe you were always meant to be here. As I was. Whatever, you are here now, and so am I. Let's see where it takes us to."

Eugenie wriggled in his arms, wincing a little as her sore bottom made contact with the duvet.

"Still hurting?"

"Mmm, it feels wonderful, Sir. Did you say a few more canings?"

"I did, *ma petite* brat." He gave her bum a playful pat. "Now, sleep. Tomorrow we hit the tourist trail."

* * * *

Aaron couldn't recall having enjoyed a day off so much in a long time. It started well enough, waking to find Eugenie still snuggled up close, warm and soft in his bed, and just got better.

She moaned her appreciation, writhing delectably under him as he made love to her while she was still half asleep, her body responding even before her brain kicked in. She opened her eyes, her smile one of welcome as she laced her fingers behind his neck.

"*Bonjour, Monsieur. Comment vas-tu?*"

"*Je vais bien. Tu?*"

"*Très bien, Monsieur.*"

"Good. And now that I have your attention, do you think you could wrap your legs around my waist?"

"Of course—oh, Sir." Her words were lost in a long, deep moan as he deepened his thrusts, fucking her very slowly and very thoroughly.

They had toast and coffee perched on tall buffets at Aaron's small breakfast bar. As he pushed a second mug in front of her, Aaron thought she had never looked more beautiful. He pondered whether to mention that, but settled on something more prosaic.

"I'll buy you a cooked breakfast while we're out."

"Out, Sir?"

"Yes. We're going sightseeing, remember? You need to go back to your apartment and get dressed. Sensible shoes. We'll be walking."

* * * *

An hour later, they were strolling along the Champs-Élysées, their fingers laced together. Although they were both familiar with this part of the city, the magic never seemed to fade. As the golden arches of McDonald's came into view, Aaron steered her inside.

"I promised you breakfast."

"Here, Sir?"

"Here. The full works—a breakfast wrap with coffee and a hash brown."

"Ah, you are so English, Sir."

"I am. McDonald's is American, though."

"True. Do they do croissants?"

"We'll ask."

They ate outside, watching the growing crowds scuttling past. Even on a Sunday morning, Paris absolutely buzzed with activity, the pavements of the city seeming to throb under their feet.

"You know, it is said that if you sit on the Champs-Élysées for long enough eventually everyone in the world will pass by." Eugenie mentioned this snippet as she contemplated the bustling crowds.

"Yeah?" Aaron was too engrossed watching her to contribute more to the conversation. She truly was exquisite. Her slim build hinted at fragility, but he knew better after yesterday. Now that he was coming to understand her emotional responses too, he really believed they could make a success of this. *He* could make a success of it.

"Sir? Am I boring?" She gazed at him, her expression quizzical as she licked crumbs from her fingers.

"No, you're being absolutely breathtaking." He couldn't take his eyes off her pretty little pink tongue as she captured a stray flake of her sausage and egg bagel from the corner of her lip. Christ, what plans he was making for that tongue.

"Sir?"

He leaned across the small metal table to brush his lips over hers. "I'm glad you're here, Genie. Here in Paris and here with me. Have you finished?"

"Yes. Thank you for the breakfast, Sir. It was delicious. I do not usually come here."

"You should. I like it. It helps to keep me grounded." He loved the luxury and perfection of the hotel, the Michelin-starred perfection of their haute cuisine. Perhaps this was why he enjoyed the contrast with the bright plastic glare offered by this star of the fast-food industry.

He stood and held out his hand again. Eugenie took it, and they resumed their stroll along the wide pavement. They gravitated toward the Arc de Triomphe, resplendent at the western end of the Champs-Élysées. They dodged the traffic to reach the island at the center of the Place Charles de Gaulle where the monument was situated, then stood to admire the architectural precision laid before them. The length of the Champs-Élysées stretched away as far as the Place de la Concorde at its eastern end. The Jardin des Tuileries continued the vista, the whole cutting a perfectly straight line through the heart of the city, testimony to the precise art of town planning. Beyond lay the palace of la Louvre, once home to the kings of France but now housing one of the finest art collections in the world.

"Should we go see the Mona Lisa?" Eugenie turned her face to Aaron, her smile eager and hopeful.

"If you like. I've never seen it."

"Me neither. Not the original anyway. Shall we walk there?"

"Of course. Ready?"

They took over two hours to reach la Louvre, stopping to window-shop under the ornate galleries of the Rue de Rivoli then lingering to enjoy the lawned perfection of the Tuileries. Eugenie declared this one of her favorite haunts and told him she often came here when she had a couple of hours off. Previously, she had always been alone, though.

Aaron squeezed her hand, reminding her that she was not alone anymore.

Leonardo da Vinci's masterpiece did not disappoint, despite being so much smaller than most of the other canvases on display. They spent a few minutes admiring its timeless beauty, the haunting image seeming to follow them with her eyes as they moved on through the galleries.

"So, how are the wedding plans coming along?" Aaron asked as they sat at a table on the wide pavement outside a café, enjoying the late afternoon sunshine. The scene was so typically *Parisien* that Aaron couldn't contain his self-conscious grin. Never much of a tourist as a rule, he'd somehow slipped into the role without even trying. He also noted that he and Eugenie were now tending to converse entirely in French and that felt natural too.

"It's early days, but good so far. It's to be a civil ceremony — that makes things simpler, perhaps. Farah has provided a long list of her preferences for music, color scheme, flowers, food. The guest list is not as long as I had expected, but there are some high-profile names on it, including some royals. Between them, Farah and Lucas seem to know everyone."

"Yeah, a pair of real A-listers. I've been looking at the guest list myself to identify any security issues that need dealing with."

"Will there be problems?"

"Not on my watch. The trick will be nailing everything down tightly, but without strangling the occasion."

"You can do it, though?"

"Yes. I'm not complacent, but I think we'll be fine. I'm bringing in a lot of extra personnel for the three days the wedding party will be with us and for the couple of weeks leading up to it. Everything's under control — or it will be. What about your end of it?"

"The same, really. I still have to source the flowers and a photographer that they both agree on, and I've yet to find enough limousines to get everyone here from the airport within a six-hour window. There are no budget issues, though. It seems money is no object. Even so, I'm not prepared to throw their cash around too much. There's no reason not to drive a hard bargain — we deal in value as well as excellence."

Aaron nodded his approval. "I'll need to vet any suppliers so let me have the details as soon as you can. Ready to start making our way back?"

Eugenie folded her napkin and stood, clasping his hand when he offered it.

"Will you be staying over again tonight?"

"I would like to, but I should not. I have to be at my office very early tomorrow."

He was aware that a delivery of wedding stationery was expected at six thirty in the morning, so her response came as no surprise. What did surprise him, however, was the pang of disappointment he felt. He wouldn't jeopardize her work, though. "I knew you'd say that. Have dinner with me, then?"

"Thank you, Sir. I would love that."

Chapter Thirteen

Eugenie had been working at Totally Five Star for nearly five weeks and those had been the busiest weeks of her life. Every day was packed to the rafters with meetings, correspondence, phone calls and Skype conversations with Farah's team in the Gulf. It was coming together, though, everything dropping into place as she plotted and planned and itemized every aspect of the coming wedding. Nothing was too minor, no detail too small for her attention.

Eugenie liked to think she ran a tight ship. She drove herself hard and expected others to meet her standards. So did Aaron. It was one of the traits she liked most about him. He was every bit as meticulous as she was, determined that there would be no loose ends, no opportunity for any disruptions. The hotel was a hive of activity as new surveillance equipment was installed, additional staff recruited, briefed, trained.

On one occasion, Eugenie had been horrified to discover a heap of discarded packaging in a corner of the ballroom. This was in direct contravention of

Aaron's rules. No unattended packages were tolerated in the hotel at any time, and right now that extended to works materials too. Eugenie had marched up to the team of electricians on their tea break in the staff cafeteria and demanded that the offending items be removed immediately. She stiffened her shoulders at their protestations that they had tidied up after themselves and insisted that their foreman accompany her back to the ballroom. Once there, he'd scratched his head and declared himself baffled. Not the word Eugenie would have used to describe such dereliction, but she'd let it go at that.

The foreman had promised to get the mess shifted. Ten minutes later, she'd checked the ballroom again to find the floor cleared and swept. Satisfied, she'd returned to her office.

This morning she was running late. She decided to take a shower before work then had trouble finding her notebook. Everything, absolutely every detail of her plans, notes from meetings, contacts, it was all in that notebook and she carried it everywhere. Not the most efficient recording method perhaps, certainly not the most high-tech solution, but it just worked for her. She always had her information at hand. There was no point setting off for her morning of back-to-back meetings without it, so she hunted around her small flat until she unearthed the slim, leather-bound volume from under a cushion. She grabbed her keys, her phone, her bag, shoved everything inside and dashed out of the door.

The deep carpeting in the hallway absorbed her rapid footsteps as Eugenie hurried toward the elevator. She offered a polite *"Bonjour"* to a petite maid dragging a vacuum cleaner along the corridor.

The woman replied in a low murmur, bobbing her head at her as Eugenie dashed past.

Eugenie jabbed her finger at the call button, checking her watch as she waited for the lift door to open. She had just eight and a half minutes to get to Elise's office for their regular morning briefing. Anton would be there. Aaron, too, probably, though he might be tied up with final details for the electronic surveillance equipment, which was still being installed in all communal areas, and some of the guestrooms. The prospect of CCTV in the suites themselves was controversial and sensitive, and she knew Aaron would require all his powers of diplomacy to get the wedding party to agree to it.

If anyone could, *he* could.

The elevator showed no sign of arriving. Eight minutes now. She'd be quicker to walk, surely. It was only seven flights and down at that. With an exasperated sigh, she turned and headed back along the hallway to the top of the stairs.

Her strappy sandal loosened as she dashed across the hall, her foot slipping from it. This was all she needed, to break her neck on the stairs. She stopped to perch on the top step, her bag beside her as she reached to refasten her shoe. Satisfied, she started to rise.

The next thing she knew, she was hurtling forward, tumbling head first down the stairs. She curled into a ball instinctively, bouncing painfully on the edges of the stairs as she rolled. Her hips, her shoulders, her knees, the pounding felt brutal as she tumbled toward the bottom of the stairs.

It was over in moments, her headlong fall finished as quickly and as unexpectedly as it had begun. She ended up in a sprawled heap on the landing below, winded and shocked, every inch of her hurting.

Christ, I must have broken something. Everything. The thought flittered through her mind as she waited for the real pain to hit her, the pain that would confirm just where the damage had been sustained. She didn't want to open her eyes, preferring to wait for the little maid from the floor above to come rushing to her aid. But the woman must not have seen her. The soft thud of muffled footsteps hurrying along the corridor above receded to be concluded by the distinct click of a door closing.

Eugenie experimented with one or two tentative movements and was astonished to discover that her legs still worked. Her arms too. Amazing. Thank God and all the saints for the ankle-deep Axminister that covered all the floors in the hotel, even the staff accommodation. It had certainly helped to break her fall. She sat up and flexed her shoulders, turning her head to peer back up the steps she had just descended in such an ungainly manner. Her bag still sat at the top, but otherwise the stairs and landing were deserted.

She dragged herself to her feet and made her slow, painful way back up to the top. As she picked up her bag, she realized she was shaking. And she ached everywhere. Good sense dictated that she should go back to her flat, phone Elise to say she'd taken a tumble and needed to lie down for a while. Their briefing could wait. Probably. Better still, she should call Fleur and ask her to come and check her over for internal injuries, a concussion or whatever.

She did none of those sensible things. Instead, she headed for the elevator. The doors now stood open, the car having at last arrived in response to her earlier summons. It waited for her, the gleaming metallic cocoon representing safety. She stepped in and pressed for the first floor where the offices were situated.

A few minutes later, she slipped through the door into Elise's office, no more than a couple of minutes late. She eased herself gingerly into a spare chair, nodding to the other directors already present—Elise, Anton, Annette. Mercifully, Aaron wasn't there. He would have noticed in an instant that she was not her usual self. She extracted her notebook and a pen from her bag and did her best to pay attention to the morning's business.

All in all, she thought she'd made a decent pass at it. Her ass hurt, her left shoulder throbbed, her knees were stiffening by the minute, but Eugenie managed to ask the right questions and answer those put to her. More or less. Elise had to repeat herself a couple of times, but Eugenie covered her tracks by appearing to refer to her notes. She was not sure why she didn't just tell her colleagues what had just happened. Mainly she was embarrassed. *Who falls over their own feet at the top of a flight of stairs, for heaven's sake, and manages not to break every bone in their body?*

Also, she knew that Elise would insist she go back to her flat and relax, take the rest of the day off at least. And Eugenie just could not spare the time. She was immersed in wedding arrangements, in daily contact with Farah's household staff as they choreographed every detail of the coming event. She had delegated nothing and did not intend to start now. The deal with Farah had been that she would devote her exclusive attention to this affair, and she had meant it.

She would be having no time off, no taking to her bed. Nothing was broken, everything seemed to be still working, just about. She would just get through this day and hopefully she'd be much better by tomorrow. A good night's sleep, a long soak and she'd be fine.

Problem was, her tiny flat boasted a small shower cubicle but no bath. She'd have to prevail on Aaron for that luxury, which would mean telling him about her mishap. And he would fuss. He'd want to know exactly what had happened, how it happened, how she'd managed to be so careless. He did seem so much more easygoing than when she'd first known him, but he was unrelenting as far as taking care of herself was concerned. He liked her to eat properly, to get plenty of sleep, to relax as well as work. He would not approve of her stoicism today.

Eugenie was relieved not to encounter him at all during the course of the day, though that was unusual. The negotiations regarding the proposed surveillance must have been more difficult than he'd anticipated, or maybe other matters had required his attention.

As the afternoon wore on, her back stiffened up and she could hardly move her left shoulder at all. She managed to complete her correspondence by typing more or less one-handed, and groaned as her phone pinged to alert her to the arrival of a text. She knew it had to be from Aaron.

Sorry, missed you today. 8 p.m., my place. Usual rules re underwear.

Normally, she'd be bouncing with excitement at such a promise. This evening she knew she couldn't do it. She would have to tell him what had happened, that she'd managed to hurl herself down the stairs then made matters worse by dragging herself through a full day's work. Shit, she hadn't even checked the bruising, let alone shown up at Fleur's clinic for a more thorough check-up. He'd have a right to be pissed off, but she just wished he wouldn't find it necessary to take issue with her over it while she felt so fragile.

She knew it would do no good to appeal to his sympathy. The fall was an accident. He might grumble, but he'd live with that. Her disregard for herself afterward, though, would earn her a spanking at least. With a grimace, she decided to make the best of it. She picked up her phone to return his text

Took a tumble earlier and feeling a bit stiff. Is it all right to use your bath? I need a long soak.

His response came seconds later.

What happened?

With a sigh, she tapped out her response.

Fell down the stairs this morning. Nothing broken but a few bruises.

His reply was instantaneous.

What does Fleur say?

Now for it.

I didn't see her. I'm fine. Really.

Go to Fleur's office. Now.

She sent the only possible reply.

Yes, Sir.

* * * *

"Some quite severe bruising, especially around the shoulders and left hip. No fractures and no obvious signs of concussion, but I really would have preferred to have seen you earlier. As soon as this happened."

Fleur's words were not unreasonable, but Eugenie knew they signaled the start of what would prove to be a difficult conversation with Aaron. He had arrived at Fleur's office a few minutes after Eugenie did and had stood in silence as she allowed the doctor to examine her. Fleur had suggested he might wait outside, but Eugenie protested at that. She needed him — it was that simple. She proceeded to remove her blouse for the doctor to see her battered torso, then she perched quietly on the edge of the examination couch while the doctor did her stuff.

Eugenie snatched a glance in Aaron's direction and her heart sank. He looked so formidable, so bloody angry with her. He leaned against the door, his arms folded across his chest, eyes narrowed. He made no comment as Fleur checked Eugenie's pulse, listened to her breathing, shone her little penlight in her eyes.

"You can go, but take things easy for the next day or so. If you experience any dizziness, any nausea, headaches — I want to know. I'll prescribe you something to ease the inflammation and reduce the pain a little, but what you really need now is rest."

"I'll see to it she follows orders. Thank you, Fleur." Aaron eased himself from the door and passed Eugenie her blouse to put back on. He held the sleeves for her as she struggled to maneuver her shoulders, then he stepped in front of her to fasten the buttons. His expression was grim.

"You said you wanted a soak?"

"Please, yes."

"Okay. Let's go, then." He nodded to Fleur as she sat at her desk to enter her notes in the computer. The doctor lifted her hand in what Eugenie felt seemed like a sympathetic wave as they exited. Odd, there was no way the doctor could even start to imagine what Aaron probably had in store for her.

They walked in silence to the elevator. Eugenie cringed as he punched the call button.

"Sir, I—"

"Save it. We'll talk in my apartment."

Eugenie followed him into the elevator, her eyes fixed on her shoes. If only she'd buckled her sandal properly that morning, then she wouldn't have needed to stop to refasten it. Her body ached, every bloody inch of it. She just wanted to lounge in a warm bath then sleep. Instead, she had an angry Dom to contend with. A Dom intent on retribution.

She'd been in a similar position before, she now recalled. Three years ago, in Newcastle. She'd felt dire then, utterly miserable, yet he'd piled on the pressure—and she'd snapped. She promised herself she would not make the same mistake this time, no matter how severe his punishment. But despite her resolve, she wished he'd just leave her alone to lick her wounds tonight.

Aaron opened the door to his apartment and gestured her inside. She hugged herself as she stood in the center of his living room feeling awkward and unhappy. Aaron marched past her and headed for the bathroom. A few seconds later, the sound of running water reached her.

Her bath. He intended to let her have that soak. With any luck, he'd let her ease some of the aching from her bones before he exacted his retribution for her careless disregard for her wellbeing. Sure enough, he re-emerged, sleeves rolled up.

"Should be ready in a few moments. Get undressed, please."

Disobedience was not an option. And in any case, she wanted that bath. She slipped off her sandals before starting to unfasten the buttons down the front of her blouse. She winced as she attempted to shrug out of it. Aaron stepped up behind her and eased the sleeves down her arms.

"Thank you, Sir."

"Can you manage the rest?"

"Could you unfasten my bra, please?"

He unsnapped it and Eugenie leaned forward to slip the lacy lingerie off. Aaron took it from her and placed it on the couch. She released the button on the waistband of her skirt and allowed that to fall around her ankles. As she started to bend to retrieve it, Aaron beat her to it. She stepped out of the pooled linen to allow him to pick the skirt up and fold it with the rest of her things. Her briefs were next, and she was naked.

Aaron walked slowly around her, circumnavigating her as he inspected every inch of her bruised body.

"Shit, girl, that looks sore. You managed to work all day, in this state?"

"Yes, Sir."

"Why?"

She glanced up at him, surprised he would need to ask that. "Because I was busy, Sir. We are all busy."

He made no comment on that. "Did Elise know?"

Eugenie shook her head.

Aaron snorted in apparent disgust. "No, I'll bet she didn't. Yeah, everyone's busy, but that doesn't mean we're expected to fucking kill ourselves. There's nothing you needed to do that couldn't have waited until tomorrow, or next week. Or someone else could have stepped in, helped you out for a bit. You're part of a team here and that's how it works. You could have taken the day off."

Eugenie raised her gaze to his, her defensive instincts kicking in. "I…"

"What?" He tipped up his chin, waiting.

"Nothing, Sir. You're right. I'm sorry." She bowed her head as she accepted the truth of his words.

"You will be. But now, your bath should be ready. I'll help you get in—you look as though you can hardly move."

Eugenie muttered her appreciation as he held her arms, steadying her as she lowered her body into the steaming water. He'd put something pleasantly aromatic in there too, and a soft, inviting foam lay on the surface. Surprised, she hadn't expected him to own a bottle of bubble bath. She sighed in relief as she sank into the warm depths, felt the heat envelop her aching limbs.

"Lie back, just relax for a while. Would you like some music?"

Eugenie nodded, her eyes closed. A few seconds later, the strains of something soft and classical drifted around the room.

"Mozart. Do you like it?"

Eugenie nodded, her eyelids heavy.

"Enjoy it, then. I'll be back soon to wash your hair— and the rest of you."

Was that a glimmer of humor in his voice? Eugenie thought it might have been, but knew better than to get her hopes up. Punishment first, play later.

* * * *

"How do you feel now?"

Eugenie opened her eyes to see Aaron crouching beside her, his arms folded on the edge of the bath. She managed a watery smile.

"It's easier now, Sir. Less stiff. Thank you for this."

"You're welcome." He stood to unhook the showerhead from its bracket. "Ready for your hair now?"

"You don't have to do that, Sir. I can manage. Really."

"Really? I think not. Sit up, girl." He slipped an arm under her shoulders to help her into a sitting position. Neither of them spoke as he sprayed her hair with warm water then worked lather into her long, curling strands. Eugenie thought this was the first time since she'd been a child that anyone other than a professional stylist had washed her hair for her. She could get to like it.

Aaron rinsed the suds away then squirted more shampoo into his palm. He massaged her scalp slowly, working the lather through as Eugenie tilted her head back into his palms.

"Is this good?"

"Mmm, yes, Sir. Wonderful."

"I have some conditioner somewhere. Would you like that too?"

"Thank you, Sir. That would be nice."

Aaron rinsed the shampoo off, then rifled through his bathroom cabinet for a miniature bottle of hotel conditioner. He grinned as he returned to the side of the bath. "I don't use it myself, but even so we can't let the guests swipe the lot. I like to keep a bit in reserve."

That explanation probably accounted for the bubble bath too.

Eugenie thought she might just fall asleep in the cooling bathwater as he stroked the slick cream though her hair, working slow circles into her scalp. He lingered over the delicate hollows just behind her ears then moved on to her neck.

By the time he reached her shoulders, Eugenie knew that any pretense of conditioning her hair was over. He was exploring her fragile body now.

"Where does it hurt most?"

"My back. And my bum."

"I see. Pity about your bum. Can you lean forward a little, love? Let me reach a bit farther down."

Eugenie obeyed, loving the feel of his fingers as they played along her spine. For a Dom intent on punishment, he was being incredibly gentle. Despite her discomfort, her pussy moistened in helpless response. Perhaps she might be able to work up some interest in fucking him after all, though he might yet manage to beat that sentiment out of her. Just as she deserved.

Eugenie gulped, biting back a sob. She felt dreadful and not just because of the physical toll this day had taken on her. She was filled with remorse for having ignored what she knew would have been Aaron's wishes and, without doubt, the wishes of her boss too. She'd let herself believe she was so indispensable that she just had to carry on, that no one else could replace her, that the whole wedding might fall apart if she missed a day's work. How arrogant, how self-important could she be? He was right to be disappointed in her. She was disappointed in herself.

It was not even as though she'd been firing on all four cylinders today. She'd most likely spend most of tomorrow putting right the errors she'd made. How could she have been so stupid? She needed that spanking. It would mean he'd be able to forgive her, and it might even help her to forgive herself.

"I'm sorry, Sir. I'm ready now." She turned to look at him over her shoulder, no longer attempting to hold back her tears.

"You're crying, love. Does it hurt that much?"

"Yes. I hurt everywhere. But it's not the bruises. I feel such a fool. I let you down."

"Yes, you did." He continued to caress her lower back, feathering his fingers across her most tender places.

"You're right to be angry."

He flashed her a lopsided grin. "Do I seem angry to you?"

"Not right now, but… You must be, Sir."

"I was angry, but now I'm disappointed. And worried about you. I need you to take better care of yourself than this. If your body is to be covered in bruises, I prefer to know I put them there and that we both had a good time in the doing of it."

"I know that, Sir. I know you care about me. More than I deserve."

"No, not more than that. So, what are we to do about this problem of yours, then?"

"I deserve a spanking, Sir."

"You do, certainly."

"Would you like me over your knee, Sir?"

"Hell, yes. But I don't think either one of us really believes that would be good idea right now. Are you ready to get out?"

Eugenie nodded, unsure how to interpret his remark about what might constitute a good idea. She tilted her head back as he sprayed warm water over her hair to rinse out the conditioner then accepted his help to stand. Aaron wrapped her in a large towel and wound another around her hair before lifting her in his arms and carrying her from the bathroom. He marched into his bedroom and laid her on the bed.

"Are you tired?"

"Yes, Sir, I am. But I'd rather get this over with now, if you don't mind. Then, if you think I deserve it, could we make love?"

"So, let me get this right. You expect me to spank you now? While you're so fragile, so sore? And follow it up with a bit of vanilla sex?"

"Yes, Sir. I need it. Please."

"Why? What is it you need?"

"I need to be rid of this, this — this guilt."

"Ah, so this spanking is for you then, not for me?"

"Aren't they always?"

Aaron smiled, and this time she knew it was a grin of genuine warmth. Still beaming at her, he stood and went over to a drawer, started hunting around inside for something. Eugenie waited, eyeing him with curiosity as he returned to the bed carrying a wooden ruler. Surely, he did not mean to stripe her bottom with that.

"Hold out your hand, Genie. The left one."

"My hand?" She was incredulous.

He nodded. And waited. Eugenie sat up and extended her left hand, palm up.

"I'd be satisfied with just one stroke. Will that be enough for you, do you think?" He regarded her from under lowered brows, waiting for her to respond.

Eugenie considered for a few moments then shook her head. "No, Sir. I need five, I think. At least five."

"Okay, five it is, then. Hold your hand still for me, please."

She did so, resting her fingers against Aaron's outstretched left hand as he adjusted his grip on the ruler. She closed her eyes, half expecting to be instructed to open them and watch her punishment being administered. The slight whoosh of displaced air was her only warning, then the sharp sting of pain as the ruler connected with her palm.

"One." Aaron usually asked her to count. She was surprised that he was doing it this time.

Another whoosh and the ruler struck her palm again. It hurt, but was not as bad as she had feared. He was taking it easy, deliberately holding back.

"Harder, Sir. I need it to hurt. Please."

"Okay. Your safe word for this is still Maupassant, then?"

"I will not require it, Sir. Please, harder."

The third strike was blistering. Eugenie cried out and it took an extreme effort of will not to hug her hand to her stomach.

"Three." Aaron waited, as though expecting her to use the safe word.

Eugenie opened her eyes to meet his dark gaze. She pushed her hand toward him.

"The last two, Sir. Please."

He flattened his mouth in quiet determination. The last two strokes were delivered with quick efficiency, but when she would have at last cradled her hand against her other arm, he held onto it, lifting it to his mouth to lay a soft kiss in her red and smarting palm.

"All done. Could you sleep now?"

"Nearly, Sir. Thank you."

"Nearly?" He lifted one eyebrow, tilting her chin up with two fingers. "Is there something else I can do for you tonight?"

"Fuck me, Sir. If you would, please. Hard. I need it to be hard. I want that to hurt too."

"No can do, sweetheart." He grinned as her face dropped. "I'm all done with hurting you for tonight. I will fuck you, if you insist, but it's going to be soft and slow and might take a while. How does that sound to you?"

"It sounds quite perfect, Sir."

* * * *

"If your bum and shoulders are the most sore, would you prefer to lie face down?" Aaron murmured the words as he nuzzled the sensitive hollow between her neck and chin. He was naked too, having undressed quickly before stretching out alongside her.

Eugenie angled her head to allow him better access. At that precise moment, her bumps and bruises couldn't be further from her mind. "Not yet. I'm just… Could we stay like this, Sir?"

"If you like. You'll tell me if you're not comfortable, though. Yes?"

"Mmm, yes, Sir. Oh. Oh, Aaron, that feels good."

Aaron didn't answer. His mouth was occupied, leaving a trail of kisses from her throat down to her left breast. He flicked her nipple with his tongue, then closed his lips around the swelling nub and sucked.

Eugenie arched her back, and he slid his hand under her shoulders to support her weight as he continued to torment first one pebbled nipple then the other. She writhed on the bed, gasping her appreciation when he scraped his teeth over the sensitive peaks, biting down but not quite hard enough to hurt.

Eugenie knew he was treating her as he might the hotel's finest porcelain, taking care not to hurt her. She loved his concern for her current fragile state, but at the same time, she craved the intensity of his usual approach. Aaron was exciting, demanding, and always left her body aching in the most intimate places. She wanted some of that ache now.

"Sir, I'm all right, really. You can—oh!" She let out a sharp cry as he plunged two fingers deep into her pussy.

"What can I do, Genie? This?" He withdrew and drove his fingers back again—three this time. "Or this perhaps?" He rubbed her G-spot as he shifted farther down to position his head between her thighs. Eugenie spread her legs wide, lifting her hips in optimistic invitation.

Aaron grabbed a pillow and shoved it under her bottom. "Another?"

Eugenie nodded, grateful for the support. Every movement hurt her somewhere, and her muscles really weren't up to the job tonight, however enthusiastic she might feel. Aaron slid another pillow beneath her.

"How's that?"

"Fabulous. Thank you, Sir."

"You're welcome. Now all you have to do is lie still. Well, fairly still. And if you feel like it, you can tell me when it feels good."

"I can manage that, Sir."

Aaron chuckled as he settled back down, his mouth just inches from her damp, welcoming pussy. Eugenie could feel the moisture gathering and longed for the penetration of his skilled fingers again. He'd promised her that this would feel good though, and she was content to wait.

She let out a little hiss of pleasure as he parted her pussy lips with his thumbs then blew on the throbbing flesh he had exposed. He trailed the tip of his tongue around the entrance to her cunt, using his fingers to hold her open. Twice more he traced the outline before dipping his tongue inside.

Eugenie jerked hard, the rush of pure pleasure impossible to contain. She knew she would come quickly — if he allowed it.

"Don't hold back, love. This is for you."

Aaron's Dom antennae were on high alert, sensing everything she was thinking and feeling before she had the chance to verbalize her needs. Moments later, she lay quivering, her pussy spasming as her orgasm pulsed through her, relaxing her tensed muscles in a way the warm bath could never have achieved.

Aaron continued to lick and tongue-fuck her until the climax was spent and she lay still under him again.

He knelt up, still positioned between her thighs.

"Nice start, sweetheart. I wonder how many more we can manage."

"One or two, I should think."

"Is that a challenge, love?"

"No, Sir. I just meant…"

"I'd like to blindfold you. Is that all right?"

"Of course, Sir. Whatever you decide. You know that." The question surprised Eugenie. Aaron never usually told her what he planned, let alone asked for her permission. Tonight was certainly different, in many ways.

He reached past her to open a drawer beside the bed and pulled out a soft scarf. He rolled it loosely then used it to cover her eyes and tied the ends at the back of her head. The effect was instant, the loss of one key sense heightening her others. Eugenie knew this was his plan. She also knew that whatever he had in mind for her next might not be strenuous but it would be intense.

Her thoughts scattered in the next moments as his hands were on her hips, caressing her then lifting her toward his mouth again. He sucked on her clit, drawing the swollen bud into his mouth and pressing his tongue against it. Eugenie felt like she might be floating.

All too soon, he lowered her back onto the pillows and began to work his way back up her body. He kissed her belly button then her breasts again, before finding the sensitive spot just below her ear. She was dimly aware of the snap of foil and settled against the pillows in happy anticipation. He shifted his hips, and Eugenie lifted her legs as the head of his cock nudged her entrance.

"Keep still, girl. Unless you're uncomfortable. Are you, Genie?"

"No, Sir. I'm fine."

"Good." He shifted again then thrust forward. His cock slid into her. He buried himself to the hilt in her warm pussy."

Eugenie moaned and resisted the urge to lock her heels behind his waist. She reached for his shoulders, though, and hung on as he withdrew and drove his erection deep into her again.

"Are you still fine, Genie?"

"Yes, Sir. Very fine."

"Mmm, and very tight too. So fucking sweet, girl…"

He delivered a couple more long, slow strokes, and Eugenie thought she might faint with pleasure. Was such a thing possible? She would soon know.

His cock balls-deep within her, Aaron stopped. Eugenie rolled her hips, her body already tightening in readiness for her next climax. Aaron ignored her wriggling and reached under her to drag the pillows away. He then shoved his knees under her bottom and arranged her legs on either side of his, spreading her out for his perusal.

Even blindfolded, Eugenie knew he was looking at her, and specifically at the point where their bodies joined. She lay still, absorbing the intimacy of the moment, vulnerable, open to him. Were it not for her injuries, she suspected he would have tied her hands behind her back for this, which would have heightened the sense of his possession still further. On instinct, she tucked her hands under her waist. And she waited.

"This is going to feel good, but if it gets too much, you're to tell me. Is that okay, Genie?"

Too much? Could there ever be too much pleasure? Puzzled, Eugenie nodded her agreement.

Even though she was expecting him to touch her, she still jerked when Aaron used his fingers to trace the lips of her pussy stretched tightly around his cock. Eugenie quivered, her body already preparing to orgasm again.

"So aroused, so ready. Would you like to come again, little slut?"

"Yes. Yes please, Sir."

"Do it, then." His tone was low and so sexy, a caress in itself.

He held her hips still as he slowly pulled back then thrust deep. He repeated the stroke, achingly gentle yet filling her entirely.

Helpless, Genie sighed her delight as the walls of her pussy contracted around him, her body convulsing as he drew her climax from her. She was still shaking as the waves of sensation died away and Aaron sank his cock deep inside her and went still once more.

"Nice?"

"Mmm, very nice, Sir."

"And this?"

She started at the faint humming sound then let out a long, low groan as sensation exploded across her clit.

"What...?"

"Shh. Enjoy."

A bullet vibrator. Must be. She had no notion where he had produced it from, but he had. Aaron was always prepared. He rubbed the toy against her clit, stroking the sides, the tip. He pressed harder, and she knew her next orgasm was just moments away. How many had that been? Two? Three?

"Oh God! Sir, I can't..."

"I think you can, love. Now."

Her body convulsed again, waves of pleasure pulsing from her clit. She squeezed her pussy around his cock, loving the feeling of fullness as she came. Aaron was relentless, continuing to stroke her clit and pussy lips with the vibrator, ramping up the intensity as she stilled.

Eugenie lost count of how many times she came, each orgasm drawn from her by his expert touch and the magic of his sweet little toy. At last, though, she answered her earlier question. There was such a thing as too much pleasure. Or perhaps that should be too much all at once.

"Enough, Sir. Please, that is enough."
"Yeah?"

The buzzing stopped.

For a few moments, Eugenie basked in the silent stillness, her body still humming. She sighed as Aaron stroked her sensitized clit with the pad of his thumb.

"All done?"

"Yes. No. Oh, that feels so good, Sir."

"Enjoy then."

She would not have believed that he might yet draw another orgasm from her, but he did. The soft, undemanding caress coaxed her back to the brink and over, sending her spinning once again. And at last, she was really done. She could manage no more.

"Stop now. Please."

Aaron said nothing, but rearranged his body so that he was lying above her, taking his weight on his arms. He brushed his lips across hers as he withdrew his cock and waited, poised to drive forward again. Ready to finish this.

"Sir, I…"

"My sweet Genie." He sank his cock into her, his entire body tensing as he held still. Then he let out a low oath as his semen spurted into her, filling the condom with his liquid heat.

* * * *

Later, as Eugenie lay wrapped in Aaron's arms in that hazy place before sleep descended, she had to admit he'd been right. It had been perfect. She had not believed it possible but now she felt even more cherished, more adored, utterly at peace with him and with herself. She knew he would not have punished her at all but for her insistence, and even then, he'd allowed her to set the limits of it. The stripes left by the ruler across her hand had served their purpose. They had released her pent-up feelings of guilt and self-loathing, exorcising her demons and allowing her to just let it all go. As for the bruises from her fall, those would fade in a few days.

But the bond forged tonight between herself and Aaron, the deepening trust and understanding that connected them, that was only going to become stronger. She promised herself that it would, and in the dark silence, she swore it to Aaron too, even though he was already sleeping.

Chapter Fourteen

The next couple of weeks flew past in a blur. Aaron became accustomed to hearing the light footsteps in the office next to his, her quiet voice as she spoke on the phone in her rapid-fire French. The arrangements continued to click into place, each and every detail subject first to Eugenie's minute scrutiny then to his. She would check quality, ensure that the wishes of their celebrity clients were honored in all matters, while it was his responsibility to handle the safety and security aspects. Theirs was a seamless operation, their teamwork effortless.

Other members of the management team played their parts too. He knew that Eugenie spent long hours in detailed discussions with Anton, poring over menus, debating the wine list, tasting desserts. She and Annette had also toured the honeymoon suite as well as the rooms to be occupied by the guests, ensuring every possible need was anticipated. The hotel facilities were already superb, every surface gleaming, every item of linen crisp and neatly folded. All that came as standard, but the added touches made the difference—color coordinated towels and bed linen to match the wedding themes, additional maids recruited to help with packing, unpacking, dressing. The hotel hairdressing service would be available twenty-four hours a day, as would the spa and fitness suites. Each guest would be pampered, treated to the very best Totally Five Star Paris could offer and more besides. They would never forget their visit here.

Eugenie and Aaron spent a lot of time together, both at work and outside of it. While they were discreet, he had no doubt that their personal relationship was no secret, though the exact nature of it remained between them. Not that she would have ever said anything, but Fleur would have put two and two together on the day of Eugenie's fall when she had insisted on his presence while she was examined. She'd undressed in front of him without a second thought.

His cock throbbed as he contemplated their relationship. Eugenie was a unique blend of contrasting qualities. He adored her cool efficiency in the office, her absolute submission outside of it.

Since the evening following her fall down the stairs, they seemed to him to have moved onto a new plane. She deferred to him, obeyed and anticipated his requirements almost before he voiced them. He believed that her desire to accept his discipline, even when he would have let the matter drop, signaled a fresh insight on her part, the realization that she could trust him not to harm her. He would never have inflicted further pain on her tender, bruised body, but she wasn't to know that and surrendered to him anyway. The ruler across her hand had been the best he could come up with at short notice to satisfy her craving. It seemed to do the trick.

They spent most evenings together and every weekend. She stayed at his apartment on Fridays and Saturdays, and had recently started to leave some of her belongings there. She had never even suggested such a thing when they were together in England, and he would have discouraged it then, he thought. Now, he found he had no objection at all.

They had breakfast together most days, usually in the terrace restaurant, and lunch when they could manage that too. As often as not, they had company, the hotel's management team were a sociable lot. But the growing bond between Aaron and Eugenie was obvious to all.

Aaron knew he loved her. Perhaps he always had. Whatever, his feelings had required very little in the way of rekindling. Within days of their first night together, he murmured the words into her ear as he slid his cock into her ass. She had sighed, her smile beatific as she lifted her bottom up to offer herself to him.

Now, the wedding was just days away. The first handful of guests had started to arrive, although most would be descending on them the day before the actual ceremony. That was when Farah and Lucas would arrive too, and the party would really get underway.

He had a small army of additional security personnel dotted about the hotel, mingling with the permanent staff, ever vigilant. Aaron was confident but not complacent. The marriage of one of the world's most popular sporting personalities to an exotic Arab princess was a romantic dream that would delight, inspire, fascinate. The eyes of the world would be on them. But viewed through his security lens, Aaron knew that this wedding was an obvious target, both for the greedy disruptive presence of the flocks of paparazzi who would try to infiltrate the event, and for the more sinister attentions of political extremists. The alliance of Farah Ajram with a high profile international footballer had not gone unnoticed or unremarked in the more traditional circles, though for the most part, the reaction had been positive. It was his job to make sure that no one and nothing disrupted Eugenie's carefully laid plans. And Aaron was good at his job.

He closed down his computer and pocketed his mobile. She should be finished briefing Elise now and he was looking forward to having lunch with his little Genie. Aaron made his way to the terrace bistro, nodding to several members of his team as he strode across the thick carpeting of the reception area and out to the gardens at the rear. He looked for her in their usual spot, the table tucked away in one corner of the patio, surrounded on three sides by fragrant honeysuckle. He smiled to himself as he rounded the corner and she came into view. She glanced up, her smile dazzling when she saw him. His heart did a little flip. He was one lucky bastard.

The firm tread on the paved terrace alerted her to his approach. Eugenie looked up. She had been watching for him and beamed in delighted anticipation when Aaron came into view. Her Dom. Her wonderful, stern, commanding Dom. She loved him, utterly adored him. And he seemed to feel the same way about her. Life was good, better than good. Life was perfect.

She stood as he reached their table, her face upturned for his quick kiss. Aaron was not overly demonstrative, at least not in public, but neither did he seek to conceal their relationship. He sat next to her, reaching for the black coffee she had ordered for him.

"It is probably a little cool now. Shall I get you another?"

"This is fine." He took a long sip. "Good briefing?"

"Yes, no problems. It is very hectic, but everything is going to plan." She lifted both hands to show him her crossed fingers.

"Never doubted it. Any idea what time you'll be finished tonight?"

"Late. Not before eight. Is that okay?"

"Of course. Come to my apartment as soon as you're done. No underwear, naturally."

She bowed her head. "Naturally, Sir. Should I eat before I come to you?"

"Was some part of 'as soon as you're done' not entirely clear, Eugenie?" He lifted one eyebrow, his tone remaining even, and all the more ominous for that.

"Of course, Sir. I apologize."

"I'll feed you. Eventually. Talking of which, have you ordered yet?"

"No, Sir. I wanted to wait for you."

Aaron signaled for a waiter. The young man scurried over, notepad in hand. They asked for a selection of cold meats and a refresh of their coffee. The next hour was spent in pleasant conversation, Eugenie's pussy moistening disgracefully as she anticipated the evening to come once the day's business was concluded.

Aaron had to leave before she did to meet with Lucas' bodyguard. He leaned in to kiss her, his breath feathering across her neck as he murmured in her ear.

"I left you a present. You'll find it in your desk drawer. Please be wearing it when you come up later."

She gazed after him as he strode away. It would be a butt plug, she was sure of that. Her ass tingled in excited apprehension. Tonight was going to be good.

The waiter came to clear the table and asked if she required anything else. Eugenie was about to say no, but decided a cup of tea would be nice. She was on top of her work, she could afford the time for once. She had a meeting scheduled with Anton, but not for another hour. Her tumble down the stairs and Aaron's reaction to it had taught her a valuable lesson about overworking. She ordered a tray and sat back to enjoy the unaccustomed solitude.

From her vantage point, she could admire the neat informality of this secluded garden in the heart of the vibrant, throbbing city. A gardener passed their table, one of Aaron's team probably, as she didn't recognize him. The hotel was full of new faces just now. She watched as the slim figure made his way down the shrubbery, clipping off errant blooms and sweeping them into a sack attached to his belt. Not so much as a stray grass cutting was allowed to clutter the pristine footpaths. For a security guard, this young man seemed to understand horticulture, but she supposed the role was all about blending in.

Her tray of tea arrived, and she drank her first cup of aromatic Earl Grey. She poured another, but decided she needed to visit the loo before drinking it. She passed the waiter on her way there and told him she was not yet finished and not to clear her table.

As she made her way back to her table and the unfinished tray of tea, her mobile rang in her pocket. She recognized Farah's caller ID from the display.

"Good afternoon, Farah. How can I help you?"

"Eugenie? I need to add four people to the guest list. Is that all right? It is not too late, I hope."

As if. Aaron would work all night if need be to follow up the security checks. And she would help him.

"Of course. May I have their names, please?" Eugenie dug in her bag for the notepad and pen she always kept at hand. She scribbled the notes, knowing it was vital to get these latest additions to Aaron as soon as possible in order for his background checks to be completed in time. She ended the call and picked up her tea cup, but thought better of it.

Her interlude was over. There was no longer time to linger if Aaron was to get to work on these extra names. She grabbed her belongings and hurried back indoors.

Eugenie put down her pen and shook her hand. It hurt. No, not hurt — it was stinging. Really sore. She turned her palm up and was surprised to see the raised red marks across her skin. It looked as though she'd scalded it, but she knew she couldn't have. She closed her hand into a fist, wincing. It seemed to be getting worse.

Ten minutes later, she could no longer hold her pen at all. She hugged her hand to her stomach, in real pain now. She was due to meet with Anton in less than half an hour, but she knew she couldn't ignore this. Using her left hand, she picked up the receiver of the phone on her desk and tapped in two numbers.

"Fleur? Do you have a minute?"

* * * *

"This is a chemical burn." The hotel doctor peered at Eugenie's hand, turning it over and comparing it to the other, undamaged one. "I would estimate not that long since you were in contact with the irritant as the effects are usually very rapid. Acid perhaps, or maybe some sort of bleach." As she spoke, she tugged Eugenie out into the corridor. She dragged her across the hall into the ladies' toilet where she proceeded to hold her hand under the running cold tap. "This may not make a lot of difference now, but we should ensure there is no trace left of whatever has caused this. Do you have any ideas?"

"Ideas about what?"

They both turned at the sound of Aaron's voice behind them. No one commented on his presence in the female toilets.

"Eugenie has injured her hand. She has sustained a chemical burn."

He stepped forward, looping his arm around Eugenie's shoulder as he leaned over to examine the damage. "How bad is it?" The question was directed to the doctor.

"It bloody well hurts, that's how bad it is." Eugenie glared at her hand, still red and now looking swollen too.

"It is difficult to tell unless we know what the cause was. It looks to be superficial, but I would like to refer you to the hospital. This is not a specialism of mine."

"But I..." Eugenie started to protest, her head whirling with all the reasons she could not leave the hotel right now.

"I'll come with you. Do you need your coat? Your bag?" Aaron was already steering her from the ladies' washroom. "Apart from your office, where else have you been in the last half hour or so? Where might you have come in contact with this stuff, whatever it is?"

"Nowhere else. I just came straight back here from the bistro."

Aaron dragged his phone from his pocket and tapped in a number.

"Pierre? It's Aaron. Could you do a check of Miss d'André's office, please? You're looking for any trace of a caustic substance, something that would cause chemical burns. If you don't find anything there, could you check the route from the management suite to the terrace bistro?" He paused, turning to Eugenie. "I assume you came back the direct way? No detours?"

She shook her head, starting to realize the implications if a guest were to come into contact with whatever substance had caused her injury. Aaron gave her a curt nod of acknowledgement before returning to his call. He never stopped walking, heading back to her office.

"No, no idea what it is. My hunch is you'll know it if you find it. Text me as soon as you have anything." He ended the call as Eugenie picked up her bag from beside her office chair. She followed him quietly from the hotel to find a limousine already outside and waiting.

"Nothing but the best for our key personnel. And this was handy. Get in." Aaron held the door open for her then slid into the rear seat alongside Eugenie.

* * * *

Two hours later, they were back, Eugenie's hand neatly dressed in a sterile bandage. The consultant at the accident and emergency department had diagnosed the burn to be superficial. Still painful and still prone to infection if not kept clean, he had assured her it was unlikely to leave a lasting or prominent scar.

"It's a good thing you don't bite your nails." The nurse who applied the bandage made her observation as he'd wrapped gauze around Eugenie's hand. "Is that okay? Not too tight?"

"It's fine. What do you mean about my nails?"

"This isn't too bad. It'll heal up just fine. It would have been a different story, though, if you'd ingested any of it. Internal burns are much more serious. So it's lucky you didn't put your hand anywhere near your mouth."

"I see. Yes." Eugenie looked up as Aaron came back into the cubicle. He had been out in the corridor taking a call.

"Was that someone from your team? Have they found anything?"

"Yes. But it makes no sense."

"What do you mean?" Eugenie flexed her hand as the nurse secured the end of the bandage.

"I'll explain when we get back. Are we done here?"

"Yes. All done. If you need any painkillers just take a couple of paracetamols." The nurse collected her instruments and equipment back onto her trolley and wheeled it toward the curtain at the front of the cubicle. "If you have any worries just go back to the hotel doctor. And you'll need to get the dressing changed in a few days. Your doctor can handle that too."

Chapter Fifteen

Aaron was deep in thought as Eugenie thanked the nurse and picked up her bag. They both followed the nurse into the corridor, Aaron intent on reading the latest text from Pierre, his deputy in the security department. His mood became even grimmer.

The limousine was waiting for them in the car park outside. Neither of them spoke on the short journey back through the city, this time alighting at the staff entrance at the rear of the Totally Five Star. Aaron offered her his hand as she got out of the car then held onto it to tug her along.

"Where are we going?"

"The garden bistro. If you feel up to it. Unless you'd rather go back to your apartment? We can do this later if you prefer."

He was relieved as Eugenie shook her head. He wouldn't push her if she was feeling too fragile but he really needed her input to help make sense of what he was learning.

"I'm fine. It hardly hurts at all now. What did your people find? Something at the bistro?"

"Yes. It'll be easier to show you than to try to describe it, though. And I want to see for myself too. Are you sure you're okay?"

"Yes. I just want to get to the bottom of this now."

"Here we are." Aaron led her through the indoor dining room and out onto the terrace.

"Where's our table?" Eugenie stared across the patio at the empty space where just a couple of hours ago she and Aaron had enjoyed their lunch together.

"Over here."

They turned in the direction of the voice. A man in a smart suit emerged from a door beside the kitchens.

"I sealed it, as you asked me to."

"Thanks, Pierre. Do you know Miss d'André?"

"*Enchanté, Madame.*" The newcomer inclined his head in a slight bow. "I would offer my hand, but…"

"No, of course. I'm pleased to meet you too, Mister…?"

Aaron took up the introductions, keen to get on. "This is Pierre Barent, my deputy for the next couple of weeks or so. He's an IT and electronics specialist. We decided we needed to beef up our team in some respects to ensure the best security possible for the wedding. Pierre came well recommended."

The pleasantries over, he turned to Pierre. "So, where is it?"

Pierre led the way around to a storage area at the rear of the restaurant. He gestured to a table, now covered in a transparent plastic sheet. "Is that the one?"

Aaron stepped forward. He circled the table then lowered himself into a crouch to look closely at its surface. "I'd say so. Do you agree, Genie?"

She came to stand beside him. "I'm not sure. It looks like it. But they're all the same, aren't they?"

Aaron chose not to reply to that. "Is the manager still on duty?"

"No. He left about an hour ago. The waiter who first spotted the damaged table is here, though. Do you want a word with him?"

Aaron nodded, still studying the tabletop. Eugenie followed his gaze. He knew from her small start of surprise the moment she spotted what was so interesting to him. A dull stain marred the otherwise smooth perfection of the varnished ebony surface.

"What is that? Has something been spilled on it?" Eugenie bent to touch the plastic covering the tabletop.

"Looks like it." Aaron straightened as a young man dressed in TFS livery hurried toward them. He recognized him as the waiter who had taken their lunch order earlier.

"*Madame, monsieur*? How may I be of assistance?"

"Tell me about this mark on the table, please." Aaron's question might have sounded curt, but he softened it with a brief tilt of his head.

The young waiter seemed eager to help. "Ah, *oui*. I came to clear away the tea tray, after *Madame* left." He paused to nod in Eugenie's direction. "I noticed the damage to the table. It is terrible. It must be repaired — or replaced. I told the manager about it and he asked me to bring the table back here until we could deal with it. It is not fit to be used like that."

Aaron frowned, trying to piece together an implausible sequence of events "No. Obviously. But how did it happen? What caused this damage?"

"I do not know, sir. I had thought that perhaps you might be able to say. Or *Madame*? It was not damaged when I laid the table this morning. I am sure I would have noticed."

"And so would we if it had been in that state when we came here for lunch. Eugenie?"

She shook her head, seemingly as puzzled as he was. "Yes, of course we would have noticed."

All TFS staff were under strict instructions to report any damage, deal with any imperfection as soon as they spotted it, no matter how slight. Those instructions applied at all times, but the usual high standards were even more rigid just now. They both knew that a damaged tabletop would not have been ignored by anyone.

"Right. So we're all agreed this table was the same one that was in the spot by the honeysuckle, where Miss d'André and I ate lunch about two hours ago? Yes?"

Eugenie and the waiter nodded. Aaron was gratified to note that Pierre was also listening to the exchange with interest, his frown indicating that he also found this more than a little suspicious. It wasn't just Aaron's police training creating the unmistakable smell of a rat.

"And at the start of our meal, it was in perfect condition. Are we also agreed on that?"

He looked from one to the other as they both nodded.

"Yet a few minutes after Miss d'André left, it was in this damaged state? Also correct."

The waiter nodded. "But it was not even a few minutes, sir. I saw *Madame* leave and came straight over to clear up."

"Right, so that covers my next question. But for the avoidance of any doubt, are you certain that no one else could have approached this table between Miss d'André leaving and you discovering this damage?"

"Absolutely not, sir. No one. I came straight out to collect the tray and the table was already ruined."

"But you were here the whole time?" This question was directed at Eugenie.

"Yes. I ordered another tray of tea after you went back to work and I drank one cup."

"You were at the table the whole time?"

"Yes. No." She looked up at him, her eyes widening. "Apart from a few minutes when I went to the loo. I took a call from Farah as I was on my way back to finish my tea. She told me she had additional names for the guest list. I made a note of them and came to find you in order that you could add them to your background checks. I did not sit again."

Aaron placed his palms on her cheeks, tilting her face upward so he could look into her eyes. "Think hard, sweetheart. Did you touch anything?"

"No, I do not think… My bag, my pen."

Pierre stepped forward. "May I, *Madame*?"

Aaron released her face and Eugenie handed her bag to Pierre. No one spoke as the deputy director of security rummaged inside and drew out a smart rollerball pen. Aaron recognized it as the one she usually used. Eugenie nodded her confirmation as Pierre held it up. "Yes, that is the one."

Pierre put it back in the bag and handed the whole lot back to her. "Nothing there, sir."

"You touched nothing else before you left? Are you certain, Genie?"

Her brow furrowed, her eyes narrowing in concentration as she reran the series of events in her mind. Suddenly she looked up at him.

"My cup. I picked up my tea cup. I had poured a second cup of tea but left it on the table when I went to the toilet. I intended to drink it when I returned, but the call from Farah changed my plans. I was in a hurry to bring you the new names so I put the cup back down and left it."

Aaron turned to the waiter. "Where is the crockery used by Miss d'André?"

"In the dishwasher, sir."

"Pierre, I want every item in that dishwasher checked and tested. If there's any trace of anything left, I want it found."

"On it, sir."

Pierre and the waiter hurried off in the direction of the kitchens. Aaron knew the chances of anything remaining once the steam wash cycle had run its course was remote, but he had to try.

"You think my cup might have had bleach on it? Or acid?"

Actually, he didn't. His suspicion was rather direr than that. He suspected her tea itself might have contained the corrosive, and but for a stroke of luck she would have drunk it. Even if she had tasted the contamination immediately, the damage would have been done. He shuddered at the thought.

Farah's timing had been perfect.

He toyed with the notion of protecting Eugenie from the knowledge of how close she may have come to disaster, but dismissed it. She needed to know.

"The cup? Yes. It's the only explanation we have and it makes sense. As I'm seeing it, while you were away from your table, someone was here. They poured the bleach or whatever it was onto the tabletop."

"But why? Why would anyone deliberately damage our furniture?"

"They wouldn't. My guess is that the damage to the table was accidental. The bleach was meant for your tea. But some was spilled. He was probably in a hurry, got careless, slopped it around a bit more than he intended."

"My tea! You think someone tried to put bleach in my tea?" Her face blanched, her eyes like saucers.

He would have preferred to have spared her this, but if he was right, she needed to be on her guard. He nodded, his gaze holding hers. "Yes. That's what I think."

"But why? Why would anyone want to hurt me?"

Why indeed? Aaron shrugged, his mind turning over the facts, as he understood them. He could come up with no convincing reason for this attack on Eugenie, but the more he considered the situation the more convinced he became that this was the only possible conclusion.

"What is happening here? Eugenie, I was informed you had had an accident. Are you all right?"

They both turned at the female voice behind them. Elise had entered the storage area and was looking around her in astonishment. She took in the table wrapped in transparent plastic, Eugenie's bandaged hand. Aaron knew his expression was grim but made no attempt to conceal it. This was serious and Elise needed to know what was going on.

"I believe someone has attempted to poison Eugenie by putting a corrosive substance in her drink. Luckily, she didn't ingest any of it, but her hand came in contact with some of the substance, probably spillage, and she has a chemical burn."

"Oh, my God. You're serious, aren't you?"

Aaron nodded.

"Why? Is this some random attack or was Eugenie the intended target?"

Now this was an aspect he hadn't considered, but it made some sort of sense. Perhaps this had been an attempt to sabotage the wedding. A case of deliberate poisoning at the hotel would soon put a stop to the ceremony. The police investigation alone would be enough, without the damage to their reputation, the sudden rush of cancelations as guests decided against coming here.

Shit! This was his responsibility. This was exactly the sort of disaster he was hired to avoid.

Elise's voice interrupted his train of thought. "Eugenie, how is your hand? Will it be okay?"

"Yes, it is fine, thank you. The burn is only superficial."

"But you are so much in the wars recently. First, you fall down the stairs, and now your poor hand. You are certainly accident-prone."

"I do seem to be, just now. My mother always said these things come in threes. I hope she was wrong."

"Me too. We must take better care of you." Elise slipped her arm across Eugenie's shoulder and gave her a quick hug. She turned to Aaron. "I prescribe a massage in the spa. Perhaps a visit to the hairdresser. A pedicure. Some girl time. You can spare her, *n'est-ce pas*?"

Aaron glanced at Eugenie, couldn't miss the flicker of hope that passed across her features. She obviously fancied the prospect of a bit of pampering with Elise but expected him to deny her permission. They were in the middle of a crisis, her sense of duty must be on overdrive. He smiled before leaning in to lay a quick kiss on her forehead.

"Elise is right. You need a break. Go. Enjoy yourself. And take care. I'll see you later."

Accident-prone. In the wars. As he watched the two women walk away from him, Elise's words ricocheted around his head. It could be bad luck, might mean nothing.

But Aaron didn't believe in coincidences.

Chapter Sixteen

If she was aware of his increased vigilance, Eugenie gave no sign of it. She carried on about her business, rushing everywhere, issuing instructions, answering questions, dealing with the constant flow of rapid-fire minutiae that filled the final days of preparation. The bride and groom would arrive in less than twelve hours' time. Over two hundred guests were already settling into the suites with at least double that number expected in the next day or so.

As far as possible, Aaron made it his business to be glued to her side. Pierre had his instructions and he was in charge of the wider hotel, would see to the protection of the guests. Aaron's sixth sense told him that if there were to be a real problem, it would occur somewhere in Eugenie's vicinity. So that was where he stationed himself. He had no idea what he was expecting, but he trusted his instincts to recognize it when he saw it. No one got to harm his little Genie. He would protect her with his life if need be.

His long, loping strides kept him alongside as she scurried along the corridor back to her office, having just resolved a dispute between two of their suppliers. The flowers were to be arranged first then the tables could be dressed. The contractors would have to coordinate their efforts, and with commendable patience she had explained to them just how this might be accomplished. Now she intended to finalize the contents of the wedding favors to be distributed to the female guests, then she had a conference call booked with several celebrity magazines who were scrambling over each other to publish pictures from the wedding.

He knew she found the media the most difficult to deal with, their demands incessant. But she fully appreciated the importance of publicity for this event if Totally Five Star Paris was to gain the international recognition and new business that they all hoped for. He was grateful for the influence of Claudette Leclerc. As head of marketing and PR, she took the brunt of the liaison with the media, but Eugenie was not immune.

Her features were pinched. He saw the stress building and knew he had a sure way of helping her with that.

As she turned to enter her office, he clasped her elbow and carried on walking. Without a word, he marched her into his office and closed the door behind them. He locked it then turned to face her.

"Strip and kneel."

"Sir?" Her expression was perplexed, but not reluctant.

"No questions. Don't speak at all. Just do it. Now."

He was gratified to note the aura of relaxation that appeared to descend on her as she drew her mental cloak of submission around herself. Even before she placed her ever-present notebook on his desk and reached for her buttons, she seemed to loosen up. Her features smoothed out, the tension evaporating. He watched in quiet satisfaction as she removed her clothing piece by piece, taking the time to fold each item and place it in a neat pile. She even loosened her hair, letting the long curls ripple down her back before she sank to her knees at his feet.

"What do you need from me right now, sub?"

"I need you to hurt me, Sir. Spank me."

"Why? Why do you need this?"

"I need to scream. I need to let it all out and, and… It will help me to focus. I need to let go of control, just for a little while."

"Good answer. Stand and bend over my desk."

His cock twitched and swelled as she obeyed him, her gorgeous peachy bottom raised for his attention. He could just make out the faint marks left by his cane a few days previously, but she was more than ready for a refresher. He stepped forward to lay both his palms on her smooth buttocks. He parted them to expose her anus, pink and puckered and so very inviting. He had no lube here in his office, otherwise, he might have been tempted. Pity. But later…

He slipped one hand between her legs to explore the dampness there. Her pussy was always wet, always welcoming. She moaned her appreciation as he shoved three fingers high inside her.

"Maybe I'll fuck you afterward. Would you like that, my sweet slut?"

"Sir, I would. Very much."

"Okay. Hold that thought." He straightened and unbuckled his belt. She trembled a little as he pulled it free, her usual reaction to that sound.

He liked it — that heady mix of delighted anticipation and fear. No matter how much she craved this — and he knew she did desire it—he knew she needed this pain with a desperation bordering on pure anguish. She still exuded an air of perfect surrender to his will. She hadn't always, so this was new. This was cultivated in recent weeks and all the more delightful for that.

His belt dangling from his hand, he leaned over her to lift the hair from the back of her neck. He trailed his lips over the sensitive hollow right below her hairline, loving the way his caress sent small shivers along her shoulders. Her responses were exquisite, so delicate yet at the same time powerful. He shifted slightly to be able to murmur in her ear.

"I'll stop when I think you've had enough. Or when you tell me to stop. Okay?"

Eyes closed, she nodded, the movement so slight he might have missed it. He missed nothing, though, not these days. Straightening, he positioned himself behind her.

"Ready?"

"Yes, Sir. Make it hard. Please."

Aaron smiled to himself as he adjusted his trousers to accommodate his swollen cock. *Too late, baby, already hard.*

He didn't share that snippet, though, preferring to let her focus remain where it was—on the blistering he was about to inflict on her tender bottom.

He started with his hand, a succession of quick, sharp slaps followed by a vigorous rubbing to dissipate the pain. Her buttocks reddened as the blood rushed to the surface, and Genie writhed against the polished mahogany of his desk. She stretched her hands out in front of her, opening and closing her fingers as though she was grasping for something. She scraped the wooden surface with her nails as her breath shifted from deep, even sighs to a soft panting. As she started to clench her buttocks in anticipation of each slap, he knew she was ready for his belt.

He paused for a few moments, caressing her bright crimson bottom to allow her the seconds she needed to ready herself for the main onslaught. She wriggled, gyrated her hips a couple of times then went still.

Aaron swung, aiming the first stroke to land at the top of her right buttock. He liked to paint his stripes evenly down one side then the other, leaving maybe half an inch between them. He was good, very accurate, and he knew Genie wouldn't move. If he'd been less certain of her, he might have tied her in place, but he hardly ever felt a need to do that these days.

She was silent for the first stroke, but the next one elicited a faint gasp. He could improve on that. The third stripe snaked across the roundest part of her bottom, causing the flesh to quiver in a way that absolutely delighted him. He would never, ever tire of watching that and the sweet way she tightened her buttocks as the pain grew and bloomed.

Her legs were slightly parted. He could see her pussy lips glistening as she became more aroused. She was loving this as much as he was.

Still, no harm in checking. He slid his free hand between her thighs to explore her moist folds. *Oh yes, so wet, so warm. So fucking beautiful.* She groaned and opened her legs more to invite him in.

"Soon, baby." He withdrew his hand and took up his position again.

The next three strokes created a mirror image on her left buttock, the stripes glowing in precise and perfect symmetry. Genie was letting out small cries as each one fell, not quite a scream, but he knew she was hurting. And he knew she needed more yet.

Shifting his stance, he was able to target the lower slopes of each buttock, and if she was still in need, he'd move on to the backs of her thighs. He was confident she would call a halt soon. This was intense, even for a pain slut like his beautiful little Genie.

He resumed his attentions on the right side, laying three more strokes in rapid succession. She needed the pressure to intensify. She needed to become one with the agony now blistering her backside. He could see her wetness gathering between her thighs, her pussy lips pink and swollen. He wouldn't neglect her cunt, though he preferred to use his hand to slap her there.

He worked his way back up her left buttock, pleased to note that her cries had built to real shrieks of pain now. He was glad of the soundproofing that he knew would prevent unwanted attention from concerned colleagues. She was sobbing too, her face wet with tears that she made no attempt to wipe away.

When he had evened up his artwork, he paused, allowing her the opportunity to tell him if she'd had enough. Her sobs subsided, her eyes remaining closed. This was her signal to him that all was well. He repositioned himself to attend to her thighs. Two strokes, maximum, each side.

She managed one, then she raised her hand to tap the desk top, two short, sharp raps on the solid surface. Aaron stepped back, surveying his handiwork as he re-threaded his belt through the loops on his trousers. Genie lay still, small sobs still sending shudders through her small frame.

Aaron picked up a box of tissues from on top of a filing cabinet and went back to his desk. He hitched his hip alongside Eugenie, still stretched out across the cool surface. He placed the tissues by her hand then laid his palm on her bottom. Heat radiated from her skin. Aaron smiled to himself as she cringed under his touch before stretching like a satisfied cat and lifting her rear toward his caressing palm.

He stroked her tender, flaming buttocks as she sighed in contented appreciation. Long minutes passed before she rolled awkwardly to one side to peer up at him. She'd made no attempt to repair her ravaged face so Aaron did the honors, grabbing a handful of tissues to dab her cheeks and smooth away the tears below her eyes. He shoved a tissue into her hand.

"I draw the line at wiping your nose, Miss d'André."

She threw him a watery smile as she shuffled to her feet then buried her face in the soft tissue. A couple of hefty blows, some frantic wiping, and at last she met his eyes again.

"That's better. So, how was that, then? Ready to face the world again?"

"Nearly, Sir. Thank you. I think I should get dressed first, though."

"Yes, probably. Soon. Wait there a sec."

He went back over to his filing cabinet, this time to extract a tube of anti-inflammatory cream from the top drawer. He returned to her and, with a brief twist of his finger, indicated that she should turn around. Eugenie did so, leaning to rest her hands on the desk as he applied the salve to her buttocks.

His ministrations completed, he gave her bottom a playful swat. "There, give it a few minutes to soak in and you'll be ready to deal with those bloody journalists."

"Ah, yes, the magazines. I am due to talk to them in"—she consulted the clock on his wall—"thirteen minutes. Is that clock correct?"

"To the second. I suppose a fuck would make you late."

Her expression was priceless. Panic, hope, regret, but mainly contrition. Her mouth worked as she contemplated what to say to him, obviously wondering if he was about to insist.

Aaron grinned. "You'll keep. The paparazzi won't. Would you like me to sit in on your call?"

She smiled, her expression now one of genuine relief. He should have been annoyed, but he wasn't. They were past that.

"No, Sir, I will be fine and I know you have work to do. I will only be next door." She started to dress, though he noticed she seemed reluctant to put her panties back on. No problem, her skirt was knee-length. He held out his hand to take the remaining underwear from her.

"I'll give you these back later. In my apartment. Maybe. What time will you be done?"

"I am not sure, Sir. I will need to finish off the wedding favors today, so I will be working late. Can I text you when I'm nearly ready to leave?"

"Sure. Do you want to eat in one of the restaurants or at mine?"

"Could we stay in, Sir? Would you mind? I could do the cooking."

"I'll cook. You just turn up." He stepped forward to cup her cheeks between his palms, holding her face still so he could look into her eyes. He could lose himself there, he knew it, just sink into those gray-green depths and never resurface again.

"I love you, Genie." He laid his mouth across hers, the kiss featherlight.

"I love you, too, Sir. Thank you for this, for just now."

"My pleasure, love. Now go."

He grinned at her retreating back, a new spring in her step. A decent thrashing seemed to have done her a world of good.

* * * *

Aaron gave his casserole a stir and turned the oven down low. He'd been back in his apartment for a couple of hours and had resisted the urge to just phone down to room service and get some supper brought up. Instead, he'd raided his small freezer for a pack of braising steak he had stowed in there and sliced up an onion, a carrot and a few mangetouts. It was nothing special, but with some herbs thrown in and a couple of jacket potatoes, he thought it was a decent enough meal.

The only missing ingredient was his sub. She should have been here by now.

He checked his phone again, reread her text.

Just finishing here. Will go back to my flat for a change of clothes, see you in 30 mins.

He checked the time since that message arrived. Fifty-five minutes. How long did it take to throw a fresh pair of pants and a T-shirt into a holdall and walk up one flight of stairs? And to make matters worse, she wasn't answering her phone or texts. He wasn't given to stalking his submissives, but he was concerned. He knew Eugenie had a casual attitude toward time keeping—or she used to. It wasn't a trait he'd seen much in evidence of late.

Once a brat, always a brat. She's angling for another spanking. He dismissed that notion as quickly as it formed. Not Genie, not anymore. She had no need to manipulate. She needed only to ask and she knew that now. They had both grown up. With a curse, he turned the oven off and headed for the door.

He jogged along the corridor and down the flight of stairs separating their floors. His phone was in his pocket but he didn't bother to try her again. He had his security passkey so would let himself into her flat. If she wasn't there, he'd go looking for her in the offices or the public rooms—she would never have left the hotel without letting him know her plans.

As soon as he turned the corner and started along the corridor toward Eugenie's studio flat he smelled it.

Smoke!

Autopilot kicked in. He lunged for the fire alarm situated on the wall a few meters ahead of him and punched the glass. A cacophony of bells filled the hallway. He ignored them as he dragged a fire extinguisher from its bracket next to the alarm button and started running. He was halfway down the corridor before he saw it, but it was with a fatalistic sense of expectancy that he registered the wisps of pale gray smoke drifting from under Eugenie's door.

The pounding of his feet echoed around the empty corridor as he raced to reach her. He dumped the fire extinguisher and tried his passkey. Nothing, the fucking key wouldn't work. Not so much as a flicker. He rattled the door but it was locked solid. He was aware, just dimly, of the sound of running feet approaching behind him. Help was on the way, but might be too late.

He stepped back the width of the corridor between him and Eugenie's door. He eyed the solid barrier before giving it a resounding kick. The wood shook, rattling the frame, but it held. He stepped back and repeated the action, desperation and naked fear lending him a strength he hadn't known he possessed. He grimaced in satisfaction as the doorframe splintered. He shoved the door, crouching to avoid the billows of smoke pouring out into the hallway.

"Genie! Genie, are you there?" He peered through the haze, seeking some shape, some clue that she was in here and alive. Nothing.

"Aaron, don't go in there. The fire brigade is on their way." He recognized Elise's voice but knew he couldn't wait. Eugenie couldn't wait. With his hand shielding his mouth and nose as best as he could, he grabbed the extinguisher from the floor and dove into the flat.

He saw at once where the fire was. The waste paper basket was alight, and flames were starting to lick along the curtains nearby. He had a few seconds at best before the entire room would be engulfed. He directed the nozzle of the appliance at the bottom of the paper bin and let out a thick burst of foam. The flames died. He waited for a moment then delivered another blast when he spotted a faint, defiant flicker. This time he killed it.

"Genie! Genie, where are you?"

He staggered to the window and threw it open, the smoke already starting to dissipate now that the source was extinguished. He leaned over the sill to heave in a couple of lungs full of sweet oxygen then turned to crouch against the wall, below the smoke. His eyes smarting, he peered around the empty room. Nothing. Where the fuck was she?

Then he heard it. A groan, faint but unmistakable. He crawled toward the bed and almost fell on her. She lay on the floor, curled in a ball on her side between the bed and the wall. He cradled her in his arms as he struggled to his feet, his lungs now burning as they filled with the remaining smoke. Head down, holding his breath, he headed for the only light source, the hallway outside.

Moments later, he stumbled back out into the relatively clear air of the corridor. He sank to his knees, still hugging Eugenie close.

"Let me see her." Fleur's voice cut through his sense of relief at finding himself alive, and Eugenie too, he hoped. She had been alive. He'd heard her voice, her soft moan. He laid her on her back as Elise ushered the growing crowd of hotel employees back along the corridor, issuing her instructions as she did so.

"Someone needs to be downstairs to direct the fire service when they arrive. Louis, could you do that, please?" One of the waiters, clad now in just jeans and a shirt, turned and sprinted for the stairs. Elise wasn't done yet. "Anton, call an ambulance."

Aaron sat on the floor and leaned back against the wall, heaving in long, cool draughts of precious oxygen as Fleur strapped a facemask across Eugenie's mouth and nose.

"The fire's out." Aaron managed to choke out the words though his throat felt to be full of gravel.

"Good. But the alarm will have connected to the fire service automatically and they'll be on their way. We need them to check that all is safe." Elise's words were matter-of-fact, though her tone and anxious expression belied this.

She knelt beside Aaron, her hand on his arm. She squeezed his wrist. He found her presence reassuring but he knew that even though the immediate crisis was over, their problems were far from finished.

"We need the police too." He coughed, leaning forward to reach for Eugenie's hand. "My passkey didn't work. It was dead."

"Well, perhaps the fire... The electrics...?" Elise sounded as unconvinced as he was.

"No way. The fire was at the other side of the room in the waste paper bin. It wouldn't have affected the security system, and even if it had, the failsafe would have unlocked all the doors. She was locked in there." His mind was racing now, assembling all the pieces. "And how the fuck did her bin catch fire? Genie doesn't smoke. There would be no reason for any naked flame."

"Okay. The fire investigators will be able to tell us more. I'm just glad you were here and spotted the smoke in time." Elise patted his arm as they both watched Fleur working on Eugenie.

Aaron groaned, leaning his head back against the wall now. "She was late. I should have come looking for her earlier. I should never have let this happen. Is she okay? Why doesn't she wake up?"

Fleur turned, her expression grim. "Concussion would be my best guess. You are right about the police." She gently probed the back of Eugenie's skull. "This head wound will take some explaining."

Chapter Seventeen

Her head hurt. Her throat felt like sandpaper. Her eyelids were heavy and it was too much trouble to open them. Perhaps she wouldn't bother. Not yet anyway. She allowed herself to drift as the dark fog descended again.

* * * *

Still hurting. Thirsty. So tired.
Eugenie could hear voices, low, whispering, somewhere close by. She tried to make out words but couldn't. It was effort, too much effort. She'd try later. Perhaps.

* * * *

"Why doesn't she wake up? It's been twelve hours. Is she going to be all right?"
She recognized that voice, that tone. *Aaron.*
Eugenie tried to open her eyes but it was too difficult. She tried to reach for him but her hand felt to

be made of lead. She was filled by a sudden sense of desperation, an overwhelming need to touch him, to feel his solid presence. She again tried to reach for him, but still her limbs would not obey her.

"She's coming round. There, look, she moved her fingers."

Eugenie was aware of the strong, warm hand that now wrapped itself around hers, the long, capable fingers she knew so well. She tried to grasp him, but couldn't move. It didn't matter, he just tightened his grip.

Secure in the contact, she allowed herself to drift away again.

* * * *

The next time her mind edged toward consciousness, she was ready. She wanted to wake up, wanted to open her eyes and see the world, needed to know she was still in it. Eugenie pried her eyelids apart, slowly opening them to let in the light.

The room was strange, not a place she knew. She lay on her back, above her the bright glare of strip lights. She turned her head, saw a white rail beside her head, and beyond that, a sleek cream-colored cupboard fixed to a plain white wall. Something caught her eye, a light flashing. She peered at it, tried to focus. It was a small screen, figures dancing across it. A monitor of some sort?

Her hands. Something was touching her hands. She lifted the left one a few inches, amazed to find that she could do so. A clip rather like a large clothes peg was attached to her middle finger, and from that, a cable connected her to the monitor.

She was in hospital. This was medical equipment. Why? Why did she need to be in hospital? What was wrong with her?

She opened her mouth to ask, but there was no one to direct the question to. She tried to lift her other hand, but this one was weighted down. She turned her head to investigate, and saw him.

Aaron was in a low chair beside her bed, his head on his chest. He was asleep, his hand clasping hers in a firm, immovable grip.

Eugenie relaxed. If Aaron was here, this would be okay. He'd know the answers. She could wait until he woke up then ask him. Her fears evaporated and she allowed herself to drift off to sleep again.

* * * *

"Genie? Can you hear me, sweetheart?"

Aaron's voice invaded her dream. She didn't mind, she loved to hear his voice. She smiled.

"Wake up, love. It's time to come round now."

No, not yet.

"Yes. Now. Come on, you can't lie around here all day." His words were firm but his tone achingly gentle.

"Sir? I'm tired."

"I know, love. You can go back to sleep soon. The doctor needs to check you over."

Doctor? Oh yes, the hospital. Eugenie remembered the white rail, the monitor. She had questions. The doctor could tell her, or Aaron could. She forced her eyelids apart again.

"Hello, darling. Welcome back." Aaron was leaning over her, his face close to hers. He was smiling, his eyes soft. Had he been crying? No, impossible.

"Hello..." Her voice rasped. It didn't sound like her at all. Her throat felt awful.

"Shh, you don't need to speak just yet. Here, try some of this." Aaron slipped his arm under her shoulders and lifted her up a little, at the same time holding a cup to her lips. It was one of those odd hospital cups like a child would use, with a lid and a spout. Cool liquid spilled onto her tongue. It was sweet, so welcome. She swallowed, lifting her hand to clutch at his.

"It's okay, baby. There's plenty. Take it slow."

Eugenie sipped at the water, relishing the cool, soothing sensation as it flowed down her throat. She felt as though her tonsils had been attacked with a cheese grater. When she'd had enough she looked up at Aaron, who understood at once. He placed the cup on the bedside table before leaning back to look at her.

Another figure appeared, this time wearing a white coat. The doctor. He leaned over the bed to peer at her.

"I'd like to examine you, Mademoiselle d'André. Is that okay?"

Eugenie nodded.

"I'll wait outside." Aaron started to rise, but Eugenie grabbed at his hand, shaking her head in desperation. He couldn't leave. She couldn't let him go.

"It's quite all right for Monsieur Praed to stay, if you want him to." The doctor's voice was kind, and calm. Eugenie liked him.

She nodded, and Aaron settled back in his chair. The doctor's checks were soon completed — heart, lungs, blood pressure, temperature. He seemed satisfied.

"Your readings are back to normal, more or less. How do you feel?"

"My throat hurts."

The doctor nodded. "You inhaled a lot of smoke. That will pass, but I know it's unpleasant right now. I can prescribe some painkillers for you. What about your head?"

"My head?" Eugenie was only now beginning to register that her head was hurting too, a dull ache at the front, behind her eyes, and a sharper pain at the back.

"Yes. You had quite a knock there. You've been out cold for nearly twenty-four hours."

"What? What!" Eugenie struggled to sit bolt upright. *Twenty-four hours! The wedding.* She was supposed to be at the hotel directing operations with military precision. She couldn't be lying around here in a hospital bed complaining about a sore throat and headache. She needed to get back there — now.

"Whoa, steady on, Genie. You need to rest."

Aaron sounded so calm. Didn't he realize? Had he entirely forgotten how vital it was that nothing be allowed to go wrong? Yet here they both were, their posts deserted. Anything could be happening. She turned to him, her desperation mounting.

"I need to get back. *We* need to get back. My clothes…"

"Your clothes are in the hotel laundry, where perhaps we might be able to get rid of the smell of smoke. I'll bring you some fresh things to wear when you need them. Which is not now." Elise's voice echoed across the small room. She stood in the doorway, her arms full of flowers. She offered a polite nod to the doctor as he left to minister to other needy patients. "We have everything under control. Farah sent these and she hopes you'll be well enough to be at the ceremony tomorrow, but not to worry if you don't feel up to it."

"What? But… How?"

"Your notebook. It's a bit grimy from the smoke but we managed to salvage it from your apartment. From there, I was able to take over. Unless you don't think me capable, of course…?" Elise's expression was wry as she arranged the showy display of glorious blooms in a vase she found on the windowsill. "These roses are beautiful."

"Yes. Yes, but I…" Eugenie watched her employer arrange the flowers. Farah had sent them. Their VIP client knew Eugenie was ill and had sent flowers, wished her well. No recriminations, no complaints that she was not available, not at her post where she should be. Perhaps this was going to be all right after all.

"You're bloody good, love, but no one's indispensable. Not even you and me. Elise and Pierre seem to be managing without us, at least for a day or so. I'm as surprised as you are, but there you have it."

Aaron was grinning at her, and Eugenie knew her expression must be one of pure incredulity. Certainly, that was how she felt. Utterly astonished. Her initial shock was followed by a wave of relief, then delight, then gratitude that so many people seemed to care about her. People who mattered.

She settled back against her pillows, shifting slightly as Aaron arranged them for her. She tried a couple of experimental swallows. Her throat was sore, felt very dry, but she could manage. And now, she wanted answers.

"What happened? The doctor said something about smoke? And my head?"

"You were in a fire. Your apartment. Aaron managed to get you out. He's quite the hero." Elise dragged a chair over to settle herself on Eugenie's other side. "Do you remember anything about it?"

Eugenie shook her head, careful to avoid any jarring movements.

"Tell us what you do recall. Start from when you left your office. You texted me to say you were almost done. Do you remember that?"

Aaron's tone was light, but she knew him too well to be fooled. This was serious.

Eugenie turned to study Aaron's face, frowning as she tried to cast her mind back. Was it really only twenty-four hours? It seemed like a lifetime ago. Maybe that was common in people who survived near-death experiences. Had she had one of those? It certainly felt like it. But she had survived, that was the important thing. She was here to tell the tale. And Aaron wanted to hear it.

"Yes. I finished costing up the wedding favors and I emailed the supplier with the final quantities. Then I texted you." She paused as Aaron handed her the cup of water again, grateful for a few more cooling sips. She settled herself against the pillows and closed her eyes as she continued. "I left my office and headed back up to my flat. I saw Annette on the way, stopped for a chat. Just five minutes or so. I was looking forward to seeing you."

She opened her eyes to glance at Aaron. He squeezed her hand. "Me too, love. I made you a casserole."

"I would have enjoyed that. I was hungry."

"You're always hungry. Go on. What happened after you left Annette?"

"I went up to my flat."

"Did you go straight there? Did you see anyone else?"

"No, I don't think so. Well, just the maid who does the rooms. She brought me some fresh sheets."

"What, she left them in your apartment for you?" This from Elise.

"No. She was in the corridor with her trolley when I went past. She knocked on my door a couple of minutes later and handed me the sheets."

Aaron's gaze was intent. "Okay. Then what?"

"I... I don't know. Nothing. I don't remember anything else after that until I woke in this room." She looked from Elise to Aaron, bewildered. How could she have just lost an entire day?

"What time was this? When you went back to your room?"

"I'm not sure, around eight, I suppose."

Aaron pulled his phone from his pocket. He tapped the screen to bring up his text messages. "That'd be about right. You texted me at seven fifty-three."

"What was a maid doing still working at eight in the evening? They usually finish by four." Elise reached for her own phone. "I'll call Annette, find out who was on duty yesterday. That maid might have seen something."

"No, wait."

Eugenie couldn't miss the sharpness in his voice, that tone of command. His words were enough to stop Elise before she had chance to hit the call button.

"We'll look at the CCTV first, see if that helps." He paused as both women stared at him, puzzled. He flattened his lips before continuing.

Eugenie knew they would not want to hear what he was about to say.

"If there was a maid on that corridor, she's just as likely to be a suspect as a witness. I don't want to alert her if I can help it."

An insider. Someone on the TFS staff might have been responsible for this. Aaron had put in place a veritable arsenal of security measures to protect them from external interference, from the malevolence of strangers. But Eugenie knew that if the threat came from one of their own, the danger was much more acute. He knew it too, as did Elise.

He put his phone to his ear. "Pierre? It's Aaron. Hi. Yes, she's conscious now, much better. Thanks. I'll tell her. Right now, I need you to do something for me. Can you check the CCTV footage from the corridor on floor seven? Yesterday, say between seven thirty and eight thirty in the evening. I want to know about every person who went along that hallway." He paused then chuckled. "I knew I was right to hire you, even though your rates are extortionate. Okay, text me a list. I'll view the footage myself when I get back."

He put the phone back in his pocket. Eugenie just watched him. Waiting.

"Pierre already checked the CCTV. He says there was a maid working, and a couple of others went by. Staff on their way to and from their rooms probably, but we'll talk to them all. For now, though…" He tapped out a text message. "There. I just asked Pierre to access the staff rosters for yesterday. We'll soon know everyone who was working last night."

"What about the police? Isn't this a matter for them?" Elise looked perplexed.

Aaron nodded, his features tight. "Oh, yes. We've already reported the unexplained head injury and they're waiting to interview Eugenie. We're still waiting for the fire investigation report too, but I'm almost certain they'll conclude the fire was started deliberately."

He reached for the half-empty glass of water as Eugenie was seized by a violent fit of coughing. She was grateful for his support, his quiet care as he sat beside her and held the cup to her lips. Her lungs heaved and contorted as they battled to rid themselves of the irritants still in her body. At last she was still again, her breathing even. She turned her face up to his.

"I don't remember anything about a fire. Is that how my throat got so sore?"

"Yeah. I found you unconscious beside your bed. The wastepaper bin was on fire and the curtains. The room was full of smoke."

She shook her head, her certainty absolute. "I didn't set fire to my bin. I don't even have a box of matches."

Aaron seemed to have been thinking along the same lines. "No. That's what I was wondering. But someone did."

"And you think it was deliberate? Who? Who could have done it? And why would anyone want to do that? To me?" Eugenie grasped at his hand again, her world tilting. What he was suggesting amounted to an attempt to murder her. And it had so nearly succeeded.

"I don't know—yet. We will solve this, though. And until we do, you won't be out of my sight, not even for a moment. I won't let anyone hurt you again."

He caught her gaze and held it. She felt steadied by his quiet determination, his unwavering confidence. She believed in him.

With a self-conscious cough of her own, Elise stood and reached for her bag. "I need to get back. I just wanted to see you for myself, to make sure you were okay. I'll let everyone else know."

Aaron turned to her. "Actually, if you wouldn't mind, could you just let everyone else think Genie is still unconscious? Best not to broadcast that this attempt failed in case it encourages whoever set that fire to have another go."

Both women stared at him.

"Do you think they might? Am I still in danger?" Eugenie could hear the tremor in her voice.

Aaron gave her a reassuring smile. "Not right at this moment. Whoever did this is probably assuming you're still at death's door, and I want to keep it that way. Apart from us three, only Pierre knows you've regained consciousness and are able to tell us anything about what happened. When the doc says you're fit to be discharged, my plan is to sneak you back into the hotel without anyone else knowing you're there. Pierre and Elise can help keep other staff away while we spirit you through. You can hide out in my apartment. We'll check out the CCTV images, see if anything jogs your memory further—if you feel up to that, of course. Or you can just get some rest."

"No, I want to help. And I want to be at that wedding. If I can…"

"It's not until late afternoon tomorrow. We'll probably know a lot more about what happened by then." He grinned at her. "I don't want to miss it either, after all the work we've both put in."

"When can I leave here?"

Elise leaned down to kiss Eugenie's cheek, a purely Gallic gesture. "I'll see if the doctor's still around and ask him to come back and talk to you about that." She turned to Aaron. "I assume you'll be staying here?"

He nodded.

"I'll see you soon then." Elise stopped in the doorway. "Aaron, let me know when you're coming back and I'll make sure the coast is clear." With a quick wave at Eugenie, she was gone.

A few minutes later, the doctor came back. "I gather you want to leave us already?"

Eugenie's smile was self-conscious. "I'm feeling a lot better now, thank you. You've been very kind, but I'd like to go home, if I can."

He smiled at her. "Ah, we have that effect on so many of our guests. I daresay your accommodations at the Totally Five Star are much more comfortable. Well, your readings were near enough normal, but I'd like to get a couple more hourly observations in before discharging you. It's after nine in the evening now, so how about you stay with us overnight and we'll look to send you on your way first thing in the morning?"

Eugenie grimaced. She'd hoped to be leaving sooner than that. Aaron's expression was suddenly pure Dom, daring her to argue. Eugenie subsided back against her pillow.

"That sounds fine, Doctor. Thank you."

On reflection, tomorrow would come soon enough.

Chapter Eighteen

Aaron much preferred her in his bed than in the hospital one, especially as she didn't find it necessary to wear any clothes. Perhaps it was the fact that he was stretched out alongside her. Certainly, that didn't hurt. Eugenie turned to nestle up against him, her nose buried in the cotton of his T-shirt. He could hear her breathing and thanked God for that sound. He'd nearly lost her.

"Thank you for staying with me."

He pulled her up his body to plant a kiss on her mouth. "I said I would. We're joined at the hip, you and me, until this is settled."

"Nice idea, Sir. And since we are here, in your bed…"

His cock twitched, but he knew that would have to wait. Still, he couldn't help playing with her. "Insatiable slut. Aren't you tired?"

"No, Sir. I've done nothing but sleep for nearly two days."

"Thirty-six hours, actually. Well, since you're so bright-eyed and bushy-tailed right now, do you feel up to watching a bit of television? Of the closed circuit variety?"

Eugenie sat up next to him, treating him to an uninterrupted view of her gorgeous breasts. His cock was taking on a life of its own.

"Can we view it from here?"

Christ, yes. We could probably view it from the moon if it got any bigger.

"Sir? The CCTV—can we watch it from your apartment?"

Aaron gave himself and his rampant testosterone a mental shake. Business first, pleasure later. Lots of pleasure.

"Yes. I can patch my laptop through to the hotel system. Wait there." He rolled from the bed and left the room. A few moments later, he returned, his laptop under his arm. He'd loosened the button on his jeans. He set the computer on top of the duvet and winked at her as he fired it up.

"Looking good there, little Genie. Maybe I should move you in permanently."

"Sir?"

"Just an idea. Your flat is uninhabitable and I don't think there are any vacant ones. At least not singles."

Her face fell. "Oh. I see. That's kind of you, Sir."

"And of course a live-in sub is so much more convenient. I could fuck you every morning. How would you like that, Genie?"

"I'd like it very much, Sir. If it's not too much trouble. Are you sure you have enough room for me?"

"I'll make space. Are you being a brat again, Genie?"

"Me, Sir? Of course not."

"Mmm, I think you are. Whatever, I'll spank you anyway. After we're done here."

"Thank you, Sir. Do I have any clothes left? After the fire, I mean?"

He glanced across at her. "I'm not sure. There was a lot of smoke damage. The TFS insurance will cover you, though. Elise sent some stuff over for you to borrow until you can replace your own."

"She's been so kind. She's a wonderful boss."

"She values her best staff and looks out for them. And she likes you."

"You too. I mean, you've been wonderful too. Did I thank you for rescuing me?"

"You did, and you will again. I intend to fuck you until you see stars later. If you feel up to it, naturally. That'll be my reward."

"I see. But even so, Sir, I want you to know how grateful I am."

He turned to face her, his expression serious. "Don't be grateful. I love you. You mean the world to me. What else would I have done? I need you. Here. With me."

"So, the live-in sub thing, it's not just for convenience?"

"Who are you talking to, Genie?"

"For convenience, Sir? I apologize."

"Accepted. No. It's not. You may be many things, my sweet little slut, but convenient is not one of them. You'll lead me a real dance, but I'll manage to control you. Somehow."

"Your belt might be useful, Sir."

"Indeed."

"And a cane. A cane always gets my attention."

"I've noticed."

"I don't much like being whipped."

"I noticed that too. I'll be needing a new whip. Maybe two."

"Thank you, Sir."

Aaron growled as she shifted to kneel on the bed, leaning forward to peer at the screen of his laptop, her pert little bottom right in front of his nose.

Later, baby. You will regret that. His cock was straining the font of his jeans. This was going to be a difficult day.

* * * *

"There. That's the maid. She was about halfway along the corridor when I got back."

They sat on the bed, Eugenie nestled between Aaron's outstretched legs, her bum pressing against his erection. His self-control was sorely tested as he reached his arms around her, his fingers on the keyboard. They had work to do. Aaron halted the recording to note the time the cleaner had come into view. Ten minutes or so before he knew Genie had returned to her room.

They watched the woman push her trolley full of cleaning materials along the deserted corridor. She paused at Genie's door and knocked. She waited a few moments then continued on her way to the far end of the hallway. There, she turned the trolley around then just leaned on the handle, waiting.

"What's she doing? She doesn't look to be doing any work."

"I'd say she's waiting for something. Or someone."

"Me? Do you suppose she was waiting there for me?"

Aaron shrugged, not wanting to give voice to his suspicions. But she was spot on. He used the zoom facility to move in for a close-up of the maid's features. His heart lurched as he recognized the face.

"Shit! That's Sara Khalid al-Fulani." Aaron leaned forward to study the image in the screen. "What the fuck is she doing pushing a bloody cleaning trolley?"

"You know her?"

Aaron nodded, reaching for his phone. "Yes. She's part of Farah's household. Deals with her personal correspondence mainly. You've probably seen her about the hotel but had no close dealings with her." He tapped his phone once and put it to his ear. It was answered immediately.

"Pierre? Can you locate Sara Khalid al-Fulani? I want to know exactly where she is at this moment. No, don't let her know we're interested, just find her and tell me."

He thanked Pierre before turning back to the computer. He tapped a few more keys to access his restricted security files and went straight to his personnel files relating to the wedding party.

"I did the checks on all the guests, but not the personal staff of either Farah or Lucas. Their own operations had that covered. Or so we thought. Here, this is Sara." He hit a key and the screen filled with an image of a young woman, pretty enough, dark-haired, dark-eyed, smiling into the camera.

"I *have* seen her."

"Yeah, you will have."

Eugenie grabbed for his arm, her fingers digging into his wrist. "No. Not with Farah. I've seen her working as a maid before—or pretending to." She turned to him, her eyes glittering. "She was there, in the corridor, when I fell down the stairs. I know it was her. I walked right past her, she said good morning to me."

Realization dawned, the final pieces started dropping into place. There was a reason he didn't believe in coincidences.

"Holy fucking shit." He grabbed his phone and in moments had Pierre back on the other end. "How far back do we store CCTV records for? Thirty days?" He turned to Eugenie. "Can you remember what date it was when you fell down the stairs?"

She did a quick tally in her head, then replied, "The twenty-second of last month, I think. Yes, the twenty-second. Definitely."

"Good. We might just be in time, then. Pierre, can you find the CCTV footage from the twenty-second of June, seventh floor in the staff wing. Particularly the area around the lifts and stairs. Patch it through to me as soon as you have it."

"Do you think she was the one who set fire to my apartment? Why would she do that? I don't understand. Why would she want to attack me?"

"I have no idea. But I intend to find out. You've been having too many mishaps for my liking, and if Sara was in the vicinity on more than one occasion, that means she has some questions to answer. Apart from anything else, I want to know why she's been sneaking around the hotel disguised as a chambermaid."

"She could be a thief. You know, using her passkey to access guests' suites."

"That's a possibility, though no thefts have been reported." Somehow, his instincts were not screaming 'thief' at him. His gut told him this was something else, something more complex.

"Maybe she's planning something…" Eugenie broke off as Aaron's phone trilled. He reached for it, saw Pierre's name on the caller ID.

"Yes?"

"Boss? I'm sending you the CCTV now. You'll want to see this."

Aaron wedged the phone between his head and his shoulder as he tapped the computer keys again to go back to the CCTV footage. This time the image was of the section of the hallway close to the lift. The maid — Sara — was clearly visible, dragging a vacuum cleaner along the carpet.

"See. That's her. I *knew* it." She peered more closely. "What's she doing? That vacuum cleaner isn't even plugged in."

"It's a prop, that's all. Look, this is you."

The image showed Eugenie walking along the corridor, her stride brisk. She sidestepped to get past the maid and the two exchanged a brief greeting.

"That's when she said good morning. She looked right at me. I recognized her as the same maid when I opened my door the other evening. That's why I didn't think anything of it, I'd seen her before."

They both watched the screen as Eugenie continued down the corridor to the lift. She pressed the call button then waited a few moments before heading for the stairs.

"My sandal came undone. I stopped to fasten it. I sat on the top step—"

"Look. Watch the maid. She's coming up behind you."

"I never heard her. I thought she was still somewhere along the hall. What is she—?" Eugenie grabbed his hand, her eyes startled. "Did you see that? Did you see what she did? She pushed me! The bitch, she actually pushed me down the stairs."

"She sure did." Aaron rewound the final few seconds of the recording and replayed it. They watched in silence this time as the maid in the image crept along the hallway and crouched a couple of feet behind Eugenie. As Eugenie started to rise, having fastened her sandal, the maid moved fast. Her hands outstretched, she shoved Eugenie in the middle of the back to propel her head first down the stairs. This time Aaron let the recording continue. Eugenie had disappeared from their view but they watched the maid as she stood on the landing for several seconds, looking down the stairs after Eugenie. Then she turned and marched off in the other direction.

"I never felt the push. How could that be?"

"Probably because you were startled and concentrating on trying not to fall. And maybe because it seemed so unbelievable you just didn't register the possibility."

"Maybe. I heard her, though, after I fell. I heard her footsteps. I thought she was coming to help me, but there was just the sound of a door closing then silence."

"Pierre? You still there?" Aaron had his phone to his ear again.

"Yes, boss. Did you see it?"

"We did."

"And the other footage? From the other night?"

"What? No, not yet."

"Look at that too. I'll wait." Pierre's tone was terse.

"You're on speaker. Eugenie is here too."

"Okay. Good morning, Miss d'André. I hope you're feeling better now." The security consultant's voice softened, his concern apparent.

"I'm fine, thank you, *Monsieur* Barent."

Aaron switched the CCTV footage back to the shots of the corridor outside Eugenie's apartment. He used the fast forward function to flick through several minutes where the maid in the image made no move to perform any duties.

"She's not there to work, that's for sure." Aaron muttered the comment, glancing at Eugenie.

The disembodied voice of Pierre Barent answered him. "You'll see what she's there for in a minute. Has Miss d'André appeared yet?"

"No. Yes, here she is." Aaron leaned forward, concentrating hard on the scene unfolding on the small screen. Eugenie came into the picture, walking down the hallway and letting herself into her room. Moments later, the maid pushed her trolley along the corridor, stopping outside Eugenie's door. She knocked and waited. The door opened, the maid seemed to be saying something, then she turned to lift a pile of bedding from her trolley.

"She told me she had fresh bed linen."

"Right. And now she's handing you the sheets. Shit—what was that? What did she just do?"

"She had something in her other hand, some sort of weapon. It looks as though she hit Miss d'André with it." The disembodied voice again.

"I don't remember anything about that. I took the sheets then… Nothing."

"Carry on watching." Pierre's tone was grim.

They watched as the maid pushed the door of Eugenie's room open and stepped inside. A couple of minutes later, she came out and closed the door behind her. She knelt beside it for a couple of seconds and looked to be fiddling with the lock.

"What's she doing now? Did she sabotage the locking mechanism?"

Pierre's reply was curt, "Yeah. She used a magnet. A strong one but wafer thin. She attached it to the underside of the lock housing and it played havoc with the circuitry. An old trick but effective. She locked the door, then she disabled the signaling system so it wouldn't respond to any more commands. It stayed locked."

Aaron let out a low whistle as they watched the maid scurrying away from the room. "Will we be able to prove it, though?"

Pierre chuckled. "We have the footage. And I have the magnet. She's not wearing gloves so her fingerprints will be on it. I reckon we can make that stick."

"You have the magnet? How?"

"I saw this footage last night, remember? As soon as I realized she'd tinkered with the lock, I went to investigate and found the magnet. It was subtle. The police and fire service both missed it. In fairness, they weren't looking."

As they watched the continuing sequence of images, they caught sight of the first wisps of smoke creeping from under the door then, seconds later, Aaron came into the picture, hurtling down the corridor carrying the fire extinguisher.

"Thank God you came."

"I wish I'd been there sooner. Christ, I was so scared. I thought I'd lost you."

Eugenie winced as she saw him launch himself at her door, splintering the frame on the second attempt. She turned to bury her face in his chest. He closed his arms around her and kissed the top of her head, oblivious for once to her nakedness. He was only aware of the warm, living, breathing woman that she was. That she still was, despite the repeated efforts of this would-be murderer.

Suddenly Eugenie stiffened in his embrace. She looked up at him, her eyes alight.

"She was in the garden too. That day. When I burned my hand."

"What? How?" The last piece of the puzzle was dropping into his grasp, the one remaining anomaly about to be explained.

"The gardener. There was a different gardener that day. I assumed it was a lad, an apprentice perhaps. He was slim, not tall. The usual guy is elderly, walks with a bit of a limp. He was nowhere to be seen and that day there was another man pruning the bushes. Except I think now it wasn't a man. It could have been her."

"Pierre, I want the staffing roster for that day. What grounds or maintenance staff did we have on?"

"I'm already checking, boss." They waited in silence as the seconds ticked by, then Pierre came back on the line. "No one outdoors that day. It was Edouard Leclerc's day off—he's the guy with the limp—and everyone else was deployed inside. Whoever was in the terrace garden that day had no good reason for being there."

"Where is she now?" His voice was cold. Arctic. Aaron had seen enough.

"In Ms. Ajram's suite." Pierre's response was immediate.

"Right, we're on our way there. Could you meet us? And we'll need a security team."

"The team's already outside the suite. I didn't want her slipping off anywhere while I brought you up to speed. I'll see you there in five minutes."

Aaron looked at Eugenie, who had already started to pull on some of the clothes borrowed from Elise.

"Better make it ten." He had no intention of leaving her behind. She stayed right by his side until he was sure this thing was over—really over.

Eugenie slanted him a quick look. "Five minutes will be fine, Sir." She pulled a loose sweatshirt over her head and started for the door.

Chapter Nineteen

"If we're right, she's tried to kill me three times. At least." Eugenie muttered the words as they jogged the length of the hallway. They veered to the left to take the stairs, ignoring the elevator.

"Looks that way."

"But why? Why me?"

"I'm working on a theory, but we need to talk to her."

"What theory?"

"Well, suppose her real goal is to sabotage this wedding, prevent it happening somehow? She might think she could do that by eliminating the wedding organizer."

"But that would never work. They would just hire someone else, or go somewhere else."

"Yeah, that's the flaw in my theory. Look, here's Pierre."

They paused to wait for Aaron's second-in-command as he marched toward them from the direction of the management suite. The three of them made their way to the executive guest accommodation together. A group of six security guards awaited them at the door to the honeymoon suite where Farah Ajram was already in residence. Her husband to be would join her there after the ceremony.

"Anyone go in or out in the last hour?" Aaron's question was curt.

One of the guards was quick to respond, "Just the bridegroom, sir. He arrived about thirty minutes ago."

Aaron grinned. "Not a traditional sort, then. It's supposed to be bad luck to see the bride before the wedding."

"They've been living together for over a year. And the Muslim ceremony took place a month ago." Eugenie leaned against the wall, slightly winded from their dash down there so soon after her close encounter with a smoke-filled room.

"Are you okay, *cherie*?" Aaron's businesslike demeanor was instantly transformed into concern. He rubbed her back as she gasped in large gulps of air. "Maybe you should sit this out."

"No way. I want to hear what that bitch has to say for herself. I deserve that much."

"Fair enough. Right, let's see what's happening, then." He knocked on the door of the suite.

Silence. He turned to the informative guard once more. "Are you certain they're in there?"

"Yes, sir. The woman Sara Khalid al-Fulani arrived soon after nine, and Lucas Belanger about half an hour later. None of them have left."

Aaron knocked again. Still nothing, He leaned against the door and pressed his ear to it. "I hear running water. Sounds as though someone's taking a shower."

"Surely not all three of them." Eugenie pressed herself up close to him, also listening for any clues.

Aaron knocked again then called out. "It's Aaron Praed, Head of Security, Ms. Ajram. I need to speak with you."

He waited a few seconds before fishing his passkey from his pocket. "I'm about to unlock the door, Ms. Ajram." He slid his key card through the narrow channel next to the door handle. An orange light clicked on then a green one. Aaron turned the handle and pushed the door open.

"Do not enter. I *will* kill her."

Sara Khalid al-Fulani stood facing them. Farah was perching on the edge of the sofa, her eyes fixed on the group in the open doorway. Eugenie's first impression was that the bride appeared to be remarkably calm given that Sara had a gun pointed at Farah's temple. Eugenie had no doubt at all that Sara intended to make good on her threat.

"Aaron, be careful. She means it."

"Me too, honey." He started to edge his way forward, his eyes fixed on the woman with the gun.

"What is all this? What's it all been about?" His voice was low, calm. Deceptive. Eugenie knew he was playing for the few seconds it would take him to reach the pair, but then what? As far as she knew, he was unarmed.

Sara glared at Eugenie, still framed in the doorway. She narrowed her eyes. "What is she doing here? She is like a cat — she has nine lives. Maybe I should drown her, that is how you get rid of cats, is it not? Or maybe just a simple bullet. I should have done that at the start."

Eugenie stiffened, transfixed, as Sara glowered at her. Somehow, she had become the object of this crazy vendetta, a target for a woman she barely knew and had no idea she had offended.

Aaron's voice remained calm as he inched closer to the center of the room. "No, Sara, you don't want to do that. So far, no one's been hurt, not really. There's no harm done, we can sort this out."

Sara switched her attention from Eugenie to Aaron. The woman's features were contorted in fury, her skin gleaming with a sheen of perspiration. Her breathing was labored, stressed. "No harm? How can you think it does no harm for this marriage to take place? This, this—atrocity? This affront to Islam." Her voice had risen to a near scream, her fury radiating from her.

"Ah, I see." Still that low, even tone, so reasonable, so unmoved by the fear and bitterness reverberating around him. Eugenie watched in astonishment as he continued to edge toward the couch, his hand outstretched in front of him. "You are not in favor of this marriage, I gather."

"It is an abomination. How can a princess of the Prophet even bear to be in the same room as, as...?"

"It's hard to understand, I know that." Still he approached, his tone now sympathetic, taking the side of this mad bitch. Eugenie was baffled.

As though recognizing a kindred spirit, Sara continued her tirade. "He is vile. A monster. Evil. We have no use for such decadence."

"We?"

"Our country. Our people. My people."

"I can tell you feel passionately about this. We have to talk. We can find a way out, a solution. But not with a gun. You need to put the gun down and we will talk. Yes?" Aaron was just a few feet from her now.

Eugenie watched his muscles tense, and sensed that he was about to make his lunge.

"No! I will end this. I will put a stop to this outrage. We want no alliance with this scum." She fixed her gaze once more on the woman seated on the sofa the woman whose stony face betrayed not a flicker of fear at the danger she was in.

Farah turned her head, fixed Sara with a withering look. Eugenie wondered if the princess was born with that gift, an aristocratic talent for putting lesser mortals in their place.

"If you intend to kill me then get on with it. Do it now, or I will rip out your lying, treacherous tongue." Farah's voice was steady, her words delivered with icy precision. Her eyes glittered with suppressed rage.

Sara seemed oblivious to Farah's contempt. "You! You accuse me of treachery? You who have betrayed our culture, our way of life. You who would defile yourself with that animal."

"Your way of life. Not mine, not that of my family." Farah ground out her reply, her teeth gritted as she tilted her chin, daring her assailant to make good on her threats.

"Well, I expect this sort of talk from City supporters, but I'm surprised at you, Sara. I'd always had you down as more of a cricket fan really…"

Sara snapped her head around to regard the man lounging in the open doorway to the bathroom. His arms were folded across his naked chest, water dripping from his hair. He was wearing only a towel knotted loosely around his hips. In that split second, Eugenie had an idea why Sara considered him decadent. She might have agreed. Add to that cocky, arrogant, and just possibly stark-raving mad.

The next couple of seconds were a blur. Lucas appeared to exchange a glance with Aaron, then he grabbed at the knot by his hip and whipped the towel from his body. The fabric unrolled and snaked across the room, the end catching Sara's gun hand to send the weapon flying. It clattered across the floor to slither to a halt by Eugenie's feet. She stepped forward and back-heeled it farther behind her, to be retrieved by the security team still clustered in the corridor.

In the same instant, both Aaron and Lucas dove toward the settee. Aaron was closest and took Sara to the floor. The two rolled across the carpet, though the struggle was an unequal one. In moments, Sara was hauled to her feet and dumped unceremoniously into a chair. Two of Pierre's men were instructed to make sure she remained there until the police could take over.

Seemingly satisfied that Sara was no longer a threat, Lucas had diverted his attention to Farah. His fiancée had dived from the sofa as soon as he started his little party piece with the towel and now crouched, poised to fly at her assailant if she showed any signs of escaping from Aaron's grip. The naked footballer offered her his hand and pulled her to her feet. He hugged her, burying his face in her hair.

"Baby, baby, I thought she was going to kill you. Fuck, are you okay?"

"I am fine. You were wonderful. Magnificent. Thank you, thank you." Her words were muffled against his chest, but Eugenie found no reason to quarrel with Farah's description of her betrothed. Magnificent was near enough the mark. Privately she had always thought that Lucas Belanger cut an impressive figure in his tailored suits, or in his football strip. But naked, he was beyond beautiful.

"Ahem." Aaron's discreet cough caught her attention as he bent to retrieve the discarded towel. He held it out to Lucas, grinning. "Yours, I believe. Nice shot by the way."

Lucas disengaged from Farah and took the towel with a relaxed smile. He seemed in no particular hurry to make himself decent.

"Thanks. Good work yourself, keeping her talking long enough for me to get in position." He took his time wrapping the towel around his midsection again before reaching for Farah. "Are you sure you're all right, love?"

"Yes, perfectly." She turned to glare at Sara, who was now reduced to a sobbing mess. "She will hang for what she did. Or worse. My father—"

Aaron shook his head. "I'd say not. Not under French jurisdiction. We'll let the police take it from here. You two have a wedding to get to." He nodded to the gendarmes now shouldering their way past his security personnel and stepped forward, ready to deal with the formalities. Eugenie somehow imagined they would take some time.

Chapter Twenty

"Do you, Lucas Etienne Belanger, take this woman...?"

"Etienne? I never knew his middle name was Etienne." Eugenie hissed her comment out of the edge of her mouth. Aaron, seated next to her in the second row, leaned toward her to murmur his reply into her ear.

"What? Some detail has escaped you? How remiss. Maybe I need to do something about your attention to the finer points...?"

"I appreciate your care, Sir."

"Do you, Farah Ajram Abdul Ariz..." The registrar continued with the ceremony as the couple stood before her, heads bowed.

"Did you know about all those names?" Aaron whispered to Eugenie, his breath fluttering over her neck in a way that made her tingle.

"Most of them. Ajram is her father. The others are her grandfather and... Well, something along those lines."

"Ah. I see. Nice service, by the way. The room looks superb."

Eugenie cast her critical eye around and was gratified to note that he was right. The ballroom had been transformed to showcase this alliance between two A-list giants. Farah had rejected any suggestion of pink fluffiness. She wanted glamour and sophistication, a setting that spoke of elegance, impeccable taste and wealth, as well as the merging of two cultures. Accordingly, the walls were hung with a blend of Arabic art and French impressionist paintings, the oriental gold and deep red resonating with the more subdued hues of European masters. The raised dais at the front where the registrar faced the assembled guests was simple in design, contrasting with a backdrop of more Eastern art in the form of richly woven carpets and tapestries.

The guests filling the rows of brocade-covered seats surrounding her were the cream of international celebrity. The rich, the famous, the powerful all assembled to witness this marriage. High-profile names from the world of sport, of entertainment, commerce, politics, several royals, all gathered to bask in the splendor of all that Totally Five Star Paris had to offer. The media were here and the pictures would be all over the world within an hour.

She had done it. They had done it.

The couple was traditionally dressed for such an occasion, he in a morning suit and she in a flowing red gown designed to bring together a fusion of styles. Her throat encircled by a high mandarin neckline, Farah looked stunning. Her gown was perfectly decent, quite proper, deceptively modest with long, tight sleeves, the sleek fall of the train artfully arranged on the floor behind her. Eugenie knew better. Farah had never turned a hair when her bridegroom took it upon himself to parade naked in a room full of people. It was without doubt a sight she had seen many times, though probably in less public circumstances. Even so, modest hardly seemed the right word to use for this enigmatic woman.

And Lucas' unerring accuracy with that towel was giving her pause for thought. Where did he perfect that trick? She supposed his profession called for quick responses, agility, speed, but to have such a proficient whip hand implied an entirely separate set of skills. Perhaps Aaron would know. But there again, perhaps it was none of her business.

"I now declare you husband and wife..." The registrar brought the formal part of the proceedings to a close as Lucas turned to kiss a glowing Farah. The room erupted in cheering. As the din quieted, the strains of a romantic violin solo swelled from the back of the room.

The guests rose to their feet as the couple turned and started walking back along the central aisle, ready to file out and continue the party elsewhere.

The banqueting suite was the scene for the rest of the formal affair, centering on an exquisite ice sculpture depicting a swan taking flight. Farah had requested it to symbolize her new life with Lucas, a journey of interest, discovery, new beginnings.

The food continued the fusion theme, a series of small courses alternating between the haute cuisine of France and traditional Eastern dishes. Poached salmon in a delicate lemon sauce, bell peppers stuffed with shrimps, strips of lamb with walnuts and orange peel, mussels cooked in white wine, stuffed squid, snails braised in parsley butter. The succession of dishes was chosen and presented to be a celebration of the best of both worlds. Guests picked, selected, sampled, enjoyed. The atmosphere was relaxed, an easy mingling of styles, languages and cultures. It was just as Farah had intended—faultlessly delivered by Eugenie and Totally Five Star Paris.

The evening's entertainment was to continue with a cabaret of music, dance, theater. Some of the finest contemporary performers from across the globe were assembled for this private extravaganza. A trapeze act from Russia that Lucas had seen once before and had been impressed by. Bollywood dancing, another less likely favorite of his. A performance by an internationally renowned mezzo soprano reflected Farah's tastes. Eugenie's personal favorite was a violin soloist who delivered a haunting rendition of *Ave Maria*.

If anyone but the bride, groom and a few others were aware of the dramatic events of earlier in the day, they gave no sign of it. The hotel did not deal in drama or fuss. The wedding went ahead exactly as planned, on time, every carefully choreographed detail executed to perfection.

"Thank you. It has been wonderful, truly superb. Just as I hoped." Farah sought out Eugenie as her guests milled back into the now cleared ballroom to continue the dancing and entertainment. "I realize how difficult this has been—for you especially. I had no idea—"

"None of us did. But it's over now."

"That evil bitch. It is a pity your man will not allow me to deal with her as she deserves."

"Oh, he's not my man. We just work together." Eugenie opted not to comment on what Sara's just deserts might consist of.

Farah shook her head, the gesture decisive. "Nonsense. He is your man. As Lucas is mine. I will dance at your wedding, no?"

"What? No. I mean, yes, of course, if we —"

"You will, you will. And I expect to be there. So, where is Sara now?"

It seemed Farah was not to be deterred. Eugenie sighed. "She's still with the police. She will remain in custody. Aaron had to go to the police station to be interviewed again. And to fill in forms. He'll be back soon, I hope."

"So much paperwork. Do we know yet what her motive was?"

"From what the police told Aaron, it's pretty much as she was ranting in your room, some sort of misplaced religious fanaticism. She wanted to keep her culture pure, free of Western contamination. She had hoped to stop the wedding. It seems she saw me as a threat because I was organizing it. We'll know more as the police question her further."

"It is clear that she is mad — quite mad. Her mother is a close friend of my aunt. That is the only reason I employed her. I always found her strange, difficult to warm to."

"Your instincts were right."

"It seems so." She linked her arm through Eugenie's and steered her toward the ballroom. "Come, let us join our guests. We have a marriage to celebrate."

* * * *

Eugenie was dozing on the sofa in Aaron's apartment, her finery from the evening's glamorous entertainment folded and placed on the armchair alongside her. She had pulled on one of Aaron's Tshirts for warmth and still wore her pants. She could have gone to bed, should have probably, but had wanted to wait for him. Eventually, she could keep her eyes open no longer and stretched out on the couch.

The click of the lock woke her, if she had even been asleep. She wasn't sure. She opened her eyes and pushed herself up on one elbow as Aaron came through the door. He looked tired, drained.

"Sir?" She sat up properly, pushing her hair back from her face.

He turned and saw her. "Genie? What are you doing there? I thought you'd be in bed. Waiting for me."

"I am waiting for you, Sir. I didn't want to go to bed without you, though. Have you eaten?"

"Yes, I grabbed a sandwich downstairs, from the night service kitchen." He walked over to the small kitchenette and picked up the kettle. He shook it, decided it needed refilling and ran some water into it. He plugged it in and clicked the switch. "I need some tea. You?"

"Yes, thank you. What time is it?" She peered at the wall clock. Ten past four. Eugenie arranged herself on the settee as she watched Aaron make the tea. Neither of them spoke until he had placed two steaming cups on the low table in front of her.

He was still in his morning suit from the wedding, though he had discarded the jacket and the tie hung loose around his neck. He flopped onto the cushion next to her and leaned back. Eugenie had never seen him look more exhausted.

"Do you need to go back to the police station?"

He shook his head. "Not for a while. There will still be statements to go over, to sign. We'll need to certify the accuracy of the CCTV images and, in due course, I suppose her defense team will try to prove we set her up somehow. None of that will stick, but I suppose they can't be blamed for trying. That's if it gets that far. I have a suspicion this will never get anywhere near a trial."

"Oh?" Eugenie frowned at him over the edge of her mug. "Why not? Surely the evidence —"

"The evidence is fine. Watertight. But she's really lost it. She was lucid enough at first but she's just babbling now. The psychiatrists need to examine her, but personally, I doubt she'll be considered fit to plead. She'll be placed in some mental health facility, though I have no idea how long she'll need to be there for."

Eugenie wriggled into an upright position, her expression anxious now. "Sara may be ill, but she's very dangerous. They can't let her out."

"No chance of that for the foreseeable. She had quite a tale to tell, though, before she stopped making sense. You were right about the gardener — it was Sara you saw that day."

"I knew it."

"But did you also recognize her as an electrician you had a run in with?"

Eugenie furrowed her brow, thinking back, "No, I don't remember that."

"Apparently you kicked up a fuss about some debris or something dumped in the ballroom, insisted it had to be shifted. Ring any bells?"

She nodded. "Yes. It was weeks ago now. Some empty boxes, I think. It was a hazard. And you know our rules about unattended packages. I went to look for the workmen who left it there. They were having their lunch. The foreman sent someone to clear up the mess but he insisted they didn't leave it."

"He was telling the truth. It was Sara who left it there. She found a pair of overalls and pretended to be an electrician because she'd hatched some wild plot to rig the overhead lighting. There were several different contractors in at that time and they all assumed she was part of another firm's team. No one questioned her presence. She'd planned to see to it that the chandelier directly above the platform would fall during the ceremony, likely killing Lucas and Farah, and the registrar too."

He gave her a wry grin. "But you spotted the gear that she left there, intending to come back later, after hours, and complete her little scheme when the rest of the men had gone. The only reason she wasn't found out then was that she was with the men when you confronted them, and she volunteered to come back and clear up. If anyone else had touched the rubbish, they'd have spotted the wiring and explosives hidden among the packaging. You wrecked her plans and from then on, she had you in her sights. She saw you as the obstacle to her scheme and wanted you gone. She would have been happy just to scare you off, or have you incapacitated. That was her thinking when she pushed you down the stairs. The attack in the garden was more serious. She followed you out there and waited until you went to the toilet. As soon as your back was turned, she laced your tea with bleach, and if you'd drunk any of it, you might not have survived." He dropped his head into his hands. "Christ, she came so close to killing you."

Eugenie closed her eyes, remembering. "I was going to sit back down and drink that second cup. If that call from Farah had been even a few seconds later…"

He reached for her and squeezed her hand. "Your number just wasn't up, love. Thank God. That didn't stop Sara trying, though, and in her twisted reasoning, killing you became an obsession. It was as important to her as preventing what she saw as an unholy alliance between Sara and her heathen footballer."

"So she decided to set my apartment on fire."

Aaron simply nodded. "Same pattern as before. She waited until you finished work and came back up to your room, then she made her move. She had a wine bottle on her trolley and that's what she hit you with. Once you were down, she dragged you back over to the bed, hit you twice more, just to make sure you stayed down, then she set fire to the waste paper in the bin. She sabotaged the lock as she left. Extra insurance, just in case you came round before the fire really took hold. The lock was disabled, so you wouldn't have been able to open the door."

"She truly intended to murder me."

"Yes, my love, she truly did."

They fell silent, each lost in their private thoughts of how close Sara had come to killing both Eugenie and Farah.

Eugenie was the first to break the silence. "I'm puzzled. Why did Sara go to Farah's room this morning? After all her plotting and creeping about, she simply walked into Farah's suite to shoot her? It makes no sense."

Aaron lifted an eyebrow in acknowledgment. It was a good question.

"I wondered about that too. It seems that was also down to you, in a manner of speaking. She became so fixated on getting you out of the way that she took her attention off Farah and Lucas. She hatched no further plans to derail the wedding, then suddenly realized the great day had arrived and she needed to take urgent action. She was out of options, basically. As a member of Farah's staff, she could gain access to her suite, so she went there intending to put a stop to the wedding one way or another."

"Thank goodness we managed to work out who was behind everything that had been happening. It would have been so easy just not to connect the various 'accidents'. If you hadn't recognized her…"

"And if you hadn't realized she was the same maid who was close by when you fell down the stairs. And better still, you connected her to the bleach incident."

"You saved Farah. And me. I owe you my life."

"You owe me nothing. Apart from perhaps a little more respect. And obedience would be welcome."

"I do respect you. There's no one I respect more. And I obey — usually."

"I accept you're making progress. But you have some work to do. As do I."

"I don't understand. What work?"

"Before I left to go to the police station, I distinctly recall telling you to enjoy the rest of the party then get some sleep. You're still on sick leave, remember?"

"I slept on your settee."

"You knew what I meant. You were to come back here when the wedding reception was over and go to bed. Yet I returned to find you dozing on my couch. It's not as though my bed is in any way unfamiliar to you. I expected you to find it without any real difficulty."

"I just… I wanted to wait for you. I would not have been able to sleep until you came back. Please, Sir, don't make an issue of this. I didn't realize it was so important to you."

"When did I ever give you an instruction that wasn't important to me? I expect you to obey. Or if you can't, to say so. And to tell me why."

"Sir?" Eugenie was desolate. A spanking was not in itself such a dismal prospect—quite the opposite, in fact. And a punishment did seem to be on the cards. But to have disappointed Aaron, tonight of all nights, left her with a deep sense of failure.

"I apologize, Sir. I wasn't concentrating and I didn't listen properly to your instructions. I realize that I was at fault and I'll accept whatever consequences you feel are fitting."

"Well, now we're getting somewhere. Tell me, Genie, what are your plans for tomorrow?"

"Most of the wedding guests are leaving, but for those who remain, we have planned a garden party at Versailles."

"You intend to be there? Working? Even though you spent last night in hospital?"

"I... I thought..."

"Elise has everything in hand. You know this. And you're officially on sick leave for another week. By all means be at Versailles if you want to be, but as a guest."

"But I feel fine now. Even my throat has stopped hurting. Almost."

"I'm delighted to hear that. But it changes things how exactly?"

Eugenie studied her hands, still clasped around her now empty cup. She sighed as the truth sank in. "You are correct, Sir. I get too wrapped up in my work."

"We all do from time to time. You are valuable, Genie. You are needed here. Which is all the more reason for taking care of yourself. That's why Elise is helping you now. She wants you fully recovered and on top of your game before you come back to work. So do I."

She nodded, tears forming behind her eyes. The care and concern surrounding her were almost palpable. She looked up at him, her vision blurring. "I need to be able to let it go, just relax and trust others to handle everything."

"Yes. I can help you with that." His tone had softened. He tilted his head to one side, waiting.

Eugenie regarded him under her eyelashes. She knew exactly what he was offering. She knew just how he would release her inner tensions, free her from the stress that wound so tight around her chest sometimes that she could hardly breathe. She reflected grimly that she had no need of a smoke-filled room to choke her, she could manage that perfectly well herself just by piling on the pressure.

"Spank me, Sir. Please. I need this."

Aaron stood and walked toward the bedroom. At the door, he stopped and turned to face her. "Coming?"

Eugenie unraveled her legs from under her, staggering a little as she realized how stiff they had become. She tottered after him. By the time she reached the bedroom door, he was seated on the edge of the bed. He had a heavy paddle hairbrush in his right hand.

"Come here, Genie. Drop your pants and lay yourself across my lap."

She had no hesitation in doing as he asked. As he commanded. He was her Dom, her Master. She slipped her underwear down her legs and stepped out of the pants before walking over to him. Her chin up, she felt confident, sure of herself—and of him. Wordless, she laid herself across his knees and reached back to lift the T-shirt. Her bottom bared for his punishment, she lay still. Waiting.

"I intend to spank you, hard. You have your safe word, but unless I hear it, I'll continue until I think you've had enough. This will hurt, little one. I intend to teach you a lesson tonight. A lesson in obedience. And trust. Are you ready to learn?"

"Yes, Sir." And she was. Truly, she was. She knew what she was inviting. What she was accepting.

Even so, it was the most painful spanking she could recall. Ever. But wonderful for that. Maybe because of her unreserved submission to Aaron, she had become more inviting, more welcoming of the pain. It felt different, the sensation more intense, unbelievably so.

The first few strokes were hard but bearable. Eugenie gasped, whimpered a little, but it took no real effort for her to resist the temptation to clench or cover her bottom with her hands. Not wriggling was more difficult, especially as Aaron ramped up the pressure.

She counted the strokes. He hadn't asked her to this time, but it had become a habit. One, two, three. By seven, she was crying out with each blow from the hairbrush, the hard plastic handle delivering a deep burst of agony that sank deep into her soft buttocks. He waited a couple of seconds between each stroke to allow the pain to radiate, extracting maximum value from every slap.

Nine, ten, eleven. Eugenie writhed on his lap. His palm in the small of her back steadied and grounded her. His leg behind her knees kept her still. Eugenie relished the feeling of powerlessness, of being quite literally his to punish as he saw fit.

"Your hands, please, Genie."

Obedient, she reached behind her for him to encircle both her wrists in his hand. The contact was comforting. She exhaled slowly, sinking deeper into her submissive mindset. She was experienced now, this feeling familiar to her. She knew that subspace was just moments away.

Aaron knew too, and set up a slow, steady rhythm, each stroke measured and executed with perfect strength. Too light, and she would have drifted out of the moment, too heavy and she would have used her safe word. He was able to pitch the spanking just within her tolerance limit and keep her there because she knew she was safe. Emotionally, mentally, physically, she was secure in the knowledge that no harm would come to her.

By the twentieth stroke, she was screaming his name, by the thirtieth, she suspected she had forgotten her own. She sobbed, cried out, her tears flowing freely, but still he didn't stop, and still she wouldn't ask him to. Her buttocks felt to be on fire, the pain blistering across her bottom and thighs. It would be days before she would be prepared to even contemplate sitting.

Still she didn't want him to stop. She needed this, yearned for it, craved the bite of his expert spanking.

After the fortieth stroke, Aaron laid the paddle brush beside him on the bed. He rested his palm on her quivering, crimson ass. Eugenie flinched, groaned and lifted her bottom up for more.

"Mmm, so hot, sweetheart." He lifted his hand to his mouth and mimed spitting on it then made a sizzling sound.

Turning her head and shoulders to face him, Eugenie answered with a watery grin, still balanced across his thighs. She knew she should move, but would wait until instructed to do so. She was happy enough where she was.

"Thank you, Sir. That was so good. Still is."

"Not done yet. Spread your legs."

"More?"

"Oh, yes. First, I want to see what effect we've had so far. Open your legs and show me your cunt."

With a small shiver, Eugenie obeyed, conscious of her swollen, sensitized folds exposed for him to view. No matter how many times she opened her legs for his inspection, the eroticism of the moment was never any less for her.

"Fucking beautiful. I think you've been enjoying yourself, haven't you, my pretty little pain slut?"

"Yes, Sir. Please, could you...?"

"Could I what? This?" He thrust three fingers deep into her pussy, curling them to caress her G-spot.

Eugenie let out a sound somewhere between a sigh and a scream as he continued to finger-fuck her. She squeezed her inner muscles around his digits, gyrating her hips as she sought more pressure, more friction, more everything. His grip tightened around her wrists, still held securely behind her back, which only served to increase her pleasure. Perhaps sensing her growing need, he increased the tempo, driving his fingers into her deep and fast as he lifted her bottom up for him.

"Please, Sir, I need to come. Now, I can't help it."

"No? You really should try, my love — unless you want more of the hairbrush. Is that it? Would you like me to spank you again?"

"No, Sir, I want you to fuck me. Please."

"Ah, I see. Have you had enough of this, then? Would you like me to stop?" He stilled his fingers inside her, waiting for her response.

It came in the form of a long, low moan. "Please, Sir, I can't stand this. I need to come. I need to be fucked. I need you inside me."

"I know what you need. I always know and I always deliver. Wouldn't you agree?"

"Please, I can't think straight. Sir, I just… I need…" Eugenie was close to tears, her desperation mounting as he slowly started to thrust his fingers inside her once more. She clenched, her pussy spasming, quite beyond her control as her orgasm bubbled and simmered, so close but just beyond her reach.

"On the bed. Face down. Now." Aaron's instructions were terse and to the point. He released her hands and Eugenie couldn't obey quickly enough, scrambling across his lap to position herself as he had commanded.

Aaron stood and stripped, the work of moments. He knelt behind her, his palms gentle on her hips as he positioned her. Eugenie moaned, her entire body tense with anticipation as he placed the head of his cock between her swollen pussy lips. Just the first inch, maybe not even that, holding her open as she felt his gaze on her again at that spot where they were almost joined.

She stopped breathing, held herself poised, desperate. Beyond pleading, past telling him what she needed, she knew he knew anyway. He always seemed to know. At last, he surged forward, filling her in one long, slow stroke.

Eugenie's muscles gave up the struggle. She would have collapsed onto the bed but for Aaron's arm around her waist. He leaned over her, his lips at her neck dropping soft, light kisses in that most sensitive spot below her hairline.

"Okay, baby?"

She managed a mumbled yes, squeezing around him in a nonverbal form of communication just for good measure. Aaron got the message, setting up a brisk rhythm of short strokes that sent Eugenie's senses spinning. Her orgasm erupted, sweeping through her in a series of pulsing convulsions which started at her center and rolled out toward her fingers and toes. Her entire body tingled, her pussy clamped hard around his cock as she sought to hold him within her forever.

Her bone-deep orgasm left her gasping. As her muscles relaxed, Aaron lowered her to the bed, but continued his long, slow strokes. He reached around her to roll her clit between his finger and thumb, eliciting another moan as she started to climax again. The second orgasm was less intense, but seemed to be endless, a series of mini-peaks sending shudders of pure pleasure shooting through her. Where the first orgasm had crackled and sparked with electricity, this was more the gentle, continuous glow of a candle, glimmering, hot, and so sensual it made her ache.

She stretched her arms in front of her, grasping at the duvet and crumpling fistfuls of it when her body convulsed around his plunging cock. Aaron increased the pace, intensifying the sensations. He drove each thrust deep and straight, his own climax mounting. Eugenie could hear his breathing become more labored. She turned her head, squinting. Her vision was blurred by tears, but she was still able to see the veins on his forearms lacing across his skin as his muscles flexed. With a final muttered curse, he buried his cock balls-deep and held still as he filled the condom with his warm, thick semen.

* * * *

Another *vol au vent*?" Eugenie reached for the plate, intending to pass it to Aaron, sprawled beside her on the manicured grass that carpeted Versailles' extensive grounds.

"No. I'm stuffed. Wouldn't mind a glass of that Chablis, though." Aaron opened one eye, squinting into the sun. His grin was infectious.

Eugenie beamed back at him as she poured the chilled wine into a delicate flute. Even while guests dined al fresco, Totally Five Star standards applied. No unbreakable plastic for them, no paper plates or polystyrene cups. Guests did not rough it. Ever.

Aaron propped himself up on his elbows so she handed him the glass and settled beside him. Together, they surveyed the remains of the wedding party milling around on the lush lawn. A handful of guests were playing a rowdy and very competitive game of boules, though from their good-natured bickering, Eugenie doubted that any of the competitors actually knew the rules. Other conversation was more muted, the excitement and intense celebrations of the previous day now giving way to quiet relaxation. Most of the remaining guests were close friends or family of Lucas and Farah so the atmosphere was one of intimacy.

Elise seemed to be everywhere, moving easily from group to group, chatting, checking, ensuring the smooth flow of conversation as well as fine wine.

Aaron turned to Eugenie, his expression warm. "You must be very proud. This wedding has been a roaring success and that was your doing,"

"I am proud. And relieved. I'm glad it's all over, but I won't know what to do with myself when I come back to work."

"Relieved? I never doubted you. Neither did Elise."

"Thank you."

"And as for not having anything to do, I reckon this is just the first of many. You'll be rushed off your feet."

"Probably. I hope so. We had a few enquiries about other functions once the news got out that we were hosting this wedding, and some of those will start to convert into definite bookings now. The media coverage will have helped us."

"Elise will be delighted."

"And me. I came here determined to start over, to reinvent myself. I so wanted to make a success of this job."

"Why reinvent? What was so wrong with the old Genie?"

"They used to call me La Brat. I wanted to leave that image behind. I wanted to grow up, I suppose."

"Well, sweetheart, I'd say you're all grown up now. And you *are* a success. You're a fucking legend."

Eugenie laughed, the sound one of genuine pleasure. She shifted her position, wincing a little as her bottom connected with the hard ground beneath her. She rolled onto her side.

"Sore?"

"A little, Sir."

"That's good. I like to leave a lasting impression."

"I believe you may have mentioned that, Sir. And you succeeded. My bottom was still pink when I got dressed this morning."

He sipped his wine, a contemplative gleam in his eyes. "I imagine so. No regrets?"

She smiled as she shook her head, the gesture emphatic. "No, Sir. It was wonderful. I feel wonderful. Thank you."

"I want to know if that changes. You've never been unduly prone to sub drop, but that was an intense session, on top of everything else that happened yesterday."

Eugenie frowned at him. "Sub drop? Oh, you mean if I get weepy, or depressed."

"Yes, could be. Any sort of negative feelings linked to being spanked until you screamed for me to stop and then some. Or fucked until you almost fainted."

"I did not scream."

"Oh, but you did, sweetheart. Believe me."

"Well, perhaps a little. But I never wanted you to stop."

"I know."

Eugenie's smile was more secretive now, her mouth curving as she relived the intensity of last night's scene. Her buttocks clenched and her pussy moistened. Aaron grinned at her, his expression wicked. He knew, he bloody *knew* what was happening to her body.

"Are you okay, girl? You don't look exactly comfortable."

"How much longer before we can go home?" Eugenie clamped her legs together, trying to create a little friction against her clit. She was sorely tempted to sidle a bit closer to Aaron, just enough to be able to rub herself against his thigh. She hoped none of the guests, or worse still, her boss, would notice her dilemma. How embarrassing to be caught humping off in a public park in front of a bunch of VIP guests.

"So, you think of my apartment as home, do you?" Aaron's expression became more serious. He was seemingly oblivious to Eugenie's plight as he watched her contortions. "Maybe we should move the rest of your stuff in—anything not smoke-damaged that is." He balanced the wine glass on the grass and lay back. "Perhaps Elise could find us a bigger place."

Eugenie stopped wriggling and stared at him. "You meant what you said then? Before. You want me to move in with you? Permanently?"

"It makes sense. As I told you, a live-in submissive has its attractions. And you don't eat much." He turned his head to catch her gaze and held it. He wasn't going to push her, but Eugenie knew he expected an answer. For her part, although the suggestion was not entirely unwelcome, she had her reservations.

"Living with a Dom could be a bit…overwhelming at times."

"It would have its compensations. I think you know that. I'm demanding, I know, but not unreasonable. Do you think you could live with me?"

Again, Eugenie took her time. She was well aware that this was a pivotal moment, a decision that would define their relationship for the future. She studied her hands as she considered, turning over in her head how she thought this latest twist in their story might pan out. Where this new chapter might take her. She shifted to face him.

"You are suggesting a permanent arrangement, Sir?"

"I am. Permanent and, of course, exclusive."

"I see, Sir. Demanding but not unreasonable, I think you said. Do you have definition of not unreasonable that I might be able to consider?"

"I'll spank you when you need it. When I think you need it. And I'll stop when you ask me to. I'll provide you with orgasms to curl your toes. Your underwear will require changing several times daily. I will not fuck you in the office, apart from exceptional circumstances. I think the rest of our rules will be familiar enough to you."

She made a thorough and careful study of her fingers, making him wait for her answer. She stroked her chin, considering. At last, she peeped up at him, her smile mischievous. "I see, Sir. I accept your terms. But you should know I would require a lot of compensating."

"Excellent. So we're agreed. I'll talk to Elise about a bigger flat. And pink bottom or not, I intend to spank you when we get back for your sassiness just now. La Brat is alive, kicking and soon to be screaming here at Totally Five Star Paris. I intend to keep her very busy."

"Thank you, Sir. And I'll try not to be too much of a nuisance."

"That's not part of the deal. I have no quarrel with brattiness, as long as you're *my* brat. I think I can manage you. You're a complicated little subbie, but I think I have you worked out now."

Eugenie rolled onto her stomach, turning her head to give him a long look over her shoulder. "Yes, Sir. I think perhaps you do."

About the Author

Until 2010, Ashe was a director of a regeneration company before deciding there had to be more to life and leaving to pursue a lifetime goal of self-employment.

Ashe has been an avid reader of women's fiction for many years—erotic, historical, contemporary, fantasy, romance—you name it, as long as it's written by women, for women. Now, at last in control of her own time and working from her home in rural West Yorkshire, she has been able to realise her dream of writing erotic romance herself.

She draws on settings and anecdotes from her previous and current experience to lend colour, detail and realism to her plots and characters, but her stories of love, challenge, resilience and compassion are the conjurings of her own imagination. She loves to craft strong, enigmatic men and bright, sassy women to give them a hard time—in every sense of the word.

When she's not writing, Ashe's time is divided between her role as resident taxi driver for her teenage daughter, and caring for a menagerie of dogs, cats, rabbits, tortoises and a hamster.

Ashe Barker loves to hear from readers. You can find her contact information, website details and author profile page at http://www.totallybound.com.

Totally Bound Publishing

Made in the USA
San Bernardino, CA
11 October 2017